Praise for th

"Wilson deftly keeps int   racter-
izations, modulating th   lay life
in the early 1980s. Crac
—Kirkus Reviews on *Jack: Secret Histories*

"A fun and exciting read that will appeal to all audiences . . .
A must-have for any library. It is a great book for general
entertainment, and it will take many adults on a nostalgic
journey to their teen years."
—*Children's Literature* on *Jack: Secret Histories*

"Readers of the adult Repairman Jack novels will enjoy bringing their background to this reading, but, luckily for kid readers, knowledge of the series is not vital to enjoying this
smart, spooky mystery adventure."
—*Kirkus Reviews* on *Jack: Secret Circles*

"Will appeal to sci-fi fans."   —*Booklist* on *Jack: Secret Circles*

"Wilson has created an engaging, fast-paced, and yet deeply
thought-provoking work that builds upon (and builds up)
the Repairman Jack mythos. It might seem like a book for
younger readers, but Wilson's many fans will want to grab a
copy right away. Strongly recommended."
—*SFRevu* on *Jack: Secret Circles*

"Wilson's final YA adventure offering a peep into the teen years
of Repairman Jack, star of fourteen adult novels (with two
more on the way) . . . Fans, teen and adult, will be in heaven."
—*Kirkus Reviews* on *Jack: Secret Vengeance*

"As with the other two entries in this young-adult series,
Wilson writes to his audience, not down to it. This series has
been a welcome way to get more out of his creation."
—*Bookgasm* on *Jack: Secret Vengeance*

ALSO BY F. PAUL WILSON

YOUNG ADULT

  Jack: Secret Histories
  Jack: Secret Circles
  Jack: Secret Vengeance

REPAIRMAN JACK NOVELS*

  The Tomb
  Legacies
  Conspiracies
  All the Rage
  Hosts
  The Haunted Air
  Gateways
  Crisscross
  Infernal
  Harbingers
  Bloodline
  By the Sword
  Ground Zero
  Fatal Error

THE ADVERSARY CYCLE*

  The Keep
  The Tomb
  The Touch
  Reborn
  Reprisal
  Nightworld

OTHER NOVELS

  Healer
  Wheels Within Wheels
  An Enemy of the State
  Black Wind*
  Dydeetown World
  The Tery
  Sibs
  The Select
  Implant
  Virgin
  Deep as the Marrow
  Mirage (with Matthew J. Costello)
  Nightkill (with Steven Spruill)
  Masque (with Matthew J. Costello)
  The Christmas Thingy
  Sims
  The Fifth Harmonic
  Midnight Mass

SHORT FICTION

  Soft and Others
  The Barrens and Others*
  Aftershock and Others*
  The Peabody-Ozymandias
    Traveling Circus &
    Oddity Emporium*

EDITOR

  Freak Show
  Diagnosis: Terminal

*See "The Secret History of the World" (page 299).

JACK
SECRET VENGEANCE

F. PAUL WILSON

A TOM DOHERTY ASSOCIATES BOOK
NEW YORK

TOR®
TEEN

JACK: SECRET VENGEANCE

Copyright © 2011 by F. Paul Wilson

A Tor® Teen Book
Published by Tom Doherty Associates, LLC
175 Fifth Avenue
New York, NY 10010

www.tor-forge.com

Tor® is a registered trademark of Tom Doherty Associates, LLC.

ISBN 978-0-7653-5813-4

First Edition: February 2011
First Mass Market Edition: February 2012

Printed in the United States of America

0 9 8 7 6 5 4 3 2 1

ACKNOWLEDGMENTS

To Keith and KRW from the repairmanjack.com forum for the tagline on a certain character's business card.

Special thanks to Susan Chang for her editorial guidance throughout the trilogy.

JACK: SECRET VENGEANCE

Weezy was attacked on a Saturday night.

1

"Jack," his mother called from down the hall. "Weezy's on the phone."

Jack poked his head out from under the covers, forced his eyes open, and checked the clock on the table next to his bed. He saw *8:13* in glowing red numbers. He squinted at his window. A cloudy morning sky peeked around the edge of the drawn shade.

"I'll call her back."

"She says it's important."

What could be important at eight thirteen on a Sunday morning?

Groaning, he slid out of bed, pulled on his jeans, and padded barefoot down the hall past his brother's and sister's empty bedrooms. Tom was finishing law school in Jersey City and Kate had started med school in Stratford. He veered right, into the kitchen where his mother was cracking eggs, and picked up the receiver lying on the counter.

"Hey."

"Jack, I need to talk to you. Real bad."

"Well, hello, stranger."

Except for brief conversations at the school bus stop, they hadn't seen too much of each other lately.

"I'm serious, Jack. I really need to talk."

Something in her voice . . . he couldn't put his finger on it, but he sensed she was upset. She didn't get along too well with her folks, especially her dad. Weezy was a little too strange for him. Maybe a lot too strange.

Not too strange for Jack. She was just . . . Weezy.

Maybe they'd had a blowup.

"Okay. Want to come over for breakfast?"

"No. I don't want anyone else listening in. Meet me on the bridge and we'll bike into the Barrens where no one can hear us."

Weezy . . . always mysterious. Well, he had some time before he was due for work at USED.

"Sure. Let me get something to eat and I'll meet you there in half an hour."

"That long?"

"I'm hungry, Weez. I'll try for twenty."

"Okay."

He smiled as he hung up. Now what? Never a dull moment with Weezy Connell. And Jack wouldn't have it any other way.

He heard voices coming from the living room—first a man's, then a woman's. Radio? TV? His folks never played either on Sunday morning. This was newspaper time. If they played anything, it was one of Mom's Broadway soundtracks. He went to check and found his father seated before the TV, leaning forward, eyes glued to the screen.

And on that screen—a pile of burning, smoking rubble with fire trucks and ambulances milling around. A caption said *Beirut, Lebanon.* The little CNN logo sat in the lower right corner.

"What happened?"

Dad looked up, his expression grim. "See that pile of concrete? That was a four-story marine barrack until some crazy Arabs blew it up."

Jack stared at the rubble. Four stories? It was barely one now.

"An air raid?"

"No. Word coming out is some nutcase drove a truckload of explosives through the front door and blew it up."

Jack blinked. "With himself still in it?"

"Yeah. What they're calling a 'suicide bombing.' Same thing happened to a French barracks a few miles away. They think the dead count is going to reach three hundred."

Jack was aghast.

"Are they crazy? I mean, blowing themselves up?"

"Well, the kamikaze pilots during World War Two went on suicide missions, but that was in battle, during a war. These kids were all part of a peacekeeping force."

"But . . . why?" He couldn't fathom anyone doing this.

"Who knows? Some reporter said it was like Pearl Harbor—a sneak attack at dawn on a Sunday morning. But the Japs had the decency to declare war first. And they had a country and an army and a navy we could strike back at. Some group called Islamic Jihad is taking credit for this. Who the hell are they? No one seems to know a thing about them, except they also claimed credit for that U.S. Embassy bomb back in April."

Jack had heard about that but had been only peripherally aware of it. This seemed different, and was so much worse. He could tell from his father's expression and tone that he was steamed.

He remembered the Iran hostage crisis of a few years ago,

now these suicide bombings. What was going on in the Middle East? Had they all gone insane?

Mom coaxed Dad away from the tube with a promise of sausage and eggs. An almost funereal breakfast followed, the silence broken only by Mom's futile attempts at conversation and Dad's muttered remarks about the "inexcusable lack of security" at the barracks.

Jack couldn't remember ever seeing his father like this. He was a Korean War vet who never had anything good to say about the army. He'd always made it very clear that he didn't want either of his sons anywhere near the armed services. But he seemed deeply shaken by the deaths of so many U.S. soldiers. Maybe he made a distinction between servicemen and the armed services. Maybe some automatic brotherhood sprouted between guys who had been to war. Like at the local VFW post.

After breakfast he went right back to the TV, and Jack headed for his bike.

2

He beat her to the Old Town bridge, a narrow, one-lane wooden span over Quaker Lake, which wasn't really a lake, just a good-size pond. It finally had returned to its normal level after all the rains last month.

He sat on his BMX and wiped an arm across his sweaty forehead. A hot day, despite the clouds, and despite it being late October. The 1983 *Farmer's Almanac* had predicted a cool fall for the area. In Jack's experience that meant keep the swimming trunks handy.

He looked around at the place where he'd spent all his fourteen years: Johnson, New Jersey, a small town in Burlington County. It began on the west side of Route 206 and ended where it abutted the western edge of the Jersey Pine Barrens. Nobody knew exactly when the town was settled, but it had changed its name from Quakertown to Johnson after President Andrew Johnson spent the night here sometime in the 1860s.

He saw Weezy round the corner off North Franklin and roll his way along Quakerton Road on her banana-seat Schwinn. Louise "Weezy" Connell was probably the best of the few friends Jack had, but he hadn't seen much of her in the weeks since the Cody Bockman fiasco. Though only four months older—she'd just turned fifteen, while he'd have to wait till January—she was a full year ahead of him in school. He was a lowly frosh, while she was an experienced sophomore.

She wore—surprise!—black jeans, a black T-shirt, and black

sneakers. Her dark, shoulder-length hair was pulled into a ponytail that swung back and forth as she pedaled.

When she got close enough for him to see her face, he knew something was wrong. First off, no eyeliner—the only makeup she ever wore. This was the first time in the past year he could remember seeing her without it. Her expression was strange.

"You okay?" he said when she reached him.

"No." She rolled past onto the bridge. "Talk to you in the woods."

He followed her into Old Town, the original settlement, which Weezy said was much, much older than anyone thought, part of what she called the Secret History of the World. They passed the boxy structure of the Septimus Lodge and skirted the filled-in sinkholes from last month's underground flood. A dozen or better pocked the pavement and some of the yards.

As they neared the end of Quakerton Road, where Old Town petered out and the Pines began, Jack spotted Lester Appleton's pickup, parked in its usual spot next to the Lightning Tree. That was the applejack spot. Depending on the day of the week, you could find either Lester or Gus Sooy there, ready to sell their moonshine. A couple of men stood by the tailgate, watching as Lester filled their whiskey bottles from a large ceramic jug.

The Appletons were an old piney family, supposedly inbred. If anyone had a doubt about that, one look at Lester was pretty convincing. Skinny, with his left eye always pointed toward his nose and tufts of wild-looking hair shooting off his scalp in all directions, he wore overalls worn through at the knees, and sneakers with no socks. His hands and his ankles were gray with grime. His back was bent and twisted, which made him lean forward and to the right. He kept licking his lips with a big red tongue.

Some people said he made the best applejack in the Pines—a secret he learned from his father, Jacob—while others preferred Gus Sooy's. All strictly illegal, but nobody complained. Applejack was a part of life in and around the Pine Barrens.

"Where we headed?" Jack called as he followed Weezy onto one of the firebreak trails that cut through the trees.

"You'll see," she said without turning.

No matter how many times he entered the Barrens—and he'd been doing it most of his life—Jack never failed to feel a little uneasy as the gnarled, forty-foot scrub pines leaned their scraggly branches over the path as if looking for a chance to grab him. The place seemed alive.

"Want to talk now?"

"When we get there."

They moved deeper into the Barrens, the million or so acres of woods smack in the center of the state that hid places no human had ever seen. Every year a few people walked in and never came out.

The familiar NO FISHING / NO HUNTING / NO TRAPPING / NO TRESPASSING signs tacked up everywhere were a sure sign they were on Old Man Foster's land. They passed the spong where a cantankerous piney kept putting out leg-hold traps and Mrs. Clevenger kept springing them. Looked like she'd been here recently because all the traps had sticks stuck in their sprung jaws.

Weezy led him deeper into Foster's land until she turned off the trail onto a path that consisted of two ruts with a grassy ridge between. Jack had never been this way but Weezy probably had. She loved to explore the Barrens.

Finally she came to a stop near a small open area where a sturdy old oak stood tall and wide among the more spindly pines.

She turned to Jack and said, "This is where it happened."

He looked around. "Where what happened?"

Her face screwed up and her eyes filled with tears. "Where Carson attacked me!"

Before Jack knew it, he was off his bike and in her face.

"He *what*? Carson Toliver attacked you?"

Suddenly Weezy's arms were around him and her face was pressed against his chest.

"Yes! I thought he was going to . . . you know!"

As she sobbed against him, Jack raised his arms, unsure of what to do with them. Finally he slipped them around Weezy's back and gently held her. He tried to think of something to say but came up blank. All he could think of was murder.

Carson Toliver, a big, studly senior, the captain and quarterback of the Burlington Badgers, and the heartthrob of South Burlington County Regional High. When he'd first shown some interest in Weezy during the summer, her IQ had immediately lost eighty points. Jack had assumed it was because of her notoriety as co-discoverer of a ritually mutilated corpse in the Barrens. He'd seen him sniffing around a few times since then, but hadn't seen any signs that it had progressed beyond that.

Apparently it had.

Weezy sobbed a couple more times then pushed away, head down as she wiped her eyes.

"Sorry. I guess I've been holding it in too long."

"Have you told your folks?"

Her head snapped up and he saw a wild, frightened look in her eyes. "No! No way! And you can't say anything! They don't even know I was out with him! They think I was at your house!"

"Swell." He remained baffled. "What . . . how . . . ?"

"He asked me to go out with him. Said it was so cool, you know, about the body we found, and about Cody, and he wanted to hear all about it."

Jack made a face. "And your brain turned into a big gummy bear."

She looked offended. "Did not."

"I've seen it happen before."

"Well, okay, when the hottest guy in school is interested in you . . . you wouldn't understand."

"Got that right."

"Anyway, I told him my folks would never let me go out with a senior, especially a guy with a car."

Toliver's car . . . a cool Mustang GLX convertible. Jack wouldn't mind a ride in that himself.

"So he told you not to tell them."

She cocked her head. "How did you know?"

"Lucky guess."

"So anyway, last night I walked over to Old Town and he picked me up and drove us into the Pines."

"Weren't you a little worried about that?"

She frowned. "Looking back, yeah, I should have been, but we were talking about the body and how it had been mutilated and about Cody and about how mysterious the Pines are and he said he'd found a cool place he didn't think anyone else knew about and would I like to see it and of course I said yes."

"Of course."

Telling Weezy about a cool new place in the Pines was like dangling a wriggling goldfish before a cat.

"So we stopped here and instead of showing me anything, suddenly he's grabbing me." She blinked. "I told him to stop but he wouldn't. His hands were all over me and I kept pushing him away but he kept on. He even tried to unbutton my blouse. Finally I hit him and he lost it. He started screaming and cursing about how 'you goth chicks are always easy' and I got so scared I jumped out of the car. But even that didn't stop him. He came after me and grabbed me and ripped my blouse but I got away and ran."

"You outran Carson Toliver?" The guy was an ace athlete.

"I got into the trees and hid. He couldn't find me, so he just stood there and screamed. Maybe because he's who he is and lots of girls are easy with him he expected me to be too, but he was . . ." She raised trembling hands to her face. "Jack, I was *so* scared. It was like he'd gone insane. Finally he left."

"He left you to walk home?" The urge to kill rose again. "You've got to report him."

"I can't! I just want it to go away."

"He attacked you. That's assault or battery or both. That's a crime. You should tell the cops."

"Ohmigod, no! If I report it I'll be in trouble with my folks and he can just say I'm crazy and that we were never together and I can't prove that we were and everyone will side with him because he's popular and I'm a nobody, and besides, who'll believe he'd ask me out anyway, and I'm already known as a weirdo, so just think of what they'll be saying about me if I say he attacked me."

When she stopped for air, Jack jumped in.

"So . . . you want me to do something?"

She looked at him as if he'd just spoken Swahili. "Do something? No. And anyway, what can you do?"

He had a flash vision of himself as some kind of Galahad defending Weezy's honor by challenging Toliver to a fight . . . and being stomped into the dirt.

Jack wasn't following. "Then why are you telling me all this if you don't want my help?"

Why else would you tell someone a problem?

"I had to tell *someone*. I couldn't tell my folks, and not Eddie of all people. And the girls at school—forget them. You're the only one I can trust. And just being able to tell someone helps, don't you see?"

Jack didn't, but that didn't matter. *You're the only one I can trust* rang through his head, leaving a warm echo.

"So you're just going to give him a pass?"

"I'm just going to keep my distance and pretend this never happened."

"Tell the cops, Weez."

"No way! I'll just make things worse for myself. It's over and done. I'm okay. And I've learned something."

"About what?"

"About getting into a car with a guy I don't know all that well." She took a deep breath and looked around. "There. I feel better already."

"Weez, a few minutes ago you were crying."

"That's because it was all bottled up. Now that I've let it out"—she gave him a weak smile and a pointed look—"now that I've *told* someone, I feel a hundred percent better."

Still baffled, Jack shook his head. "You're crazy."

Her wavering smile faded. "Don't call me that, Jack. Please. Not you."

Her intensity took him aback. She was awful sensitive about the word.

"Okay. Sure." He smiled. "How about 'goth chick'? Can I call you that?"

She batted him on the arm. "I'm not goth!"

"No? Let's see . . . you dress in black and you love Bauhaus and Siouxsie. Like my father likes to say—"

"Please don't!" She jammed her fingers in her ears and began making nonsense noises that sounded like "Bobbitta-bobbitta-bobbitta."

"—'If it walks like a duck and quacks like a duck, odds are it's a duck.' "

She removed her fingers from her ears. "Finished?"

"Yeah."

"Good. Those are simply my choices. They don't mean I've joined a club. I don't like labels."

Neither did Jack, so he dropped it.

3

They'd walked their bikes back to the firebreak trail and were readying to head back to Johnson when Weezy held up a hand.

"You know, I've never been through this area."

Jack smiled. "You mean there's someplace on Old Man Foster's land you haven't seen?"

She shrugged. "He owns a *lot* of land. Let's take a look around."

He looked at his watch. "We should be heading back. I've got to get to USED—"

"Come on, Jack. Just a little. I'd go myself but . . ."

Jack knew what she didn't want to say: After last night, she didn't want to be alone in there.

"Okay. Just a few . . ."

But she was already walking her bike back up the path. He brought up the rear until she stopped and pointed.

"Looks like some sort of clearing over there."

He followed her through a line of trees and, sure enough, a clearing.

A creepy clearing . . . almost perfectly square, the size of half a football field, with nothing growing in it.

Nothing at all.

"What's the story here?" Jack said, inspecting the sandy soil. "Does somebody come by and weed this place? Or spray weed killer?"

"Weed killer would leave dead plants."

Jack looked again. She was right: no sign of vegetation, living or dead.

"Check this out," she said, kneeling to examine a bright green fern along the edge. She stretched one of the fronds and gave it a close look, then muttered something that sounded like "warts."

"What?"

"Ebony spleenwort. It doesn't usually grow in the Barrens because the soil's too acid."

Jack felt his eyes roll of their own accord. "How do you know this stuff? And *why*?"

She rose and faced him. "Because the Pines have lots of lost towns—villages and such that just up and disappeared."

"Or were built over, as we well know."

She nodded. "But one way to spot where a town once stood is ebony spleenwort. Pinelands soil is acidic and ebony spleenwort doesn't like acid. So it grows over buried foundations because the old limestone and mortar reduce the acidity in the soil over them." She gestured around. "We're standing in an old foundation."

Jack looked at the big square of naked soil. "Of what?"

Weezy stepped onto the bare earth and wandered toward the center of the square. Jack followed, scuffing the ground as he followed. Not a sign of life. Not a beetle, not a worm-hole, not a single anthill. Looked like nothing had *ever* grown here. Something else seemed to be missing from the soft soil but he couldn't say what.

Weezy stopped and turned in a slow circle, pointing. "See? The spleenwort runs all around the edges. A building once stood here—a big one."

"Big is right. What *was* this place? And why won't anything grow in the center? It's like it's some sort of dead zone."

"Dead zone . . ." She looked at him. "Why does that sound familiar?"

"It's a movie coming out." Jack had seen a preview when he'd gone to see the animated *Fire and Ice*. "I think it's about—"

"Shhhh!" Weezy said, pointing.

Jack looked and saw a pair of young Pineland deer walking their way. He froze and watched as they approached the clearing. It looked as if they were going to step into it when both abruptly turned right and followed the spleenwort to the corner, then turned left and followed the far edge. At the next corner they made another left until they came even with their path on the far side, then turned away. Jack watched their white tails disappear into the trees.

"Did you see that?" Weezy said, her voice hushed.

Of course he'd seen it. And now he knew what else was missing from the bare square.

"Tracks."

Weezy stared at him. "What?"

"Look." He pointed to the ground around them. "It hasn't rained for at least a week but the only tracks here are our footprints. The only explanation for that has to be that animals won't cross this space. It's really and truly a dead zone. What's going on here?"

"Or maybe, what *went* on here. I don't know, but . . . it doesn't feel right."

Jack knew exactly what she meant.

She gave him a sickly look. "I don't think I want to be here anymore."

Neither did he, but he put on a carefree expression. "Whatever. I've got to go to work anyway." He looked around. "You think this place might be part of your Secret History of the World?"

She nodded. "Definitely. But maybe some things should remain secret. Let's get out of here."

Jack didn't argue. If nothing else, the dead zone seemed to have chased Carson Toliver from her thoughts.

But not from Jack's.

1

The first clue that something was wrong came on the school bus.

Jack waited with Eddie and Weezy at the intersection of Route 206 and Quakerton Road with four other Johnson kids who attended South Burlington County Regional High School—SBR for short. They stood in front of Sumter's used car lot. A FOR SALE sign hung in the showroom window. The place had been closed since Mr. Sumter's mysterious death a couple of months ago and didn't look like it was going to re-open. Joe Burdett's Esso station and a Krauszer's convenience store occupied two other corners.

The grammar and middle-school kids clustered by the vacant lot across the street. He saw Sally Vivino and her mother waiting for the northbound school bus. Mrs. Vivino wouldn't look at him. Jack knew why.

He and Weezy stood apart. Eddie hung with the others but was in his own world, lost in whatever music his Walkman was pumping through his headphones.

"You okay?" Jack said.

Weezy had her eyeliner back on and was dressed in a sweatshirt, skirt, and tights, all black.

"Fine. Just glad to be out of the house."

"Your dad?"

She nodded. "He just shakes his head and keeps saying, 'What are we gonna do with you, Weezy? What are we gonna do?' That's all he ever says. I think I embarrass him. No, I'm *sure* I embarrass him. He still thinks I should be wearing pink."

Jack didn't get the whole black thing, but he never gave it much thought. Just something Weezy was into.

"Weez . . ."

Her lower lip trembled for an instant. "You know, if I ran away like Marcie Kurek, I wonder if he'd even care."

Marcie Kurek was from Shamong and had been a soph at the high school last year. One night she told her folks she was going out to visit a friend and never showed up. No one had ever seen or heard from her since.

"Hey, I know you two don't get along, but that's crazy."

She looked at him. "Didn't I ask you—"

"Yeah, okay. Right. Sorry." Touchy-touchy-touchy. "What about Toliver?"

"What about him?"

"What are you going to do when you see him?"

And she *would* see him. SBR wasn't all that big.

"I won't see him. If we wind up in the same hall or in the caf at the same time, I won't look at him. As far as I'll be concerned, he won't be there. He won't exist."

The big yellow school bus pulled up and clattered to a stop. Jack and Weezy hung back and were last on. He said hello to Karina and Cristin. He found Karina interesting and, well, attractive too. He wished she and Cristin weren't joined at the hip. He'd like riding the bus next to her.

Not that it was a long ride. SBR was only three miles from Johnson. He could have ridden his bike there easily in good weather like today's, but his folks were dead set against that. Jack saw some of the girls and guys grinning and pointing at Weezy. They whispered among themselves and one girl giggled. Weezy was oblivious.

Jack wound up next to his usual seatmate, Darren Willmon.

The bus pulled into the parking lot ten minutes later. Weezy got off ahead of him. He was hanging back, waiting for Karina and Cristin, when a trio of older girls, a blonde and two brunettes with high hair and stick-up bangs, breezed by him and flanked Weezy.

"So," the blonde said with a grin that looked as friendly as a great white's, "I hear you were out with Carson Saturday night."

Weezy stopped and reddened. "Where'd you hear that?"

"From Jerry." She gave Weezy a frank up-and-down. "You don't seem his type."

Eddie waved as he walked by, still lost in his headphones.

"I'm not," Weezy said.

"Yeah? Cars says you showed him a real hot time."

Weezy gaped. " 'Hot time'?"

"Yeah," said the heavier of the two brunettes, "we hear you were all over him. He, like, couldn't stop you."

Weezy's face turned a deeper red. "Me all over *him*? I had to fight *him* off."

They all laughed.

The third said, "When a girl like you gets near a guy like Carson Toliver—and will someone *please* tell me how that happened?—you don't fight him off. It just doesn't work that way."

"So we came up with a name for you," said the second. "Easy Weezy."

As they all laughed and repeated it, Jack saw Weezy's stricken expression and wanted to punch them. Just to shut them up.

"Who'd've thought," said the blonde, giving her another up-and-down. "But I guess if you want to look like that you've gotta make up for it some way." She waved and started to walk away. "Bye, Easy."

The other two followed, but not before the heavier one said, "And don't start thinking you're Carson's type. You're not. You're just . . . *easy*."

Weezy, mouth still open, stood and gazed at their retreating backs. The red faded to a sickly white. Finally she turned to Jack.

"How . . . what . . . ?"

"Obviously he's been spreading lies about you."

The urge to hurt, maim, maybe even kill Carson Toliver returned, stronger than ever. Not only had he attacked her, he was now smearing her.

"But why?"

Jack hid his anger and hurt with a shrug. "Who can figure a walking turd like that? Maybe he figures every girl should have the absolute hots for him. Maybe he doesn't hear 'no' too often. So instead of letting you talk about how you had to fight him off, he launched a preemptive strike."

"But it's a lie! It makes me sound like a slut."

"He's not worried about your rep, he's worried about his."

Two guys about a dozen feet away stopped and pointed. Jack recognized them as a couple of starters on the football team. Friends of Toliver's, no doubt.

"Hey, it's Easy Weezy!" one cried. "Wanna go out? You can have us both—two for the price of one!"

They must have thought that was a riot because they laughed all the way to the front door.

"It's all over school," she whispered, looking sick. "It's not even first period and already everybody's calling me Easy Weezy."

Jack didn't say it, but none of this would be happening if she'd reported him.

He touched her shoulder. "Not everybody. Just some big-hair airheads and a couple of Toliver's jock friends. The girls are jealous he asked you out instead of them, and the guys are just being jerks." He gave her a gentle squeeze on the shoulder and tried to lighten things up. "Us guys like to act like jerks whenever we can. It's in our nature."

She looked at him then at the two jocks disappearing inside. "I can't imagine you ever saying that."

"Maybe not, but maybe I simply haven't found the right outlet for all my pent-up jerkiness. When I do—duck and run for cover. Because it's gonna be ugly."

That won half a smile from her. He walked her in through the entrance, then they had to part ways. Jack's first period class was to the right, hers to the left.

He'd gone maybe a dozen feet when he heard a guy call out somewhere behind him.

"Hey! It's Easy Weezy!"

He cringed and turned. He couldn't see who'd said it, but saw Weezy moving away with her head down and her shoulders hunched.

"What an awful religion," Karina said at Jack's side as they left Mr. Kressy's class.

"I'm sure there are worse."

The Thuggee cult he'd seen in *Gunga Din* and *Indiana Jones and the Temple of Doom* seemed lots worse.

The Beirut suicide bombings had come up in Mr. Kressy's civics class and someone had asked what Islamic Jihad was all about. Mr. Kressy hadn't known anything about the group, but explained that *jihad* was an Arabic word for "holy war." And then he'd had to explain what he knew about Islam—which he admitted was very little.

"But their treatment of women," Karina said. "I mean, they're like little better than slaves."

"Slave girls!" said Matt Follette, moving up beside them in his trademark slouching walk. "I want to be a maharajah with a whole harem of slave girls."

He'd become the class's unofficial comedian. His humor tended toward black, which suited Jack just fine.

Karina said, "They're called 'wives,' but that's what it sounds like a harem is—nothing but a bunch of female slaves to cook, clean, feed, and pamper the man while having his children."

Sounding totally sincere, Matt said, "And the problem with that is . . . ?"

She gave his arm a playful slap.

From what Jack had heard about Islam, it sounded like it had been dreamed up by someone like Matt Follette.

They ambled along the echoey tiled hallways toward the caf. SBR's class building was a one-story box with an open quadrangle at its center; the caf was a connected square without a quadrangle. Once there they shuffled through the lunch line. Jack picked up a couple of burgers and added a slice of cheese to each. He noticed Karina making a salad.

"Aren't you going to be hungry?" he said.

She shook her head. "This'll hold me."

"A burger'd hold you better."

"I don't eat meat."

"No kidding?"

She smiled. "No kidding."

He realized then that he'd never seen her eat meat. He'd heard of vegetarians but had never met one. Truth was, living in Johnson, he hadn't met a whole lot of people in his fourteen years.

They found a table and Eddie joined them—physically, at least. He had his Walkman running into his ears.

Matt must have overheard the no-meat conversation because he turned to Karina and said, "So, are you, like, a Hindu or something? Cows are, like, holy?"

He said it with his usual sardonic tone, but Jack sensed genuine curiosity.

"No. I just don't like the idea of animals being killed just so I can eat."

"But that's sort of the way nature works," Jack said. "One thing dies so another can live. Plants die to feed deer, deer die to feed wolves. What's left of the dead deer feeds insects or seeps into the ground to feed plants, which other deer eat. And around and around it goes."

Matt grinned. "Where it stops, nobody knows."

Karina pointed to her salad. "It stops right here." She looked at Jack. "Does that make me weird?"

Jack had to smile. Not eating meat weird? He didn't get it, but so what? He'd hung out with Weezy Connell for years and years. Karina had no idea what weird could be.

"Not to me. Now, if you were eating worms or dirt, *that* would be weird."

She made a face. "Ew-ew."

"But it still wouldn't be any of my business. It's only my business when you try to keep *me* from eating meat." He grinned. "Or worse, start eating it off my plate."

She glanced at his cheeseburgers. "No way, José."

"I should bring you home for dinner."

She reddened, hesitated a heartbeat or two, then gave a noncommittal, "Hmmm?"

Jack realized that hadn't come out quite the way he'd intended.

"Uh, yeah. We could be an eating team. I'd take your meat and you could have my vegetables."

She smiled. "Yeah. That'd work—as long as the vegetables didn't touch the meat."

"Oh, you're one of those."

"Yep." Her brown eyes sparkled. "One of those."

They laughed. Yeah, Karina Haddon was pretty cool. So was Weezy, but in a different way.

Weezy . . . he wondered how she was doing.

3

They had the same lunch period on Mondays, so after finishing his burgers Jack looked for Weezy in the caf. They'd never once eaten together here—the class barrier was hard to cross. Lots of barriers in this room.

The caf was like a medieval kingdom with all sorts of fiefdoms. The jocks had their domain, which cut across classes but kept out non-jocks. The brainiacs had their groups, the bow-heads and big-hairs had theirs.

And then there were the pineys. They didn't seem to fit in anywhere. Jack guessed it was because they looked different.

A dozen or so sat at two tables in one of the corners. All wore odd, mismatched, ill-fitting clothes—no Swatches, Puma sneakers, parachute pants, or Jordache jeans at that table. Their biggest sin, Jack figured, was being too poor to afford all that stuff.

Some kids, like Jake Shuett, seem to have it in for the pineys, calling them retards and inbreds. A lot of folks talked about brothers and sisters or first cousins getting together and having kids. Jack didn't know if that was hot air or not. He did know that some pineys—Lester Appleton was a good example—sure didn't look right.

He spotted Elvin Neolin, a pint-size frosh from his civics class, getting up from his seat next to a girl with snow-white hair. They exchanged nods as they passed. Elvin had ruddy skin, black spiky hair, and dark eyes. A lot of Lenape Indian in him from the look of it. Not much of a talker, but he seemed like a good kid.

But where was Weezy? He wanted to hear how her morning had gone. This "Easy Weezy" stuff could last only so long before everyone got tired of it.

Or so he hoped.

He found a table with the girls she usually ate with, but she wasn't there.

"Where's Weezy?" he said.

A couple of them glanced up and looked through him like he wasn't there. Another said, "You mean Easy?"

The others giggled.

Jack gripped the end of their table and leaned on it. It took all his will not to tilt it and tip their lunches into their laps.

"No. I mean *Weezy*. Where is she?"

Maybe he was radiating something, because the nearest girl leaned away and said, "She disappeared between algebra and social studies. We heard she went home sick."

"Hey, maybe it's *morning* sickness!" someone else said, and this cracked up the table.

Jack stalked away before he said or did anything stupid. He wandered into the locker area that lined the hallway running between the main class building and the caf. There he saw Carson Toliver, in the flesh, closing his locker door, spinning the dial on his combo lock, and sauntering down the hall.

Jack felt his anger come to a boil but held it in check. No point in starting something he couldn't finish. And no point in drawing attention to himself as Weezy's defender. Who knew? Some odd accident might befall this guy, or something bad might happen to his precious car, and Jack didn't want any suspicion—unwarranted, of course—aimed his way.

He had a few minutes before his next class, so he followed.

Didn't take long for Jack to start shaking his head in wonder. The guy was amazing. Mr. Popularity. Girls would go, "Hiiii, Carrrrsonnnn," as he passed and he'd wave and smile back to one and all, pretty or not. Jack could watch the googly-eyed, weak-kneed, ga-ga reactions in his wake. The heartthrob of SBR. Made him sick. If only they knew.

But girls weren't the only ones after his attention. Guys looked for high fives, or even a simple nod, anything to be acknowledged by Carson Toliver, varsity hero. And Toliver ate it up. All he needed was a white suit coat draped over his shoulders and he could have been playing Don Fanucci from *Godfather II*.

Jack remembered with relish what the young Vito Corleone had done to Don Fanucci.

Then a surprise. They came upon Teddy Bishop and his goon buddy Joey hassling little Elvin Neolin, pushing him around. Jack had had a run-in with them over the summer. Nearly got his face rearranged. Everyone else in the hall was ignoring the scene, but as Toliver passed he made a sudden turn and shoved Teddy against the wall.

"He's kinda little for a big guy like you to be messing with, don't you think?" he said.

Teddy was a junior and probably weighed as much as Toliver, but he was a lard bucket. And knew it. He looked instantly cowed. Especially since everyone in the hall had stopped to watch.

"Aw, he's just a piney."

"I don't care if he's a Martian, you're a lot bigger."

"We wasn't doin' nothin'."

"Yeah? That's not what I saw. Wanna try a little of that *nothin'* on me? Huh? How about it?"

"Hey, no, we was just—"

Toliver shoved him again and turned to his blond-haired buddy Joey. "How about you? You up for a little *nothin'*?"

Joey raised his hands and backed away. "Hey, no, man. We didn't mean nothin'."

Toliver turned to Elvin. "These guys hassle you again, you come to me." He pointed to Teddy and Joey each in turn. "And you two . . . I'll be watching."

With that, Toliver continued his stroll as if nothing had happened, leaving Elvin staring after him with absolute, total hero worship in his dark eyes, while Teddy and Joey slunk away in the other direction.

Amazing, Jack thought.

He wondered if Toliver cared a bit about Elvin. Maybe he'd simply seen the situation as an opportunity to put on a performance.

On the other hand, maybe it wasn't completely a performance. Maybe he'd been sincerely ticked at seeing a little guy being pushed around by the likes of Teddy and Joey. Whatever the case, he'd made the most of it.

"You okay, Elvin?"

He nodded but said nothing. He rarely said anything.

Jack felt a sudden shove from behind. "Hey, you botherin' Elvin?"

He turned to see one of the older piney kids, looking ready to fight. He'd met him before. Levi Coffin, tall and lanky with unruly brown hair. His gangly arms stuck out of his too-small shirt. He had one blue eye and one brown and both flashed anger.

Elvin waved his hands and pointed back down at the retreating bullies.

"Oh, them," Levi said, his tone dripping contempt. "One of these days somethin' real bad's gonna befall them two."

Like many pineys, his voice had an almost Southern twang. Maybe that was why some people called them hill-billies without hills.

He looked at Jack. "Sorry. Got my signals crossed."

He looked at Elvin, then at Toliver's receding figure.

"Don't you go thinkin' he's your buddy and all." He jerked a thumb over his shoulder. "You know what Saree says about him."

Jack looked and saw the white-haired girl from the piney lunch table standing a few feet away, staring at him with an odd expression. He realized with a start that she had pink irises. White hair . . . milk-white skin . . . what was that called . . . ?

Albino . . . she was an albino.

Elvin and Levi joined her and the three of them walked off. Before they rounded the bend, the albino girl—Saree— stared at him again over her shoulder. What was so interesting about him? And Elvin and Levi . . . Jack had a weird feeling those two had had a conversation without Elvin saying a word.

But they weren't important. Toliver was.

Being the gridiron hero wasn't enough, apparently. Not only was he the guy who could do no wrong on or off the athletic field, but he'd set himself up as godfather of the whole damn school as well.

And clearly he liked the role. He ate up the adoration like candy.

But if people could see what lay beneath that Mr. Wonderful façade, it would be a way different story.

The problem was, how could Jack expose the real Carson Toliver without involving Weezy . . . or himself?

4

"I'm heading for the Connells'."

His father looked up from where he sat sipping a beer and listening to Mr. Bainbridge rant about Beirut. His fellow Korean War vet had come over in a rage and hadn't stopped talking since he stepped through the door.

"Homework done?"

"Every bit."

"Don't be late."

USED was closed on Mondays, so Jack had had the afternoon to himself. The first thing he'd done when he got home was call Weezy to see how she was, but Mrs. Connell said she wasn't feeling well and couldn't come to the phone. He tried a few more times through the afternoon but the answer was always the same.

He often wished they'd invent something like the *Star Trek* communicator that you could carry in a pocket and call people when you needed to speak to them, or tell Scotty to beam you up. If he and Weezy each had one, he could have called her directly.

Maybe someday . . .

"Nuke 'em!" Mr. Bainbridge was saying as Jack ducked out the front door. "Kill 'em all and let Allah sort 'em out! Who'll miss 'em?"

He'd really built up a head of steam. Dad was simply sitting there letting him blow it off.

He biked over to Weezy's and was just setting his kickstand in the driveway when he heard a girl scream.

He froze and listened.

"No! I'm not going!"

Weezy . . .

"The hell you aren't!" Her father's voice.

And then her mother's. "Weezy, you can't just quit school. Did something happen?"

Weezy . . . screaming: "Nothing happened! I'm just never going to school again and no one can make me!"

Weezy never going to school again? He couldn't imagine what it was like for a fifteen-year-old girl to be called "easy" by everyone. Bad enough if it was true, but when it wasn't . . .

And worse, no one would believe it wasn't. Jack had seen the Carson Toliver charisma running full throttle today and it was awesome. No way anyone would believe he'd force himself on Weezy Connell. He was too good a guy. And besides, why would he force himself on any girl when there were so many of them drooling over him?

Even so, it would all blow over eventually. But Weezy probably couldn't see that. She was an all-or-nothing sort. No half measures for her. When she got into something, she was into it all the way. So from where she stood, everyone thought she was a slut and would think of her as a slut for the rest of her life. She couldn't face that on a daily basis so she was never ever going back to school.

Sooner or later she'd come around, but her parents didn't seem to see that. Her father kept yelling that she was going back to school tomorrow and she kept screaming that she wasn't.

The screams bothered Jack. He'd never heard that tone from Weezy, hadn't imagined she was even capable of it. She sounded totally out of control, maybe even a little crazy.

Crazy . . . she'd been on his case about calling her that, and he remembered her getting in Eddie's face for it a few times.

A door slammed, and then her father's voice again. "Weezy! Open up! You open this door this minute!"

Jack heard Mrs. Connell say, "All right, that does it! I'm calling Doctor Hamilton."

"Not again!" Weezy wailed.

Something about the way she said it gave Jack an uneasy feeling. Dr. Hamilton? Who was Dr. Hamilton? Jack had never heard of him.

Sad and worried, he turned his bike around and headed home.

5

Mr. Bainbridge was just going out as Jack came in.

"He sure was mad earlier," he said to his father when he was gone.

"Well, he has a right to be. We all do. But he's mad at just the Arabs. It's more complicated than that."

"How? Those marines were there just to keep the peace, right? They shouldn't have been killed."

His expression turned bitter. "*Murdered* is more like it." He sighed. "But that 'keep the peace' bit is a big part of the problem. I just don't see why every time there's a dustup somewhere in the world, we have to put our guys in harm's way. Those boys died for nothing. Absolutely nothing. It's the law of unintended consequences."

" 'Law'?"

"Well, not a law, per se, but it happens enough that it's seen that way."

Confused, Jack shook his head. "I don't get it."

His father leaned forward. "Used to be, if you wanted to steal a car, you'd cross a few wires under the dashboard to get it started, then drive off. To prevent thefts, car makers installed safeguards against hot-wiring. So what are car thieves doing now? They're waiting for drivers to get in and start the car, then attacking them and pulling them from the car, and driving off. So, measures to prevent hot-wiring had the unintended consequence of replacing simple theft with violent carjacking."

Jack got it . . . sort of.

"But Beirut?"

"The peacekeeping force had the best intentions: Calm the violence so cooler heads could prevail. But the fanatics saw it as an invasion. The result: An attempt to save Middle Eastern lives results in the slaughter of the U.S. peacekeepers. An unintended consequence."

Shaking his head, Jack wandered into the kitchen and pulled out the phone book.

Mom came in then, drying her hands on a towel. She had hair and eyes the same shade of brown as Jack's. The weight she'd gained over the past few years had made her face rounder than Jack's.

"How's my miracle boy doing?"

Jack snapped the phone book closed and suppressed a groan.

Miracle boy . . . he hated that almost as much as "Jackie." He'd broken her of calling him Jackie—at least he hoped he had. It had been a whole month since she'd said the word. But he didn't think he'd ever break her of the "miracle boy" thing. On the plus side, she used it when only family were present.

"Fine."

"What were you looking up?"

"Just browsing through, looking at the yellow pages and stuff."

The "stuff" he'd been looking for was a doctor named Hamilton.

She gave him an amused look. "Since when are you more interested in the phone book than football?"

Oh, yeah. The Monday night game. Normally Dad would be glued to it. Jack loved watching football but the voice of one of the Monday night announcers, Howard Cosell, got on his nerves at times. The guy had made some comment a couple of weeks ago that upset lots of people, but Jack had already forgotten what it was.

"Forgot about it." No lie there. This thing with Weezy and Toliver had blown it out of his mind. "Who's playing?"

She gave a dismissive wave. "How should I know? I don't understand what anyone sees in grown men fighting over a silly ball."

"You play tennis with Dad, and that involves a ball."

"Yes, but we're *hitting* the ball, not fighting over it."

As Mom puttered in the kitchen, Jack peeked in and saw the light from the screen reflecting from his father's glasses and balding head. The Dolphins were playing the Raiders. He wasn't a big fan of either team.

He wondered when the Eagles would make the Monday night game again. He was still stinging from the Phillies' World Series loss to the stupid Orioles. People had called it the I-95 series, but Jack called it the Crap Series. Just a week ago they choked in the fifth game—a five-nothing shutout, of all things—and went home losers. A black day for Phillies fans like Jack and his dad.

Well, at least they'd made the series. No hope of the Eagles making the Super Bowl this season. They were awful.

He heard Mom go upstairs, so without saying anything to his dad he returned to the kitchen and reopened the phone book. He found the *Physicians* section again and ran through the names. His finger froze when he came to the only Hamilton.

Selena Hamilton, MD
Child and Adolescent Psychiatry
Medford, NJ

Psychiatry? Weezy was seeing a shrink? No. Couldn't be. And yet . . . Weezy had said, *Not again!* And Medford . . . she and her mother had made a trip to Medford every Friday throughout the summer. Weezy had never said what for and Jack had never asked, assuming they were shopping trips.

So many things fit together now, especially her sensitivity about the word "crazy."

But what was wrong with her head? Her moods bounced all over the place. When she was up she was flying and when she was down she was in the basement, but she wasn't crazy.

Although she'd sure sounded crazy tonight. Maybe she'd been standing on the edge of some kind of psychological cliff and this "Easy Weezy" business knocked her off.

Only one person to blame for that.

Jack felt a surge of dark and cold sweep through him, as if a latch had suddenly lifted, freeing something that should remain safely locked away. He closed the phone book and slammed out the back door. He headed for the garage and went straight to the corner where they kept all the sporting equipment—tennis racquets, tennis balls, birdies, badminton racquets, footballs, baseballs, mitts . . . and bats.

He pulled a Louisville Slugger from a bin and hefted it.

Yeah.

6

Jack crouched in the shadowed shrubs along the side of the Toliver garage and waited for Carson.

The Tolivers lived on Johnson's western boundary, at the tip of the cul-de-sac that capped Emerson Lane. People who lived in this relatively new and ritzy development on the far side of Route 206 liked to call it "New Town." The name hadn't stuck.

But Jack hadn't arrived via Emerson Lane. He'd hidden his bike among the used cars in Sumter's lot and hiked through the sprawling orchard on the north side of the development. Along the way he'd passed Professor Nakamura's house; through the rear windows he'd seen the professor sitting at the desk in his study. Here was another guy who'd let Weezy down, but not on purpose.

From the orchard it had been easy to slip through the Tolivers' backyard to the side of their garage where he peeked through the window to check out what cars it held. He found two: a Cadillac DeVille and a Mercedes sedan. No Mustang convertible in sight. Which meant the Boy Wonder wasn't home yet.

Good.

Jack wore dark jeans, a navy blue sweater, and a knit watch cap. He stoked his rage as he planned his moves.

When Toliver arrived, Jack would wait till he got out of the car, then pull his cap down over his face, sneak up on him, and crack his kneecaps—good, hard, solid shots to one, then the other, ending his sports-hero days. Then, if time permitted, maybe he'd smash the hands that had groped Weezy. That done, he'd hightail it back through the orchard to his bike and be back home before the sheriff's office got the call.

Yeah. That would work.

But the longer he waited, the more he thought about it. And the more he thought about it, the less he liked it. But he wouldn't back down. Someone needed to put the hurt on this guy, and Jack had elected himself to the job.

He crouched lower as he saw lights flare down the street. They reached the end of the cul-de-sac and swept into the driveway as a Mustang pulled to a stop before the garage doors. Jack stretched the cap down over his face and watched through the weave as the convertible top rose from its hiding place behind the rear seat, then lowered itself into place. As he waited for the driver's door to open he felt sweat collecting in his armpits and on his palms where he white-knuckled the bat. Finally Carson Toliver stepped out. He stood and stretched, and Jack knew here was the perfect time to make his move.

Yet he remained in a crouch as Toliver strolled up to his front door and stepped inside. When the door slammed shut Jack slumped onto his butt with his back against the wall.

His first thought was that he'd chickened out, but it hadn't been that. With darkness, surprise, and a baseball bat against a barehanded kid, even if that kid was older and bigger, Jack had had nothing to fear. But as he'd readied to spring, he thought about cowardice. And he'd realized that making no move wouldn't be cowardly—but *attacking* would.

If he'd gone through with it, he'd have been nothing more than a thug. Yeah, he'd have gotten even for Weezy, but with a sneak attack and brute force. Not the sort of thing he'd take pride in afterward. In fact, he could see himself feeling pretty crummy about it later.

Besides, Weezy deserved better.

He rose and trotted back to the orchard. As he reached it he glanced back and saw a light go on in a bedroom. Toliver stepped to the window and pulled the blinds.

Sleep tight, you rotten . . .

As he wove through the droopy trees, their branches lighter now since the recent apple harvest, he searched for a way to balance the scales. He knew he'd eventually find one, because he wasn't giving up on this. His rage at Toliver hadn't dissipated one speck, it had simply gone from hot to cold.

And revenge, they said, was a dish best served cold.

But how to balance those scales? Or better yet, tip them the other way?

On one side was Weezy, afraid to go to school and perhaps teetering on the edge of some emotional abyss. From the sound of her earlier, maybe she'd already slipped over.

On the other side was Toliver, riding high.

And in the middle . . . Jack, with very few options.

Weezy's refusal to let anyone know about the attack was tying his hands. That had been a bad decision on Sunday morning, and here, on Monday night, it was no longer an option. Toliver had made a preemptive strike, and no one would believe her now.

Had to be a way.

Carson Toliver, looked up to and admired by all. The guy must love to come to school every day; walking through those doors had to make him feel like a king entering his court.

But what would happen if the king lost his crown? What if things changed to make *him* afraid to go to school?

That would be cool.

Yeah, but how? How to change the hallway buzz from Easy Weezy to Creepy Carson . . . or Cowardly Carson? And all without even a hint that it had anything to do with Weezy.

Tall order. This would take some thought.

Jack wasn't going to let this ride. One way or another, Carson Toliver was going down.

And if Jack worked it right, maybe, just maybe the creep would end up wishing someone had busted his knees instead.

1

"What the hell is going on in this world?"

Jack was lying in bed, semi-awake, when he heard his father's raised voice.

He hopped out and padded down the hall to find him standing before the TV.

"Dad?"

His father turned to him, his expression distraught. "We've just invaded Grenada. What the hell?"

Jack looked at the TV—nothing but talking heads there. He'd heard of Grenada but had no idea where it was.

"Is that in the Middle East?"

Dad gave him a look. "The Caribbean—near Venezuela. Apparently some commies took over and executed the prime minister and a bunch of others."

"So we're peacekeeping again?"

Dad shook his head. "Not this time. There's a bunch of American kids in the medical school there. It looked like they were in danger—at least that's the reason given—so the troops hit the beach this morning."

"Everything okay?"

"Don't know. They're still fighting." He shook his head. "What's going on in the world these days? You never know what you're going to find when you wake up. Bombings, invasions . . . what a world. What a world."

2

Jack figured it best to play dumb.

"Where's Weezy?" he asked when Eddie showed up at the bus stop without her.

His red Izod was tight on his overweight bod. He turned off his Walkman and pulled his headphones off his ears to let them rest on his neck.

"Not coming." He looked uncomfortable.

"She's still sick?"

He kept his eyes pointed north on 206, the way the bus would come. "Sort of."

Jack didn't know how hard to push. Weezy was his best friend and he craved information on how she was doing, but he didn't want to step on her privacy. She obviously didn't want anyone to know about her psychiatrist.

"'Sort of' how? Is she running a fever, is she contagious, what?"

Eddie turned and looked Jack in the eye. "Don't say I told you this, but she says she's never going to school again."

Jack faked shock. "What? Why not?"

"She won't say. But she locked herself in her bedroom this morning and wouldn't come out."

Jack shook his head. "I don't get it."

"Neither do I. All I know is—and after hanging around her all these years, you've gotta know it too—she takes some things real hard."

Jack nodded. He'd seen it before, but never this hard.

"Well," Eddie continued, "something must have happened in school—probably something minor that she's blown up into something majorly hellacious."

Obviously he hadn't heard the Easy Weezy remarks. Jack didn't think Eddie would consider them minor. He and Weezy didn't always get along, but Jack sensed he'd turn tiger if he thought anyone was hurting her. Might go for Toliver and wind up hurt.

Better he didn't know.

"She going to be all right?"

Eddie smiled. "Sure. You know her—up and down, up and down. She'll get over it and things will go back to normal." He shook his head. "At least as normal as things can get with Weezy."

Jack hoped so. What if she got so low she couldn't bounce back?

Eddie was slipping his headphones over his ears again.

"What's on?" Jack said.

"SRV."

"*Texas Flood*?"

He smiled as he clicked his Walkman back on. "He's the greatest."

As Eddie started nodding his head in time with the music, Jack tried to guess which song.

" 'Pride and Joy,' right?"

Eddie shook his head. " 'I'm Cryin'.' "

Jack grinned. "Same thing."

He too liked Stevie Ray Vaughn, and he had a Walkman of his own, but he usually reserved it for late-night listening when everyone else was asleep, or when he was pushing the lawn mower around.

As they got on the bus, some girl in the rear called out, "Where's Easy Weezy?" to no one in particular.

Jack glanced at Eddie and saw no reaction. SRV was drowning out the real world. At times like this, Jack almost wished he could live inside the headphones like Eddie was doing lately. But sometimes he had to listen to his own voice.

Especially now when he was plotting the overthrow of King Carson.

3

Mr. Kressy, Jack's favorite teacher, was discussing next year's presidential election in civics class, talking about the Democrats who would be vying for their party's nomination to challenge President Reagan for the White House.

"Listen to the candidates when they appear on television," he was saying, "and maybe—just maybe—you'll be able to determine their guiding principles. If one of them has principles in tune with yours, he may be the man you want for your president."

He turned quickly and snapped his fingers.

"Wait . . . you each *do* have a guiding principle, don't you? You know—a fundamental law, doctrine, or assumption that guides you. Quick: Somebody give me a good guiding principle."

Dark-haired Liza Escovedo said, "Do unto others as you would have them do unto you."

"Ah, yes. The Golden Rule. That sounds great, but when you think about it, it means the decision of how to treat other people originates with you, rather than with them. What if you're, oh, say, a very guilty person who feels a great need to be punished, so you want people to hurt you— punch you, kick you, curse you. That makes you feel better. By the Golden Rule, you'd be free to punch, kick, and curse other people, because that's the way 'you would have them do unto you,' right?"

Liza slunk lower in her seat. He noticed and said, "It's a good thought, Liza, and probably works well for ninety percent of people, but we've got to think our guiding principle all the way through." He looked around. "Anyone else?"

Matt Follette, the class cynic, said, "What's in it for me?"

This got a laugh.

Mr. Kressy pointed to him and grinned right back. "You've got the makings of a great politician. Or an even better lobbyist."

Another laugh.

Mr. Kressy turned Jack's way. "Anybody else?"

Deciding to go for it, Jack raised his hand and said, "How about, 'Do the right thing'?"

Mr. Kressy beamed. "Perfect." Then frowned. "Except . . . who or what determines the right thing?"

"God," said Liza.

He shook his head. "Sorry. I'm not allowed to discuss theology in this class beyond the concept of separation of church and state. I will say that if 'God' works for you, fine, but as far as politics goes, you should remember that a lot of different religions are practiced in this country, worshipping different gods. I don't know about you, but I definitely don't want this class arguing about whose god is best.

"So we need to approach from a different angle. By what process do *you* arrive at the criteria for what is 'right'? For that, you have to dig deep. You need to have a first principle to work from. So let's think about that for a couple of days. Ferret out your prime or first principle, the touchstone belief to which everything you think or do must answer. Searching for that is going to take you places in your head most of you have never been before. We'll see what we come up with." He picked up the civics text. "And now for the easy stuff."

Jack frowned as he thought about a first principle. Did

he have one? He'd never thought about it. He always tried to do the right thing, but he'd never thought about the path he took to deciding what was right.

The frown eased into a smile. Mr. Kressy was right. This was going to take him places he'd never been before.

Cool.

4

After finishing lunch, Jack again went in search of Toliver. As he passed the table where Weezy usually sat, one of the girls said, "Weren't you looking for Easy Weezy yesterday? Guess what? She's out again."

Jack realized with dismay that the "Easy Weezy" thing had legs. It wasn't going to fade away anytime soon.

"Maybe she's morning sick!" said the same one who'd said it yesterday.

Jack stopped and looked at her. He wanted to get in her face and tell her it wasn't funny the first time and how about straining the two sporadically connected neurons that passed for her brain to come up with something new and perhaps even remotely clever.

Instead he moved on. Drawing attention to himself was the last thing he needed.

What those girls needed, though, was something else to talk about.

And Jack was going to give it to them.

He scouted the halls till he found Toliver, then followed him again. As before, Toliver strolled around like the school's godfather. Finally he stopped at his locker, removed a couple of books, and moved on.

Jack let him go. He slowed his pace to a crawl as he passed the locker. Number 791. He checked out the lock: a regular spin-dial combination model. He didn't think he'd have any problem getting past that, but first things first: He had to be able to sneak back into school when no one was around.

He looked up and stifled a yelp when he found himself inches from the white face and pink eyes of the albino piney girl, Saree.

"Why can't I see you?" she said.

"What?"

"I can't see you."

Jack waved his hand between them and she flinched.

"You can see me."

"No." She looked at Toliver's locker. "I can see him. He's all sorts of dark, almost black as night."

Jack remembered Levi's warning to Elvin about Toliver yesterday: *You know what Saree says about him.*

"What's that mean?"

She shook her head. "But you . . . you're hiding from me."

What was this girl talking about?

"Gotta go," he said.

No lie. Lunchtime was winding down and he had to get to the boys' room pronto.

SBR had two of them, one on the east side, one on the west. Jack stood in the east room and washed his hands at the sink closest to the windows. But instead of paying attention to his hands, he was studying the windows: identical top-hung casement types, four feet wide and maybe eighteen inches tall, set a good five feet off the floor. Each had two latches. He didn't know if they were ever opened, but he could tell from the hinges that they swung out. One overhung his sink, the other looked over the last stall.

That stall was empty, so Jack dried his hands and slipped into it. He stood there, waiting. Lunch break was almost over. He hung out until the bathroom emptied, then he stood on the seat for a closer look. The handle on the bottom told him this was a simple push-pull window. If it had been the kind of casement that needed to be wound open and shut, he'd have been sunk.

He studied the latches—simple levers on the bottom of the frame with blades that swung up and down, in and out of slots in the casing. He tugged on one but it wouldn't move. He tried harder, grunting with the effort, but the thing wouldn't budge. He tried the other with the same result. Obviously they hadn't been opened in a long, long time.

He was going to need some sort of tool for prying. He searched the stall. Nothing. He returned to the sink area and looked around. More nothing. A screwdriver would have been perfect but not the sort of thing he carried around . . .

But he did carry a pen.

He fished out his ballpoint as he returned to the stall. He wedged it under the latch handle, and using it as a lever, managed to budge the latch. It moved only an eighth of an inch, but that was enough to allow him to open it the rest of the way by hand. As he was prying at the second latch, the hard plastic of the pen shattered, but not before it had succeeded in doing its job. Jack pried the latch the rest of the way by hand. He was about to push on the handle when he caught a flash of movement off to the right. He pressed his head against the glass to see who or what it was, but saw nothing. Had someone been out there? Had someone seen him messing with the window?

Couldn't worry about that now. He pushed on the handle, and with a squeak and a groan, the window opened an inch.

But something else opened as well—the door to the boys' room.

Jack ducked and crouched with his feet on the toilet seat. He hadn't bothered to latch the stall door, so it stood half open. If whoever it was wandered this far down . . .

He heard a couple of voices and recognized one of them.

Oh, crap—Toliver!

If he found Jack here and spotted the open window, it would be more than embarrassing. Jack's whole plan would be shot.

Heart pounding, he listened to Toliver talk to whoever was with him, their voices low, casual . . . something about football and North Burlington Regional.

Right. Friday's game was the big rivalry—the South Badgers against the North Greyhounds.

Their voices were drowned out by flushes and then the room went silent. Jack stayed put until he was sure he was alone, then he rose and pulled the window closed. But left the latches undone.

Seconds later he was in the hall, hurrying for his next class, not knowing if he'd been wasting his time back there or not. Because he didn't know if the window opened wide enough to allow him to slip through. If it didn't, he'd have to go to plan B.

Trouble was, he didn't have a plan B.

5

USED started out slow, even for a Tuesday.

Jack had worked in the store over the summer and into the fall. It sold a mishmash of antiques and junk, with a blurred and wavering line between the two: One person's precious antique was another's junk, which some people spelled *junque*. Whichever way it was spelled, USED had tons of it, all stashed here and there in a seemingly willy-nilly pattern. Jack knew the place held loads of goodies he hadn't yet seen, and might never see, but Mr. Rosen, the owner, knew where everything was. Or pretended to.

Jack had been surprised when the old man asked him to stay on into the fall. He'd wondered why at first. Customer traffic had been pretty good during the summer, but dropped off steeply after Labor Day. Weekends still saw people coming through, but during the week, almost nothing. After a while he realized that Mr. Rosen, a pretty frail-looking guy, got tired in the afternoon and liked to hit the cot in the back room for forty winks. Well, more like eighty.

Turned out to be a good deal for Jack. After he'd done his dusting and polishing and straightening up, he'd man the counter near the front and do his homework, something Mr. Rosen encouraged. Through it all he collected $3.50 an hour—just above the minimum wage

Today was different, though. After finishing his busy-work, he went to the cabinet at the rear of the store and pulled the lock-picking kit from the top drawer. Mr. Rosen had taught him how to use it so he could open cabinets and such that came with locked doors and drawers but no keys. Along with the tension bars and rakes, the kit included an assortment of padlock shims. These were little half cylinders of thin metal with a point on one end and two flanges on the other. He pocketed the kit. He'd return it when he was finished with Toliver.

He'd just settled himself at the counter, readying to practice on an old combination lock Mr. Rosen had for sale, when the door chimed. He looked up and saw Walt Erskine stepping in. He shoved the shims and the padlock under the counter.

Weird Walt, as he was known, had a gray-streaked beard and long dark hair tied back in a ponytail. His eyes were semi-glazed from the applejack he sipped all day. He wore his uniform of jeans, T-shirt, olive-drab fatigue jacket, and black leather gloves. Word was he even ate dinner with those gloves. Jack had seen him without them only once— just last month on the weirdest night of his life.

Walt looked around. "Got anything new?"

Jack deadpanned him. "No."

"Oh," Walt said with a grin and a wink as he wandered toward the rear of the store. "I get it. Right on."

As Walt disappeared down an aisle, the door chimed again and Mr. Drexler walked in. Like Walt, he had his own uniform: a white three-piece suit with a white tie and white shirt. He carried a black hide-covered cane.

"Hey, Mister Drexler," Jack said.

He had black hair combed straight back from a widow's peak. His cold blue eyes regarded Jack with mild irritation.

" 'Hey'? What sort of greeting is that?"

Jack resisted an eye roll. He and Mr. Drexler had smoothed things out after Jack's misadventures last month, but that hadn't made the man any less of a stickler for formalities.

"It's sort of like 'hello.' "

"Well, then, instead of *like* hello, let's try for the real thing next time, shall we?"

"Sure. Can I help you with anything?" he said, wishing he could add, *Like helping you out the door?*

"I stopped by to tell you not to wait until the weekend to cut the Lodge's lawn. I want everything top shape by Friday night."

Mr. Drexler worked for the Ancient Septimus Fraternal Order that owned the Lodge in Old Town—his card said he was an "actuator"—and last month he'd hired Jack to cut the lawn and keep the grounds tidy. He paid well, but the job took hours.

"I'll have to check with Mister Rosen to see if I can have the day off."

"See that you do."

"What's going on? Special meeting?"

"That's none of your—"

The door chimed yet again as a young woman stepped in carrying a baby wrapped in a blanket. She looked like she was in her early twenties—maybe just barely twenty—with long chestnut hair, pale skin, and gray eyes.

"Hello," she said, smiling at Jack. "I was told I could find Walter Erskine here."

Walt suddenly appeared from the back. "Whoa! Who told you that?"

She smiled at him. "An old woman in black. Oddly enough, she was wearing a scarf in this heat."

That could only be Mrs. Clevenger. She always wore black and always had a scarf around her neck. Some people said that was because she was the reincarnation of Peggy Clevenger, the witch of the Pines, who was beheaded way back when. People said Peggy wandered the Pines, looking for her head, but others said she'd found it and wore the scarf to hide the old cut.

Jack didn't buy any of that, but Mrs. Clevenger did seem to know an awful lot about the Pine Barrens and was often seen entering and leaving at odd hours, always accompanied by her three-legged dog.

The young woman was staring at Walt. "You're him, aren't you."

Walt hesitated, looking like he would have denied it if no one around knew better. Finally he nodded. "Yes, I guess I am. Do I know you?"

Her gray eyes shone with welling tears. "My name is Miriam. We met, once, but I'm sure you don't remember."

"When was that?"

"Ten years ago this past June, when I was eleven. You were with a tent show that came through my hometown."

Walt paled and glanced around. "I don't know if that was me. Coulda been somebody else."

She beamed at him. "Oh, it was you. Your hair was shorter, so was your beard, and it had no gray then, but I'd know you anywhere. I'll never forget the man who healed me."

"Healed?" Walt looked sick, like he wanted to be anywhere but here with this woman. "I . . . I don't know what . . ."

She raised her free arm, the left. "See this? I didn't have one—just a little flipper-type thing in its place. You touched me back then, and it started to change and grow. It took a whole year, but now look: It's perfect."

Jack stared at that raised arm, and yes, it looked perfect—as perfect as the silence in USED. Even Mr. Drexler seemed to be holding his breath.

Last month Jack had seen Walt touch someone with an ungloved hand. He still wasn't sure what had happened then.

Finally Walt swallowed and said, "I think you've made a mistake."

"*Mistake?*" Mr. Drexler said. "She's deranged. Grow an arm? That's a medical miracle. You'd be famous the world over, young lady!"

She shook her head slowly. "My hometown is small, high in the West Virginia hills. My folks thought it might be the work of the devil, so they hid me from the neighbors. And when I had my new arm, they sent me to live with kin on the other side of the state."

"Why did you come looking for me?" Walt said.

She smiled again. "To thank you. And to ask you . . ." Her smile faded as she unwrapped the blanket from her sleeping baby to reveal the left shoulder. ". . . if you would do the same for my little girl."

Jack couldn't help gasping: The baby had no arm, just a fleshy little flap, maybe two inches long and an inch wide. Like a tiny flipper.

Walt looked panicked as he began sidling toward the door, giving Miriam as wide a berth as possible.

"No . . . I can't . . . don't ask me . . . you can't ask me."

In a single quick move he jerked the door open and darted through.

Miriam dashed after him, calling, "Mister Erskine! Please, my baby. You've got to help her! I'll pay you! Mister Erskine, *please!*"

Jack watched, stunned. What a crazy—

And then he realized that Walt hadn't denied that he could do it. He'd said, *You can't ask me.*

Just then Mr. Rosen shuffled in from the back, rubbing his eyes.

"Such *tumel*. Who's making the racket?"

Jack stepped to the window and saw Miriam and Walt facing each other by the front fender of a beat-up old Ford station wagon. He noticed Mr. Drexler's Bentley parked a dozen feet away.

Miriam was offering Walt an envelope. Money? Jack couldn't read her lips but remembered her offer to pay him.

Walt pushed it back, shaking his head as he said something.

Jack edged toward the door as Miriam pulled a slip of white paper from the envelope and stuffed it into the pocket of Walt's fatigue jacket. He pulled it out, looked at it, then threw it away.

As Walt waved his hands and walked off, Jack pulled open the door in time to hear Miriam call after him.

"I'll be there till Sunday, Mister Erskine! Please reconsider, I beg you! If you change your mind you can come anytime. I'll be waiting."

She began to cry then, and her sobs tore at Jack's heart. He watched her place her baby in the car seat in her old station wagon, then get in and drive away.

Jack jumped as Mr. Drexler spoke over his shoulder.

"Most entertaining." He straightened and smiled. "I must make a note to come here more often." He turned and nodded to Mr. Rosen. "Good day to you, sir. You have the most entertaining clientele." Then to Jack: "Remember: the lawn and beds taken care of before Friday night."

Jack looked at Mr. Rosen. "Can you spare me Friday?"

He shrugged. "Sure. Somehow I'll manage."

"Friday, then," Mr. Drexler said and stepped out the door.

A big man hopped out of the Bentley and held the rear door for him. He seemed to be a combination of driver and bodyguard, although why Mr. Drexler would need either, Jack couldn't imagine. Mr. Drexler called him Eggers.

He saw a piece of paper flutter in the wake of the car as it roared off—the slip Miriam had tried to give Walt. Jack ducked out and chased it. He checked it out when he caught it.

Lonely Pine Motel room 3

He stuffed it in his pocket and hurried back inside.

What an afternoon. Jack couldn't get Miriam and her poor baby out of his head. He remembered his father telling him that Walt had worked as some sort of faith healer in a show in the south, but had been kicked out for drinking too much. He'd heard about faith healers who could make the blind see and the deaf hear and the lame walk, all things that could be faked.

But he'd never heard of a faith healer curing an amputee . . . or causing someone born with a bad arm or leg to grow a good one.

Had Walt done that? Could he really heal with a touch? Maybe. After all, there'd been that strange incident last month. And if he could, why would he refuse? Jack had a flash of insight: Was that why he wore gloves day in and day out?

The *ding!* of the cash register roused Jack as Mr. Rosen popped it.

"A store full of people and they bought nothing?"

"I guess they weren't in a buying mood," Jack told him.

Anything but.

6

"Oh, Jack," Mrs. Connell said, "I'm so glad you're here."

Jack had decided on a direct approach to contacting Weezy. Rather than calling first, he rode his bike over and knocked on the front door. Mrs. Connell had practically hugged him.

"How's Weezy doing?" he said, playing dumb like he had this morning. "She still sick?"

Mrs. Connell chewed her lip for a second, then said, "She's not sick. She just won't go to school."

Jack feigned surprise—Eddie had told him in confidence—then put on a smile.

"And it works? Maybe I should try that."

"It's not funny, Jack. She's very upset about something. I'm sure it has to do with school. Do you know what happened?"

He shrugged. "She's a year ahead of me. I hardly see her at all during the day."

No lie there.

"I know," she said, nodding. "Eddie has no idea either. Look, I know you came over to see Eddie, but do you think you could talk to Weezy? You two are friends. Maybe she'll tell you what's wrong."

He didn't correct her about coming over to see Eddie.

"I'll give it a try."

He took the stairs up to her door and knocked.

"Hey, Weez, it's me."

"Jack? Come in." As he opened the door and stepped through, she added, "Close it behind you."

The room was dim, lit only by a tiny bedside lamp. Dressed in a black T-shirt and black jeans, looking paler than usual, Weezy sat cross-legged on her unmade bed.

"What's it like at school?" she said.

Jack shrugged. "Same old same old."

"Still talking about 'Easy Weezy'?" She spoke the words as if they tasted bad.

Jack wanted to tell her it was already yesterday's news, but couldn't lie to her . . . couldn't have her step on the bus tomorrow thinking she wouldn't hear those words.

"A couple of people asked about you . . ."

"Asked about 'Easy Weezy'?"

He had to tell her. "Yeah."

Frowning and shaking her head, she folded her arms and leaned back against the headboard.

"Damn them," she said through her teeth. "Damn them all."

"It's going to get old real quick, Weez. This is 1983, not . . . not colonial times. You're not going to have to wear a big red 'A' on your shirt."

"But why me? Why do *I* have to be known as a slut? Me of all people? I don't even date!"

"We both know why."

Weezy stared at him. "Yeah, we do. I wish there was some way to get back at him."

Jack felt his mouth opening, felt the words forming on his tongue. He so wanted to tell her his plan, but he pulled back. No . . . no one could know. This was between him and Carson Toliver, and Toliver especially could not know.

"You ever think you might be making it worse—I mean, prolonging it by not going to school?"

"I don't care, because I'm never going back."

"Weeeeez . . ."

"I'm serious. I'm not going back to a place where they all hate me or look down on me."

The words shocked him. That wasn't anywhere near true—at least in real life. But maybe to Weezy it was. She couldn't see how she'd blown everything out of proportion. He sensed she was beyond reason. Was this the sort of thing she'd been seeing the psychiatrist about?

"Weez, that isn't true. You—"

"It is." Tears started rolling down her cheeks. "That's why I'm never going back. And they can't make me. No one can make me. They can drag me to the bus stop but I won't get on. And if they force me on, I'll get off at the very next stop. And if they drive me to school, I won't get out of the car. And if they drag me out of the car and into the school, I'll walk out the first exit I see."

"But aren't there laws—?"

"I don't care. I don't care about anything. I just want to be left alone."

"Does that mean you want me to leave?"

"I'm tired. I need to sleep."

That stung, and would have hurt more if he hadn't known she wasn't really herself now.

Desperate, he fabricated a surefire way to get her moving.

"I saw a couple of pine lights earlier. Want to chase?"

Jack thought he saw a spark of interest in her eyes—
yes!—but it died so quickly he wondered if he'd imagined it.

"Like I said, Jack. I'm really tired."

She turned out the light.

His heart sank. This was awful. She wasn't Weezy anymore.

He sighed. "Okay, Weez. Get some sleep. I'll stop by tomorrow." He paused with his hand on the doorknob. "Hey, Weez, you gotta know you've got at least one person at school who doesn't think you're Easy Weezy."

"You mean you?"

"Yeah."

"You don't think so because you know the truth. But what if you didn't? What would you think then?"

"Depends on what you told me. If you said it wasn't true, that would settle it."

A sob came out of the darkness.

"You'd better go."

"Sure?"

"Please."

As he stepped out into the hall he heard her say, "I'm sorry, Jack."

" 'Sokay."

He shut the door.

Sorry . . . The word nearly broke his heart, but it also removed any misgivings he might have had about the risks of his plan.

Weezy was sorry?

Before he was through, someone else was going to be much sorrier.

7

Jack's chest felt heavy as he walked the block and a half home. He turned his thoughts from Weezy to planning his first move against Toliver. The key, he figured, was to make it look like innocent mischief. Nothing harmful. Its impact would come from the simple and inescapable realization that someone had targeted Mr. Wonderful for a prank.

By the time Jack reached his house he had an idea or two. Inside he found his mother puttering about the kitchen.

"Where's all the Halloween stuff?" he said.

His mother looked up. "You must be psychic. I was just going to ask you to bring it up from the basement."

"Okay. But where in the basement?"

The storage area was so crammed he needed a Sherpa guide to find anything.

"Right rear corner, middle shelf."

Sure enough, the box was exactly where she'd said— right next to the Thanksgiving decorations. She liked to dress up the house for each holiday, and Halloween was only a week away.

Jack pulled out the box and pawed through it until he came across the big fuzzy black spider she liked to hang by the front door. It had huge white, googly eyes with black pupils that rolled around when it moved, and was attached to an elastic string. It looked kind of goofy and cute, almost snuggly.

Jack pulled off the eyes and set it on the floor. Suddenly

it was anything but snuggly. It looked like a humongous tarantula.

Perfect.

After bringing the box upstairs, he slipped out the back door to the garage. An old backpack hung on a hook. He slipped the spider inside and added a penlight, a roll of masking tape, and a screwdriver from his father's tool shelves.

Then he removed the padlock shims from the lock-picking kit. He had four of them, each slightly larger or smaller than the others. He'd never done this before, but he'd studied the booklet that came with the kit—*Lock Picking Made Easy*—and it looked, well, easy.

He removed his bicycle padlock from the chain and snapped the shackle closed. Then he tried different shims until he found the one whose half cylinder best fit the shackle. When it was snug against the metal, he worked it down into the shackle hole. Then, with his thumbs against the flanges, he rotated the shim to the right.

The shackle popped up.

Jack stared in joyous wonder.

That's it? That's *it*?

He did it again—just as easily.

It took all his will to keep from pealing a loud *Mwah-ha-ha-ha!*

Operation Toliver was a go.

1

Jack stopped on the shoulder of Route 206 and squinted at the glowing dial of his watch: just shy of quarter to two in the morning.

He'd left his bike on the side of the house before going to bed. That way it had been right there and ready to roll when he'd climbed out his bedroom window. He'd gone as far as he could on off-road paths. Now he was going to have to ride most of the rest of the way—maybe a mile—on Route 206.

Here he faced the greatest risk of exposure. The good news was that 206 ran pretty much arrow-straight along this stretch. He'd be able to spot approaching headlights a long way off, giving him plenty of time to find cover along the roadside. Even better was the fact that hardly anybody in these parts was out at this hour.

He felt his gut crawl as he looked up and down the road. Was he out of his mind? This was one crazy stunt he was pulling. So many things could go wrong. The worst would be getting caught inside the school—he could be arrested for breaking and entering.

Then he remembered the tears on Weezy's face as she told him she was never going back to school. All because of Carson Toliver.

Some things you could let slide, and some things you couldn't.

Sometimes, when it mattered enough, when a friend was involved, you had to go out on a limb. Weezy was that kind of friend. He had a feeling she'd do the same for him. And even if she wouldn't, so what? He needed to do it for her.

He just hoped this particular limb didn't break.

Jack avoided a road-killed raccoon as he crossed to the west side of the highway near the Lonely Pine Hotel. An apt name: It consisted of a short strip of seven rooms and an office, all in the shadow of one huge, lonely pine. Everything was dark except for the small neon sign at the road's edge. Only one car in the lot—Jack recognized Miriam's beat-up station wagon parked outside a door marked *3*.

He wondered again at her story of growing an arm after Walt touched her. Maybe Walt *had* touched her at the tent show. And maybe she *had* grown an arm during the following year. That didn't mean one caused the other. He heard his father's repeated warnings about the commonest logical fallacy: *Post hoc, ergo propter hoc.* Just because one thing followed another didn't mean the first caused the second.

And besides, if Walt could truly heal with a touch, he'd be world famous. Certainly wouldn't be hanging out in Johnson, New Jersey.

He hopped on his bike and began pedaling.

2

He needed to jump off the road only twice along the way, so he arrived at the high school in good time. He pulled off the road a hundred yards or so shy of the entrance, and approached through the trees.

The buildings were dark and abandoned looking, the parking lot empty. He made a circuit of the building anyway, just to be sure no janitors were still about. He knew they did most of their work after school, but doubted any would be working at this hour. Still, he'd never done anything like this before and didn't want to run into any ugly surprises.

Nope. All clear.

The starlight was enough to guide him to the boys' room window. He glanced up at the dusty glow of the Milky Way arcing overhead. He pulled his bike behind the juniper hedge that ran along the wall. He'd known about the hedge, and its thorns were one of the reasons he'd worn his nylon track warm-up. Another was because its fabric was smooth and slippery. He wanted every bit of help to slide through that window. Yesterday afternoon he hadn't had the time to check how far it opened. If he couldn't slip through, all his plans and this entire trip would be for nothing.

He leaned the bike against the wall and shrugged out of his backpack. He removed a plastic baggie containing the penlight, shims, and spider. Clenching it in his teeth he stepped up on the seat. After swaying precariously for a second or two, he steadied himself and removed the screwdriver from his back pocket. He worked the flat tip between the window casing and the bottom of the frame.

The window wouldn't budge.

His heart sank. Had one of the janitors spotted the open latches and relocked the window? He hadn't considered that possibility.

He tried again, levering harder, and this time the window moved.

"Yes!"

He worked the screwdriver tip farther in, put more weight behind it, and soon the edge of the frame had moved out far enough to allow him to work his fingertips behind it. He yanked back and it swung open with a squeak that echoed through the enveloping silence like an elephant honk.

He stood silent, listening. All quiet, and yet . . .

. . . a feeling that he wasn't alone.

He looked around, expecting to see someone standing behind him in the starlight. But no. No one there.

Still . . . a vague feeling of being watched.

Shrugging off the unease—really, who'd be out here at this hour?—he pulled the window open to the limit and began to wriggle through. For a gut-wrenching second his warm-up caught on the frame and he thought he might be stuck. His head filled with visions of hanging half in and half out all night, then being discovered and becoming the focus of a laughing, jeering crowd of kids until some fire-man extricated him like a stray kitten from a tree.

He'd have to move into Weezy's room and neither of them would ever show their faces here again.

But he managed to get free—maybe the warm-up hadn't been the best idea—and lowered himself into the bathroom stall.

Wasting no time, he made his way into the hall and hurried toward the senior locker area. When he arrived at 791, he turned on the penlight and held it in his mouth as he reached for the shims.

His fingers trembled as he tested one after another against the shackle of Toliver's lock until he found a snug fit. Then he did just what he'd done with his own lock: thumbs on the flanges, push down, rotate right—

The shackle popped open.

So easy, it was almost criminal.

Then again, breaking into someone's locker was, in a way, sort of a criminal act.

Did that make him a criminal?

Whatever. Not as criminal as attacking Weezy.

He shoved the lock into his pocket and opened the door. He pulled the spider from the baggie and wedged it lightly behind a few books on the top shelf, then taped the elastic string firmly to the inside of the door, leaving very little slack.

He closed and relocked it, then stepped back to examine his handiwork. He played the penlight up and down the locker but could find no sign that it had been tampered with. Satisfied, he headed back to the boys' room.

Sliding out feetfirst was easier than crawling in headfirst. He pushed the window shut, pulled his bike free, and hit the road.

His heart pounded with elation. He'd done it. Or at least he'd finished the setup without being caught.

Now all he could do was be on hand tomorrow morning to see if Operation Toliver turned out to be a boom or a bust.

3

The first thing Jack did upon getting off the bus and entering school was to make a beeline for the last stall in the boys' room where he closed the latches on the window. No sense in risking the chance that someone might notice them open and wonder why.

After that he positioned himself as far as possible from Toliver's locker while still maintaining a line of sight. He pretended to be reading, leaning against a wall as if doing a last-minute cram for a test, but all the while keeping careful watch from the corner of his eye.

He didn't feel as tired as he'd expected this morning. Not a hundred percent by any stretch, but the adrenaline of anticipation was driving off any effects of sleep deprivation. It also seemed to have driven off his appetite. Mom had been on his case about having only toast for breakfast, but he hadn't felt like eating anything more.

He'd heard another "Where's Easy Weezy?" when he'd got on the bus, which made him glad Weezy had stayed home. Again, Eddie had been too lost in his headphones to notice.

About five minutes before first period, Toliver strolled by, performing his mayor-of-SBR routine. As soon as Jack spotted him, his gut tightened. He closed his book and began drifting his way. Eddie appeared at his side as if from nowhere.

"Why're you heading this way?" He jerked a thumb over his shoulder. "Kleiner's our first and he's back—"

"Just taking the long way," Jack said.

This earned a funny look. Taking a single step more than absolutely necessary was simply not part of Eddie's lifestyle. To do so willingly was for Klingons or seriously deranged people.

"I'm going the not-long way."

At that point they were maybe ten feet from Toliver as he spun the dial on his combo lock. This was hit-the-locker-before-first-period time and the area was crowded.

"Okay, okay," Jack said, putting on an exasperated tone, "I'll come with you. Just let me tie my sneak."

He leaned his back against the wall and raised his foot, untying and then retying the laces on one of his Converse All-Stars, but all the while watching Toliver . . .

. . . popping the shackle and removing the lock . . .

. . . opening the door . . .

. . . stretching the elastic string . . .

Though Jack had been expecting it, even he jumped when the big black spider came flying through the air, straight at Toliver's face. Toliver dropped the book he'd been carrying and loosed a loud yelp as he jumped back. He bumped into a passing girl, knocking her in turn against the girl beside her. Both girls went down amid flying books and papers.

"I don't believe it!" Eddie cried. "Did you see that?"

"See what?" Jack said, straightening and looking around. He focused on the two girls, kneeling on the floor and gathering their scattered things. "What happened to them?"

He hurried over, not so much to help—they didn't need any—as to get closer to Toliver who was staring at the dangling spider, still bouncing on its elastic.

"Son of a bitch!"

Gotcha!

Jack wanted to pump a fist but restrained himself. Stay off his radar—stay off *everybody's* radar.

Toliver grabbed the spider and ripped it free of the masking tape, then threw it down the hall. Red-faced, teeth bared, he turned and scanned the crowd of passersby who had stopped to watch. He looked ready to explode but, with visible effort, caught himself. Instead of raging, he swallowed and laughed. Jack didn't know what his real laugh sounded like but was pretty sure that wasn't it.

"Okay, okay. You got me. Very funny. Who was it? You look over my shoulder and steal my combination? Good one."

No one said anything and Jack was very careful not to make eye contact, afraid the dark elation bubbling within would seep through and give him away. Instead he concentrated on helping the two girls pick up the last of their spilled belongings.

As Toliver turned back to his locker and started to pull out a couple of books, he looked down and froze. Jack craned his neck to see.

A dirty, pink scrunchy sock had fallen out. After staring at it a second or two, Toliver snatched it up and shoved it into his pocket. He looked around, as if to see if anyone had noticed. His expression seemed embarrassed but tinged with something else Jack couldn't identify.

The embarrassment Jack could understand. Physically Toliver hadn't been touched, but his pride was wounded. Someone had dared to play a practical joke on the much-admired and beloved Carson Toliver. This demonstrated a humongous lack of respect.

The guy loved attention, but not the kind he'd received in the past few minutes. Soon it would be all over school that he'd been pranked, and everyone would know that someone at SBR didn't love Carson Toliver.

And worse, his spaz reaction had been anything but cool.

Think you're embarrassed now? Jack thought as he watched him relock his locker. Wait. This is just the beginning.

Jack had an escalating series of embarrassments planned.

"That was really stinkacious," Eddie said as they turned away and headed for class.

"Yeah?" Jack tried to sound as noncommittal as possible. "How so?"

"What sort of dork does something like that to Carson? I mean, he's the coolest guy around."

Jack glanced at his clueless friend, thinking, If you only knew, Eddie.

"Maybe it was one of his football buddies," Jack said. "You know how those guys are always goofing on each other."

Eddie nodded, looking relieved. "Yeah, that has to be it. Who else would have the nerve to try something like that?"

Jack shook his head. "I can't imagine."

4

When lunchtime rolled around, Jack went looking for Toliver to continue his shadow routine, but couldn't find him at first. Not in the caf, not in the halls, not by his locker. Jack even wandered over to the gym to see if he might be working out. But no Carson Toliver anywhere.

He was about to end his search and head for class when he spotted Toliver striding in through the front entrance. He looked his usual confident self as he strolled toward the senior locker area, nodding and smiling, bouncing a new-looking combination padlock in his palm.

When he reached his locker he removed the current lock and replaced it with the new one, then made a big show of tossing the old one in the nearest trash can.

Toliver walked off with a satisfied, I've-got-everything-under-control expression. As he passed a white-haired girl, she shrank against the far wall, as if to stay as far as possible from him.

That odd, albino piney girl, Saree . . . she seemed afraid of him. Jack remembered what she'd said about Toliver . . .

He's all sorts of dark, almost black as night.

Whatever that meant.

Jack was strolling toward locker 791 to check out the new lock when he saw Saree stop before it. He slowed, watching as she reached a hand out toward the door. Her palm approached it in slow motion, hesitated, then pressed against the metal surface.

With a sudden small cry she snatched it away and rubbed

it furiously against her other hand. Jack was practically on top of her now and his curiosity got the better of him.

"Did you cut yourself?"

She looked up at him with a surprised expression—surprised because someone had been watching, or surprised that Jack had spoken to her?

"No," she said. "It's cold . . . so cold."

Jack caught a glimpse of her palm before she hurried off. It looked bright red.

He glanced around—no one watching. He touched the door briefly, just long enough to feel that the metal was room temperature.

He looked at the retreating Saree. What was she talking about? One strange piney, that one.

Before moving on he scoped out the new lock: same model as the old one.

Think a new combination's going to solve your problem, Toliver?

Think again.

5

"I'm going to rest my eyes awhile," Mr. Rosen said as he headed for the back room. "You mind the store."

Jack waved the rag he was using to polish an old oak table. "Take your time. I'll let you know if things get too busy."

"I should be so lucky." He turned and looked at Jack. "Your friend, that Drexler man, he'll be back?"

Jack laughed. "He's not my friend."

That seemed sort of like being friends with Skeletor.

"I'm glad to hear that."

He couldn't read Mr. Rosen's expression. "I don't understand."

Mr. Rosen sighed. "Neither do I. I simply have a feeling he's not a nice man, that he's . . . dangerous."

Jack stiffened, surprised. "What do you mean? Like a killer? An assassin?"

Mr. Rosen laughed. "Too many pulp magazines you read already!" His smile faded. He raised a hand and tapped a finger against the side of his head. "I mean dangerous here. Dangerous ideas."

Jack still didn't get it. "Hey, all I'm doing for him is mowing the Lodge's lawn."

"Yes, well . . . be careful."

With that he turned toward the back room. Jack wondered at the vague warning, then shrugged it off as he remembered Mr. Kressy's assignment.

"Hey, Mister Rosen. Do you have a first principle that guides your life?"

He stared at Jack. "Why for you ask me this?"

"It came up in school. I'm looking for a good one. Can you help me out?"

The old man shook his head, his expression bleak. "I've got one, but it won't help you."

"Try me."

" 'Never again.' "

He turned and shuffled off to his nap.

Jack didn't have a chance to ask for an explanation because in walked an older couple and a boy about Jack's age. The woman was thin, wore a worn-looking housedress, and was puffing on a cigarette. The man was heavyset with a thick neck and short red hair. The boy looked like neither.

"Got any marbles?" the man said.

Jack pointed to a fishbowl half filled with all shapes and sizes. "Take your pick. Ten cents each."

The boy's eyes lit. "How many can I get?"

The man handed him two dollars. "Let's start with twenty."

As the boy reached into the bowl, the man wandered toward the back. "Gonna take a look around."

"Looking for anything in particular?" Jack said.

"I'll know it when I see it."

The woman smoked and looked out the window while the boy poked around the shelves by the counter.

"You collect marbles?" Jack asked for want of anything better to say as he bagged the chosen marbles.

The boy raised his hands and mimicked firing a rifle. "Target practice. Twenty-twos."

"Marbles? Where do you shoot marbles?"

"In the woods."

"Around here?"

He shook his head. "We're from Little Egg Harbor. Just riding around."

Little Egg Harbor was on the east side of the Barrens.

"You must be a good shot if you're hitting marbles."

He grinned. "Getting there. Sarge is a great teacher. Gave me a Ruger seventy-seven. It's really cool. Been shooting pinecones but now we're looking for something smaller."

Jack felt a pang of envy. He'd love a rifle. Not to hunt, just for target practice. He was sure his own dad could teach him to shoot as well as this Sarge. Maybe better. After all, hadn't Mr. Bainbridge called him "Deadeye"?

Guns were common in and around the Pines. Lots of hunters. Deer season opened last month, and small-game hunters were waiting for pheasant and quail season to start in a week or two. Almost everyone in Johnson had a rifle or a shotgun somewhere in the house. Or so it seemed.

But despite countless requests—at times he felt as if he were living *A Christmas Story*—Dad hadn't even let him have a BB gun.

The man returned to the front.

"Nothing else here, son." He nodded to Jack. "Be seeing you."

The boy said, "See ya," and the three of them left.

Jack pondered how to talk his father into letting him have a rifle—he'd pay for it himself—but he had more important matters to address. Like Operation Toliver.

He headed for the bin where Mr. Rosen kept all the toys—*used* toys, of course. He began emptying it item by item. He remembered some months ago when he had been cleaning it out he'd found—

Here it was: a small tin, the size of a beer can, labeled PEANUT BRITTLE.

But Jack knew it wasn't peanut brittle.

He pulled off the cap, and even though he was ready for it, the four-foot green spring snake that launched itself from the can sparked a laugh.

It wobbled through the air and landed on the far side of the room. Jack retrieved it and inspected it. The snake's polka-dot fabric was faded and worn in spots that let the metal coils of the internal spring show through, but it still worked. And that was all that counted.

He stuffed it back into its can and recapped it. Then he took it to the counter. As he began to write it in the sale book, he glanced out the window and recognized the Connells' car. Mrs. Connell was behind the wheel, and slunk down in the rear, her head barely above the lower edge of the window, sat Weezy. Almost looked like she was hiding. Somehow she'd been pried out of her room. They were coming in from the highway. Jack wondered where they'd been. To that psychiatrist?

He sighed. Poor Weez. Sure, she wasn't like everybody else, but did she need a shrink? She wasn't crazy, just . . . different.

When they'd passed out of sight he returned to business, peeling the $1.50 price tag off the spring-snake can and sticking that next to his written entry. He fished two bucks from his wallet, placed them in the cash register, and removed a pair of quarters.

He was now the proud owner of a novelty spring snake. But not for long.

He'd heard it was better to give than receive and so he intended to make a gift of it to someone real soon.

6

"I can't go anywhere, Jack," Weezy said.

He'd got off early and had swung by Weezy's instead of going straight home. They sat in her darkened bedroom.

"Sure you can. We can take a ride in the Pines. No one will see you there."

"No. My folks won't let me out. They say if I'm not going to go to school, then I can't go anywhere else."

Jack debated mentioning it, then decided why not?

"Um, then that wasn't you I saw with your mother earlier?"

She reddened. "Oh, that. She dragged me somewhere. That was different."

Jack didn't press. He had an idea where.

"You can't sneak out?"

"Kind of hard with my mom checking on me every two seconds asking how I feel."

"I was thinking maybe checking out the pyramid and—"

Tears rimmed her lids. "I can't go *anywhere,* Jack. Don't you get it?"

Yeah, he got it.

And so he got going. Their talk had started him thinking about that pyramid in the Pines. He hadn't been back since last month. Maybe he could find something else out there to interest her, something she couldn't refuse to go see.

As he rode through the trees and neared the spong, he spotted a fairly new blue Ford F-150 pickup—maybe a 1982 or '83—parked off the fire trail in the brush. The piney trapper's? He doubted it. Then whose?

No sticks in the traps this trip. The piney must have reset them. He speeded up as he approached, planning a quickie spong flyby, and was halfway past when he glanced over and thought he saw something wriggling on the ground. He looked again and no doubt about it: something moving there.

He skidded to a halt and stared. Jack wasn't sure what it was, but a furry little something appeared to have got itself caught in one of those nasty traps.

Jack's stomach tightened as he had a sick flash of how much those steel jaws had to hurt when they closed on a little leg. He scanned the spong area for signs of the piney but it looked deserted.

Knowing he might regret it, Jack leaned his bike against a tree and trotted over to the animal, watching for other traps. The last thing he needed was to step in one himself.

He stopped a few feet from the struggling animal. Its ringed tail and black-encircled eyes identified it as a raccoon. A young one, probably heading to the spong for a drink when it stepped on one of the traps.

Not right, he thought as anger spewed acid into his already turned stomach.

Okay, one thing dies so another can live. That was the way nature worked. But was the piney going to eat this coon or just strip off the pelt and throw the meat away? And even if he did eat it, he should kill it clean. Don't torture it like this.

How long had it been here? Raccoons were nocturnal. Probably got caught last night. That meant it had been suffering all night and the whole day.

Not right.

As he stepped closer it tried to crawl away, scratching frantically at the dirt with its forepaws. But the trap's jaws had its left thigh and right lower leg vised. It must have closed pretty hard because both legs were bleeding. And from the angle of the left thigh, Jack was pretty sure it was broken.

Slowly, carefully, he edged his hands toward the trap. The coon must have thought he was coming for it and scrabbled faster in its futile efforts to get away.

"Easy there," Jack said in a soft, soothing tone. "I'm not out to hurt you. Just going to try to help."

He grabbed the jaws and tried to spread them but his fingertips kept slipping off. He looked around and found a twig. He forced that between the jaws to spread them just enough to relieve the pressure on the raccoon's legs.

Finally its scraping and scratching with its front paws paid off. It pulled itself free and away from the trap, but not very far. Its rear legs were broken and wouldn't hold it. It stopped and lay panting, looking at Jack over its shoulder with its big black eyes as if to say, *What now?* It looked exhausted, probably from dehydration and loss of blood.

Unsure of what to do next, he rose and stared at it. He didn't feel right just leaving it here. Maybe he could—

He heard a noise behind him and turned in time to see the piney trapper swinging a tree branch at his head.

"I knew it was you kids!" he screamed, his unshaven face a mask of rage. "I *knew* it!"

Jack's instincts overcame his shock and he ducked. He heard the branch whistle through the air where his head had been. Keeping in a crouch, he turned to run away but the branch slammed against his thigh before he could get started. His foot slipped in the sand and he went down on all fours. As he was scrambling back to his feet the branch caught him across the back, knocking him flat.

Terrified now, he rolled onto his back and saw the piney standing over him, looking like a maniac as he raised the branch for a two-handed blow.

"This'll learn ya!"

But then Jack saw something else—a tall, broad silhouette looming up behind the crazed trapper. The piney cried out and stumbled back as the branch was ripped from his hands. When he turned the big figure grabbed him by the throat and lifted him off the ground.

"Jameson!" it roared as it shook the piney like a rag doll. "I should have guessed!"

Jack squinted against the low sun and saw a big man holding the kicking, struggling trapper. He had broad shoulders and a thick but neat gray beard. A soft hat with a wide, down-turned brim—something like the Shadow or the Spider might wear—hid most of his upper face.

"Let me go!" the piney rasped—it might have been a screech if he'd had more air.

The big man shook him again. "How many times have I warned you? How *many*?"

With that he shoved him through the air as he released him. The piney—Jameson—landed on his back, clutching his throat and gasping.

But the big man wasn't through. He grabbed Jameson by the back of his shirt and dragged him kicking and struggling toward the spong. Before he reached it he dropped the piney and knelt next to him. Jack saw him grab his right arm. He didn't see what was happening, but a faint *clink!* followed by a shout of pain pretty much told the story.

The big man dragged him another half dozen feet, dropped him, and grabbed his left arm this time. Another *clink!* and another cry of pain.

The big man ripped two trap anchors from the ground, then stood and stepped back. Jameson rose to his knees and began trying to remove the leg-hold traps from his hands, whimpering as he found it impossible.

"You can't do this, Foster!" he screamed. "You have no right!"

Foster? Was this Old Man Foster himself?

"No?" Mr. Foster said. "If I catch you trapping on my land again, you'll go home with one of your traps on your face. Now get!"

He held up the traps locked on his fingers. "But my hands!"

"Get!"

"My traps!"

Mr. Foster growled and took a step toward him. Jameson jumped and hurried away, dragging the trap anchors and their chains with him. Mr. Foster watched for a moment, then turned and strode toward Jack, his expression fierce.

"And who are you? Related to him?"

Jack jumped to his feet and backed up a step. This guy was scary—scarier than that piney by a couple of light years.

"N-no way! Just passing by."

He could see now that the man had blue eyes and olive skin—the two didn't seem to go together. He wore green work pants, a blue work shirt, and a worn brown corduroy jacket. His blue gaze bored into Jack.

"You had to be doing more than that for him to start beating you—although anyone who angers Jeb Jameson can't be all bad."

Jack pointed to the young coon, still panting and cowering on the ground.

"I was just freeing that little guy when he jumped me."

Mr. Foster stopped when he saw the animal. His expression softened as he squatted for a closer look.

"Broken legs." He shook his head. "Damn him."

In one smooth motion, with a gentleness in jarring contrast to the violence he'd inflicted on the piney, he scooped up the terrified animal and tucked it inside his jacket. As he rose he glanced at Jack.

"Follow me."

Something in his tone made disobedience unthinkable. Jack followed and they wound up at the pickup he'd spotted on his way by.

"I was wondering who owned this."

"I found the traps and I've been waiting around to see who set them. I figured it was Jameson and wasn't surprised. Mark my words, he's going to come to a bad end, that one."

"I've run into him before. He said he was your son."

Mr. Foster barked a harsh laugh. "That's rich."

He opened the passenger door and gently placed the injured coon on the floor in front of the seat. Then he pulled a knife with a gleaming blade at least ten inches long from a sheath attached to his belt.

Jack stiffened and stepped back. "You—you're not gonna kill it, are you?"

"This little fellow?" He stared at it. "A good argument could be made for that—it will never survive on its own—but I feel somewhat responsible. I'll bring him home to my wife. She's good with animals."

He grabbed a paper coffee cup from a holder and sliced off all but the bottom inch of the base. He opened a bottle of water, rinsed out the shortened container, then filled it and placed it before the little coon. The creature drank greedily.

"The lord of the land returns," said an old woman's voice. "Finally."

Jack turned to see Mrs. Clevenger and her three-legged dog approaching. The elderly woman wore her usual long black dress and a black scarf, which made no sense in this heat. The dog moved with odd efficiency despite its missing foreleg. Jack realized that Mrs. Clevenger's cane was sort of an extra limb, giving the pair the normal complement of eight limbs between them.

"Is that you?" Mr. Foster said, squinting at her, then the dog.

She nodded. "It's me."

"You turn up in the oddest places."

"No place is odd for me."

"I suppose you're right."

Weird conversation, Jack thought. But then, every conversation with Mrs. Clevenger was odd.

As she and Mr. Foster continued talking, her three-legged dog stepped forward and nudged Jack aside. It stuck its head inside the pickup cab and sniffed the raccoon. Jack expected the little animal to freak but it only stared up at the mutt. Then the dog began licking the coon's bloody legs.

"He's not going to eat it, is he?"

Mrs. Clevenger looked up with a surprised expression. She tapped her dog gently on the back with her cane.

"You know you're not supposed to do that. Remember the natural order—no interfering."

The dog looked at her.

She sighed. "You've gone and done it, haven't you."

The dog moved away and sat at her side.

Jack felt a hand on his shoulder and looked up to see the big man staring down at him.

"You're trespassing on my property."

Uh-oh.

"Just riding through."

"You can't miss the signs."

"I know, but—"

"No buts. I'm going to have to fine you."

"What?"

"Don't you think that's fair?"

Fine? What was he talking about?

"Come on," Mr. Foster said. "It's my land. You've used it without my permission. Fair or not? Yes or no?"

"Well, I guess . . . what do I owe you?"

He smiled. "Hard labor."

"What?"

"Spring all of Jameson's traps and pull them up. Think you can do that?"

"He already has," Mrs. Clevenger said. "More than once. And then he's thrown them into the spong."

Mr. Foster gave him an appraising look. "Have you now? Well, seems there's more here than meets the eye."

"Oh, there is," Mrs. Clevenger said, her gaze fixed on Jack. "There most certainly is." She looked at Mr. Foster. "There's something I need to discuss with you in private."

Now they both looked at him and the message was clear.

"I guess I'd better get to work."

They both nodded.

"Bring them to the truck," Mr. Foster said.

As Jack hurried toward the spong he wondered what they'd be talking about and why he couldn't hear.

7

"That's all of them," Jack said as he tossed the last of the piney's leg-hold traps into the back of Mr. Foster's pickup.

The bearded man nodded with approval from where he leaned against the passenger door.

"Good job. You've worked off your fine. Now, don't let me catch you trespassing again or I'll have to think up something else. Mrs. Clevenger says you come here often with a couple of your friends."

Jack glanced at the old woman where she stood down the trail with her dog, staring into the spong area.

"So does she."

"She has my permission to be here. You do not. I want the trespassing to stop."

No way, Jack thought. The Pine Barrens were like an extension of his backyard. He didn't care who had official title to the land, he reserved the right to explore it.

"We don't hurt anything."

"I'm not worried about that. I'm worried about *you* being hurt."

"We know the Pines. We're careful."

Mr. Foster shook his head. "Nobody *really* knows the Pinelands. It's been a dumping ground for a long time."

"You mean like bodies? I've heard the Mafia—"

Mr. Foster chuckled. "Ah, if only bodies were the worst of it. Things—some not always dead—have been deposited here for millennia."

" 'Deposited' or dumped?"

"Let's just say 'hidden' and leave it at that. Especially in this area. That was why I bought this particular parcel—back in the day when you could still buy pieces of the Barrens."

"So . . . you know your land pretty well?"

"Pretty well, I guess. I haven't been over every foot of it."

"Do you know about the men who dug up the mound east of here?"

His eyes narrowed. "Mrs. Clevenger told me. They had no right."

"They said the body we found made it a crime scene and they didn't need permission to investigate."

"Did they look as if they were investigating?"

"More like excavating. Do you know who they were?"

"Yes."

Mr. Foster offered no more, so Jack was forced to ask, "Who?"

He looked away, toward the lowering sun. "No one I can do anything about."

Jack looked too, and saw Mrs. Clevenger and her dog approaching. He was a little miffed at her for tattling to Mr. Foster, but supposed she thought she was looking out for him.

All water under the bridge. What he really wanted were answers, so he turned back to Mr. Foster.

"What were they looking for?"

"Remember I told you about things hidden in the Pinelands? That was what they were after: hidden things, lost items. And don't ask me if they found any. I don't know."

This wasn't getting anywhere. Jack took a gamble and said, "Could any of it have been part of the Secret History of the World?"

Mr. Foster trained his blue gaze on him. "Where did you hear of that?"

"From a friend."

"The girl Mrs. Clevenger told me about? She seems quite fond of her. She's the one who found the mound?"

"Yeah. But I'm the one who found the cage."

"What cage?"

"The one made of big stones and shaped like a pyramid."

Mr. Foster stared at him. "You *have* been exploring, haven't you?"

Jack only shrugged.

"What makes you think it's a cage?"

"Just a guess . . . I mean, from the way it's built. Am I right?"

He nodded. "You haven't told anybody about it, have you?"

Jack shook his head. "We didn't want it dug up. We learned our lesson the first time."

"You're wise beyond your years. Some people live entire lives without ever once learning from experience. I thank you for that."

Jack shrugged again. "I don't like trespassers either."

Mr. Foster laughed. "You're quite something."

"What was kept in the cage?"

The old man's smile vanished. "Something long gone."

"A lion? A tiger? A bear?"

I sound like someone from *The Wizard of Oz*, Jack thought. His mind flashed back to the shadowy thing he and Weezy had encountered last month.

"Take your pick."

That wasn't an answer. He seemed to be taking a cue from Mrs. Clevenger. Why couldn't anyone give a straight answer?

"But it escaped."

"How do you—oh, I see. The broken stone. Yes, it probably did. But it doesn't matter. It's gone. Extinct."

"It could have bred—"

"Forget about it. It's gone." He glanced at where the sun was kissing the treetops. "And speaking of gone, that's what you should be. It will be dark soon."

Mrs. Clevenger arrived then.

"I should be going too," she said.

Mr. Foster nodded to her. "Good seeing you, as always."

Jack wondered why he didn't offer the old woman a ride. Then again, Mrs. Clevenger always seemed to prefer moving about the Pines on her own. Mr. Foster turned and gripped the handle of the passenger door.

"Let me check on our little friend here . . ."

But as he pulled open the door the young raccoon leaped out and darted at full speed into the brush. In a flash it was gone.

Jack gawked at the spot where it had disappeared.

"But . . . but its legs! How—?"

"Couldn't resist, could you?" Mrs. Clevenger said in a scolding tone. Jack turned and realized she was talking to her dog. "You know about the natural order."

The dog stared up at her, panting, then shook itself.

"But its legs were broken," Jack said. "How did it run—?"

Mr. Foster shrugged. "I guess they weren't as bad as they looked."

They were *just* as bad as they looked, Jack thought. Bloody, bent the wrong way . . . as broken as broken could be.

Then the dog had licked them.

Jack looked at the dog. The dog looked at him. Suddenly he felt creeped out.

"He's not magic, is he?"

"Hmmm," Mrs. Clevenger said, her lips flirting with a smile. "Let's think about that. If I had a magic dog, that would make me a witch, wouldn't it."

Jack felt a chill. All those stories about Mrs. Clevenger being the reincarnation of the famous Witch of the Pines. Nonsense, of course. Fun to joke about, and scare little kids—he remembered being scared when his brother Tom had told him about it—but not to be taken seriously at his age.

Well . . . easy to joke about when hanging out at someone's house. But here in the Pines, standing with these two strange people and an even stranger dog, with the sun setting, and a definitely crippled animal jumping up and running away, it didn't seem the least bit funny.

Mr. Foster laughed. "She's only teasing you, Jack."

"Of course I am," she said. "Dear boy, I'm no more a witch than your own mother."

"And speaking of your mother," Mr. Foster said, "I've never met the woman, but I imagine about now she'll be wondering if you're going to be late for dinner."

Jack knew that wasn't true. They always ate later than most people. But he took the hint.

"Yeah, I guess I'd better be going."

Mr. Foster offered his hand. "A pleasure meeting you, Jack, but that doesn't mean I hope we meet again. And I say that with only the very best of intentions."

Jack's hand seemed to disappear inside Mr. Foster's as they shook. On the surface he seemed to be referring to his warnings about trespassing, but Jack couldn't escape the feeling that he might have been talking about something else.

"Company," Mrs. Clevenger said.

Jack looked and saw Weezy stopped about a hundred feet away.

"Is that the girl?" Mr. Foster said.

Mrs. Clevenger nodded. "That's her."

He tapped Jack on the shoulder. "Tell her what I told you: For your own good, stay off this land."

Jack nodded as he hopped on his bike and rode toward Weezy.

"What are you doing here?" he said when he reached her. "I thought you said—"

"My mom went out and I needed to escape the house. Who's that?"

"Mister Foster."

Weezy's eyes widened as she studied the man. "He's real?"

"And how. And I just saw the weirdest thing."

"Tell me about it as we ride back. I need to be there when my mom gets home or she'll think I pulled a Marcie Kurek."

"Run away? You—"

"Can't say I haven't thought about it."

"Aw, Weez—"

"Don't worry. I've got nowhere to go and no way to get there."

That was a relief.

"Okay, let's go."

As they rode away Jack felt three pairs of eyes on his back.

8

A violent thunderstorm swept in from the west just before dinner and knocked out the electricity. Jack looked out his bedroom window and saw that the whole town was dark. He heard a tap on his door and saw his father standing there with a flashlight.

"Can't read, can't watch TV," he said. "Only one thing to do in a storm like this, don't you think?"

Jack pumped a fist. "Lightning Tree!"

As he followed his father down the hall and through the living room, he heard his mother say, "Be careful."

They dashed through the pelting rain to the car. After a quick drive through the eerily dark town, they parked at the end of Quakerton Road in Old Town, about a hundred feet from the Lightning Tree.

At some time in the past, before the memory of anyone living, it might have been a stately oak, but it was hard to tell now. Lightning had hit it so many times that most of its branches were gone, leaving only a tall, thick, charred trunk. It looked like a giant used wooden matchstick.

No one knew why, but something about the tree attracted lightning. It didn't take a hit from *every* storm, but often enough to make the trip worthwhile. Sometimes half a dozen cars would be parked around the tree, waiting.

Theirs was alone tonight. Jack's father used to drive him out here a lot when he was younger. Some fathers and sons went fishing or hunting together; Jack and his dad watched storms, though not so much nowadays. Maybe Dad thought

Jack was too old for it, or not interested, or too busy. Maybe all that was true, but Jack felt good coming out here again. Like old times.

"We're kind of late," Dad said. "It might have been hit already."

Jack squinted at the top of the trunk, a tall shadow in the dim light. "I don't think so."

Dad turned off the engine. "Well, if that's true, then we shouldn't have too long to wait."

As they slid back in their seats, Jack figured this would be as good a time as any to ask. But how was he going to slide into the subject?

He tried, "You've taught me a lot, Dad."

"Hope so. And I hope it's worthwhile stuff."

"Oh, it definitely is." Here goes, he thought, taking a breath and speaking as quickly as he could without garbling the words.

"Howaboutteachingmetoshoot?"

Jack concentrated his gaze on the tree as he waited for the reaction. It took a while coming. Finally . . .

"Shoot? Where did that come from?"

"Oh . . . just talking to a kid today whose father had been teaching him to target shoot. They were looking to buy marbles for targets—that's how good he was getting."

"You're getting a little old to still be wanting a BB gun."

Still studying the tree, he said, "Yes. I agree."

Another pause, then, "Oh, no. Not a chance."

Finally he looked at his father and found his blue eyes cold, his features like stone.

"Come on, Dad. I'm in high school. Guys I know have been shooting since they were little kids."

"Yeah. Hunting. Is that what you want to do? Hunt?"

"Well, no."

Locals often gave his folks venison or game birds when they had more than they could use, and Jack enjoyed eating them, but centering a deer in his sights and pulling the trigger, or blasting a pheasant out of the sky . . .

He'd have to be *really* hungry before he could do that. And maybe not even then.

"I was thinking of just a twenty-two. You know—for target practice."

"A rifle is a killing tool. You do target practice to improve your killing skills. If you're not going to use it to kill, you don't need target practice."

"Come on, Dad. It's an Olympic sport. I—"

His father held up a hand. "Let me save you some breath and both of us some time: No guns in my house. Ever."

"But—"

"I repeat: No. Guns. In. My. House. Ever. Is there any part of that you don't understand?"

"Not even for home protection?"

"That's what we pay the police for."

"But what if someone's in the house and—?"

"No, Jack. No."

"I heard Mister Bainbridge call you 'Deadeye.'"

"When?"

"Back in the summer. That must mean you were a good shot and—"

His father gripped Jack's shoulder and gave it a squeeze—not painful but hard enough to ensure his attention. He locked his blue eyes with Jack's.

"Look, Jack, I understand that you think guns are cool and fascinating and maybe even fun. I suppose I did too when I was a kid. But you get older, you have some experiences—"

"Like what?"

He looked away. "Like seeing men die from having half their head shot off, or worse, slowly bleed to death." He looked at Jack again. "Let's not bring up the subject again, okay? When you're grown and living on your own, you can buy all the guns your heart desires. Live in an armory if you want. But here? No. Never."

Jack wondered what had happened in Korea to affect him like this. Mr. Bainbridge had been over there with him and he hunted at every opportunity, and always seemed ready to talk about the war. Not Dad. He treated it as if it never happened.

The answer, Jack was sure, lay in that lockbox in Dad's closet. If he could just get past that crummy little lock.

He decided to change the subject.

"Hey, Dad. Do you have a guiding principle?"

His father glanced at him. "A what?"

"You know, an idea or something that guides your life."

"You mean like a philosophy?"

Jack shrugged. "I guess so."

Dad was silent a moment, then said, "I guess I believe that all men are created equal, with unalienable rights to life, liberty and the pursuit of happiness—or something like that. Not original with me. You know where that comes from, right?"

"Sure. The Declaration of Independence."

"Good. I think it pretty much says it all. A lot of good people have died to protect those rights. And I do believe they are unalienable. You know what that means?"

"They can't be taken away."

"Right."

"But what if you're a slave?"

"Just because some thug prevents you from exercising those rights, doesn't mean they no longer exist. You have to—"

They both jumped as a bolt of lightning split the sky and lit up the inside of the car as it hit the top of the tree, loosing a shower of multicolored sparks. The immediate blast of thunder shook the car and rattled Jack's teeth.

He slapped the dashboard and shouted, "Yes!" as his father whooped. They'd timed it just right.

Jack held out his hand for a five slap, but his father shook it instead.

"This was good, Jack. I'm glad we came."

Except for the no-gun part, Jack couldn't agree more.

1

Jack pried at the window to the boys' room. It moved a lot more easily this time. At least something was going right. For a while tonight he'd thought he wasn't going to make it here at all.

The earlier thunderstorm had worried him. If it stalled and hung on through the night, he'd have to cancel his planned trip to the school. But it petered out shortly before midnight.

And so here he was in the wee hours of Thursday morning, standing on a bike seat in the middle of sopping bushes and yanking on a window.

The last thing Jack had done before leaving school earlier was slip into his now favorite bathroom stall and unlatch the window again. He didn't know if anyone was noticing his recurrent trips—he doubted it because different guys were in the boys' room whenever he came through—but anyone who did might think he had colitis or something.

Oh, well. Small price to pay.

Again, that uneasy sensation that eyes were on him, but when he looked around he saw no sign of life. Shrugging, he turned back to the window.

He wore only jeans and a rugby shirt this time and found he slipped through with much greater ease. The nylon warm-up had been perhaps a tad too clever. He guessed you could overthink things. Best to always remember the KISS rule: Keep It Simple, Stupid.

Toliver's new lock opened just as easily as the old one. A shim didn't care what the combination was.

Now, decision time: How to set this up?

He could simply leave the can inside on the top shelf and hope that Toliver would open it and make a fool out of himself. But he'd be suspicious as all hell. He'd probably notice that the can was too light to be full of peanut brittle and didn't rattle when he shook it. It would take a real dummy not to guess it held something other than candy, and Toliver was no dummy.

Another option was to take the snake and coil it behind the locker door so that it popped out as soon as Toliver opened it. But that was exactly what had happened with the spider. Yeah, it would spook Toliver that someone had invaded his locker again, but anyone watching would have a feeling of déjà vu or been-there-done-that.

Jack liked a third option best: Set up the snake for a delayed deployment. It would be tricky but he thought he could bring it off.

He got down to work . . .

2

On the way home, as usual, he passed a variety of roadkill and the Lonely Pine Motel. He'd noticed Miriam's station wagon there on the way out, but now he noticed something else.

A man stood by the car, staring at the door to room three.

Jack slowed his bike and stopped, squinting through the dim blue light from the roadside neon sign. Something familiar about him . . .

And then he recognized Weird Walt.

Jack backed his bike deeper into the shadows. He didn't want to be seen, and was curious what Walt was up to out here at two in the morning.

Had he come to try to cure the baby's arm? Did he really think he could make it grow? But even if he did, why now? Why not in the light of day?

Maybe he didn't want anyone else to know.

Walt took a step toward the door, then stopped. He seemed uncertain, and radiated something Jack couldn't quite grasp. He took another step, then abruptly turned and started walking away—north along 206, toward Johnson.

Jack waited until Walt had gone at least a hundred yards before cutting across the highway and taking the back paths home.

While he waited he wondered about what he had just witnessed. Why had Walt walked a couple of miles to get here, only to turn around and go back? What had just happened? Or not happened? Or almost happened?

And then he realized what he had sensed in Walt as he'd stood outside that door: fear.

Walt had been afraid. But of what? Certainly not Miriam or her child. What, then?

3

Jack yawned as he stood with the group. The yawns had started a few minutes ago and now he couldn't stop. So tired.

No mention of Easy Weezy on the inbound bus today. An encouraging sign, but that didn't mean the story was dead.

First thing after leaving the bus, he'd dashed to the boys' room to relock the window, then hurried back to the senior lockers. The area seemed more crowded than usual, and then Jack realized that some of the kids were hanging around near Toliver's locker. So Jack hung too.

Just a face in the crowd.

When Toliver arrived he noticed the crowd as well. He didn't seem to mind. In fact, he played to it.

"Come to see if my secret admirer's left me another present?" he said with a grin.

This earned smiles from his audience.

"Sorry to disappoint you, but it ain't gonna happen. How's that old saying go? 'Fool me once, shame on you, fool me twice, shame on me.' Well, nobody fools me twice." He pointed to the lock. "New lock." He pulled a slip of paper from his pocket and held it up. "The combination to the new lock. Not even *I* know it."

This earned a gentle laugh from the crowd which had grown larger as he spoke.

With a flourish he studied the paper, then turned and spun the dial. When the shackle popped open, he removed it, grasped the door handle, and without an instant's hesitation, yanked it open.

You've got no doubts, Jack thought, watching avidly. Supremely confident. Let's see how long that lasts.

When nothing happened, Toliver turned to his audience and gestured toward his locker.

"See? Nobody fools me twice."

Keep it up, Jack thought, biting his upper lip to keep from grinning.

This was perfect.

He glanced at the thick semicircle of faces and saw mixtures of relief and disappointment. They didn't want anyone picking on their beloved Carson, but a part of each of them thought another spider would have been undeniably cool.

As the crowd began to break up, Toliver reached for the books on his top shelf. As soon as he moved them, the trapped snake uncoiled, flashing right at his face. He let out a high-pitched squawk as he dropped his books and raised his arms to protect himself.

Those in the crowd who were looking cried out in alarm, and then everyone began laughing when they saw the spring snake on the floor.

Jack plastered on a smile and faked surprised laughter—just another face in the crowd.

The delay had been crucial: Give Toliver and the onlookers a brief respite in which they all thought he'd beaten whoever had set up yesterday's gag. A few heartbeats of self-satisfaction for Toliver before the boom lowered.

At one thirty this morning it had taken what seemed like forever to adjust the cap of the can just right: not tight enough to hold back the snake on its own, but assisted by the weight of a few books in front of it. Once those books were removed . . .

The laughter continued, but Toliver didn't think it was

funny. He'd managed to brush it off yesterday, but this morning his red-faced embarrassment exploded into rage.

"God *damn* it!" he shouted as he kicked the snake. "Who's *doing* this?" He turned in a slow half circle. "Show yourself, you son of a bitch! Step up and face me like a man!"

A female voice giggled. "What if it's not a man?"

Toliver turned toward the direction of the voice. "Who said that? Do you know something? *Who said that?*"

The first period bell rang then, and everyone started moving.

"Hey!" Toliver shouted. "I asked a question! Who knows anything?"

But people had places to go and weren't listening.

"Somebody's got to know some—"

Jack had turned away with the rest but turned back when he heard Toliver's voice cut off. He saw him staring at a dirty sneaker that had fallen out of his locker. It looked way too small to be one of his. He seemed weirded out. He kept staring, then suddenly bent and tossed it back into his locker, looking around as he had yesterday with the sock.

As Jack turned and started walking away, he heard a couple of guys behind him start a conspiracy theory worthy of Weezy Connell.

"Who'd do something like that to Carson? Can you think of *one* person?"

"No way. Unless . . ."

"Unless what?"

"What if . . . what if it's somebody from North trying to spook him?"

"You mean because of the game?"

"Hell, yeah. Nobody 'round here would do it."

"Yeah, but—"

"Think about it. He's our MVP, man."

"Yeah, one who screams like a girl."

They both had a laugh at that, and Jack couldn't help smiling too.

"But seriously, what if they're trying to get him all distracted and everything before the game? He's the quarterback. If his mind isn't a hundred and ten percent on the game tomorrow night, we're screwed."

"Man, you could be right. North could be trying to green-light him."

Jack wanted to tell him the term was "gaslight"—after one of Mom's favorite movies—but resisted the temptation.

He also figured Carson Toliver had too high an opinion of himself to let any of this rattle him enough to blow the Badger-Greyhound game.

Still, the idea of NBR trying to drive the SBR quarterback crazy before the big game . . .

A whacky theory, guys, Jack thought. But as long as it doesn't involve Weezy or me, go for it.

He spotted Levi Coffin, one of the older piney kids, staring at him as if trying to see right through him. He had a strange, knowing look that unsettled Jack. Did he suspect?

No way.

Jack chanced a last glance back and saw Toliver slam his locker door closed and start to relock it. But he stopped, staring at the lock.

Suddenly he hauled back and pitched it against the nearest wall where it cracked a tile. As the lock hit the floor, its black combination dial broke off and rolled around in a wobbly circle.

Toliver stalked off, leaving his locker latched but unlocked.

No! Jack thought. You can't do that.

Booby-trapping an unlocked locker would have no impact. It was nothing—less than nothing. Anyone could do it.

Toliver had to get another lock.

4

At lunchtime, Jack made a point of stopping by the table where Weezy usually sat.

"Any questions for me, ladies?"

They gave him weird looks. No one mentioned Easy Weezy.

"Come on, girls. I'm the answer man."

"Okay," said a blonde with sky-high bangs. "Who's sneaking into Carson's locker?"

The question was good news, but Jack hadn't expected it. He didn't know what to say until he remembered . . .

"I heard someone say that NBR might be trying to spook him before the game."

"Ohmigod!" one of them said and suddenly he was forgotten as they leaned together and buzzed.

Looked like Easy Weezy had become yesterday's news. His plan was already successful. But it wasn't enough. The scales wouldn't be balanced until Toliver was experiencing what he'd put Weezy through.

He'd planned to spend the rest of lunchtime bird-dogging Toliver but, just like yesterday, he was nowhere to be found until classes were about to resume.

Jack spotted him walking toward his locker. Two other guys from the football team were coming the other way. One nudged the other and they both let out high-pitched screams.

Toliver didn't appreciate the joke. As they broke into laughter he shoved one of them.

"Something funny, Warner? Huh?"

Temper, temper, Jack thought. Careful. That's not a skinny "goth chick."

Warner pushed him back. "Lighten up, Cars."

"Hey, yeah," said the other. "We're just funnin' ya."

"It's not funny, man. Someone been stealing my combination. Nothing funny about that."

"Well, don't look at us," Warner said. "Got better things to do."

The other nodded. "Damn straight."

Toliver held up his right hand to show them a new lock. "Well, whoever it is, his combination-stealing days are over." He held up a pair of keys with his left hand. "No combination. And I've got the only keys."

They exchanged high fives and continued on their various ways. Jack followed Toliver to his locker and strolled by as he secured it with his new lock. After wandering into the caf, he doubled back and slowed as he passed 791.

A bright brass lock gleamed from the locker latch. *Mr. Lock* was engraved into the metal.

Jack suppressed a grin as he moved past.

Tonight—or tomorrow morning, rather—he would introduce Mr. Lock to Mr. Shim.

5

"I'm not feeling so well," Mr. Rosen said, rubbing his stomach.

He looked a little green and Jack felt a flash of concern.

"You okay?"

"The tuna fish salad I had for lunch—it's not sitting so well. Stay open maybe another hour, then close up. Unless of course—I should be so lucky—we're jammed with people in a buying frenzy, then you call me and I'll come back."

Jack laughed. "You got it. But before you go, I need to buy something."

The kid from yesterday had given him an idea.

"Again? You bought yesterday, and now you're buying today. With business the way it is, you're going to be the week's best customer. What now?"

Jack indicated the round fishbowl full of marbles he'd brought to the counter.

"These."

Mr. Rosen made a face. "Marbles? Why? You've maybe lost yours?"

Jack forced a polite laugh.

Mr. Rosen shook his head. "Sorry. Couldn't resist. So why does a boy your age want marbles?"

Jack searched for an answer . . . and found one.

"They're a gift."

"For that Connell girl you pal around with?"

"No. This person barely knows I exist, and won't know who they're from."

His eyebrows rose and his dark eyes twinkled. "Like from a secret admirer, maybe?"

He's got it way wrong, Jack thought, but wasn't going to straighten him out.

"Sort of."

At least the "secret" part was right.

"How many you want?"

"I was wondering what's your best price for all of them."

He smiled. " 'Best price,' eh? You've been listening to me haggle?"

Jack returned the smile. "Learning from the master."

"How many you think are there?"

"I'd guess a hundred or so."

"Well, here's the list price." He tapped the 10 ¢ EACH sign taped to the glass. "So let's see . . . with volume discount plus employee discount . . . five dollars will make us even."

"Deal."

Jack pulled out a five-dollar bill and handed it to Mr. Rosen.

"Be sure to write it in the book."

Jack nodded, staring at the bowl.

Yes, sir. These marbles were going to make a fine gift for a certain someone.

6

Mr. Rosen had said to close early at five, and Jack was getting ready to do just that when Mrs. Clevenger walked in with her dog.

"Hi, Mrs. C. Long time no see."

She smiled. "I trust you will take Mister Foster's warning to heart."

Rather than answer that he had no intention of doing anything of the sort, he said, "Can I help you find anything?"

He didn't want her browsing around. He wanted to close up and go home.

"Actually, I came to see you."

"Oh?"

"Yes. One of your schoolmates sought me out with a rather odd question."

One name leaped immediately to mind. "Weezy?"

"No. The Toliver boy."

"Carson?"

"I don't believe there is another."

"Oh, right." Yeah, Carson was an only child. "What did he want with you?"

"He seems to suffer from the prevailing notion that I'm a witch."

Jack glanced at her three-legged dog and remembered that raccoon running off with a pair of broken legs.

"Did he . . . want you to cast a spell or something?"

Like one that would protect his locker?

She shook her head. "Nothing like that. No, it was the oddest thing: He wanted to know if I could tell whether or not a person was being haunted."

"Haunted? I've heard of houses being haunted, but people?"

She only shrugged.

Jack pressed. "Did he say who was haunting him?"

"You're putting words in my mouth. I didn't say he told me *he* was being haunted. He simply asked if I could tell."

"Well, can you?"

She sighed and shook her head. "I'll tell you what I told him: I am not a witch. I do not cast spells, I do not tell fortunes, I simply live my life and mind my business."

Not exactly a solid *no,* he thought.

Did she know what Jack was up to? Was it Mrs. C he sensed watching as he'd sneaked into the school these past two mornings? She had a habit of showing up without warning in the oddest places.

He noticed her watching him now with an appraising stare. It made him uncomfortable.

"What?"

She said, "Do you have any idea why he would ask me that?"

Now he was *really* uncomfortable.

"Well, someone's been messing with his locker. Maybe he thinks it's haunted."

Come to think of it, Toliver's expression had been kind of haunted this morning when he'd found that dirty sneaker.

"He didn't mention a locker. He asked about some*one* being haunted."

Jack shrugged. "Sorry. Can't help you on that."

"Very well," she said, nodding. "I just thought I'd ask."

On her way out, a stranger stepped through the door and held it for her. As it closed behind her, he approached Jack.

Swell, he thought. He was never going to get out of here.

"You're the proprietor?" he said with a New York accent. He was heavyset, maybe mid-thirties, with a double chin and a receding hairline. "So young to own such an interesting store."

"I just work here."

"Ah. A wage slave. I used to be one, but no more. *Nu?* Where is your slave driver?"

Jack debated answering that. It wasn't anybody's business, especially a stranger's, that Mr. Rosen wasn't feeling well.

"He stepped out."

"Back soon?"

Jack shook his head and pointedly looked at his watch. "No. And we're sort of past closing time."

"So soon? I have a minute for a quick look around?"

Jack shrugged. "If you're really interested in something, I'll wait."

"Oy!" He raised his hands as he started down the center aisle. "Like a rabbit I'll run."

Something about this guy—Jack wasn't sure what—was putting him on alert. Nothing particularly sinister about him, just that . . . he seemed to have an agenda. Jack just wished he knew what it was.

The man returned with an armful of old comic books. Mr. Rosen kept a few boxes of them in the back. When Jack had first come to work here the old guy had handed him a copy of something called *Overstreet's Comic Book Price Guide* and told him to look up each and every issue to see if it might be rare and valuable. No luck. Mostly the likes of *Archie* and *Hot Stuff* and *Little Lotta*. Kids' stuff. Not valuable, simply old.

"Here," the man said, plopping the stack on the counter. "I'll take these." He handed Jack a five-dollar bill. "That should cover it."

"Hang on," Jack said, doing a quick count. "You've got twenty here. You're five dollars short."

The man's eyebrows rose. "For these you want ten bucks? They're junk. I'm only buying them for my daughter because she likes *Archie*."

"They're fifty cents apiece."

"*Nu?* You make me a deal."

"Can't do that. If I write down twenty, he'll expect to find ten bucks paid."

"That's robbery. A *ganef* you work for. Look, does he know how many comic books he's got back there? I mean, the exact number?"

Jack shrugged. He'd gone through them issue by issue himself and hadn't the faintest. "I doubt it."

"Good. Then we can do a little business here. We're both men of the world, right?"

Jack stared at him, wondering where this was going. "I've been as far as Philadelphia a few times. Does that qualify?"

"Not by a long shot, but we'll say it does. Such a deal I'll make you. This guy probably underpays you, right?"

"I get enough for what I do."

The man gave him an intent look. "If you do, you're the first person I've ever met who admits it. So here's the deal: I give you seven dollars, you write down ten comics—"

"I'm not allowed—"

"Hear me out. You write down ten comics, you put five dollars in the till, and keep two for yourself."

Jack shook his head. "Can't do that."

The man's voice rose half an octave. "Why not? I get a bargain, you get a couple of extra bucks in your pocket. It's a win-win situation."

"You forgot the owner. He loses."

"That's where you're wrong. Not even *he* loses. He probably paid pennies for these. I'll bet he doesn't have more than a dollar invested in this whole stack. So five bucks leaves him with a profit too. That makes it a win-win-*win* situation!"

Jack shook his head again. He'd had enough of this guy.

"You'd better put them back. We're closing."

"You're either very stubborn or shortsighted. He'll never know."

Jack thought about looking Mr. Rosen in the eye after being part of a cheesy scam like this. He couldn't think of any amount of money that would make it right to cheat someone who trusted him.

"But I will."

The man stared at him long and hard, then broke into a smile that changed his whole face.

"What a kid you are." His wheedling tone had vanished. "You're how old?"

"Fourteen—fifteen in January."

Still smiling, he shook his head. "Fourteen, and already a mensch. My uncle Jake left his store in good hands."

"Uncle? Mister Rosen's your uncle?"

"Distant. My mother's side. Thought I'd catch him here on my way to Baltimore. How is he?"

Jack's head was spinning. He pointed to the stack of

comics. "You mean you weren't serious? You were testing me?"

"Such a look on your face. You think that's not fair? I shouldn't test you? Why not? How else am I supposed to know the mettle of the man watching over my beloved uncle's enterprise? *Life* is a test, *boychick*. Every day, a test of what's here"—he tapped the side of his head—"and here"—he tapped his chest. "You passed this one—with flying colors."

"Well, hooray for me," Jack said dryly.

"You'll get over it. In the meantime . . ." He pulled out his wallet and withdrew a card. "If you're ever in New York and you need anything—if you're tired or poor or homeless or just yearning to breathe free—you call that number." He patted Jack's cheek. "You got a friend in the big city, kid."

He tucked the card into the breast pocket of Jack's shirt, waved, then headed for the door.

Jack pulled out the card and noticed a ten-dollar bill with it.

"Hey, you forgot your comics."

"Comics, shmomics," he said without turning. "I hate comics. That's for your trouble. Tell Uncle Jake I said hello."

And then he was out the door and gone.

Jack looked at the card.

ABRAHAM GROSSMAN
ISHER SPORTING GOODS
Level the playing field with our high-caliber gear

He tucked it in his pocket. He couldn't imagine any circumstances that would cause him to call this Grossman fellow, but you never knew.

As usual, Jack approached through the trees. On his last two early morning trips he'd seen no signs of life on the school grounds, but you never knew. Some couple may have parked in a dark corner of the lot to make out.

He walked his bike to the treeline and scanned the grounds. Nope. Just as empty as ev—

"Stop right there."

Jack froze at the whispered words. Oh no! Toliver?

He turned and saw a tall, lean figure detach itself from the shadow of a nearby tree trunk.

"It's me—Levi."

Jack released a breath he hadn't known he'd been holding. "What are you—?"

"Shhh," Levi said, pointing.

Jack followed his point to a gleam in the shadows along the western edge of the parking lot. The glow from the solitary streetlight on the road at the other end was reflecting off something metallic. Jack squinted through the dark and made out the lines of a car.

And just then, behind it, a match or a lighter flared in the front seat of another car.

Two cars in the dark.

"Who are they?" Jack whispered.

"Don't know. They was parked when I got here. Wanna go see?"

Jack had a pretty good idea who it was. But . . . he turned to Levi. He couldn't see his mismatched eyes and that was okay. He found them distracting.

"Why are you here?"

Levi shrugged. "Don't sleep much. How 'bout you?"

Good question, one for which Jack had no answer.

"Um, returning a library book."

"Heh. Right. Let's get a closer look at who thinks they's hidin'."

Jack leaned his bike against a nearby trunk, then followed Levi as he circled around through the trees. They managed to creep within a hundred feet of the cars. When he recognized the Mustang GLX, he stopped. No need to get closer. He knew who was in that one, and could guess why.

He felt tension tighten his shoulder muscles as he realized what would have happened had Levi not stopped him. Beaten silly.

He should have expected something like this—should have put himself in Toliver's shoes and asked himself what he'd do in his situation. He'd have done just what Toliver was doing: staked out the school to catch whoever was sneaking in to get at his locker.

Jack was about to retreat when someone got out of the second car—it looked like a Honda hatchback—and walked up to the Mustang. A cigarette dangled from the corner of his mouth.

"Hey, Cars, this is gettin' old, man. How long we gonna hang out here?"

Toliver's voice replied, "Till the son of a bitch shows up."

"Maybe he ain't coming. Maybe he saw you don't have a combination lock now so he's called it quits."

"Maybe."

"You stopped him, man. Let's get home."

"Another fifteen minutes," Toliver said. "He doesn't show by then, we call it a night. Deal?"

Jack heard palms slap.

"Deal."

Fifteen minutes? Jack thought. I can hang another fifteen. He signaled Levi to retreat.

"So tell me," Levi whispered when they reached Jack's bike. "How'd you get Toliver's combinations?"

Oh, jeez. He knows.

Jack could see no course but to play dumb.

"What are you talking about?"

"I been watching you. I seen you open that window and seen you goin' in and out of it at night."

So . . . it hadn't been his imagination. Someone *had* been watching. Jack's gut twisted. Damn. This was bad.

"You tell anyone?"

"Nobody else's business. But you tell me: How about his lock combinations. You read his mind? You got a talent?"

Talent? What was he talking about?

"I don't know a single thing about his combinations." Which was true.

"Then what? You just look at a lock and open it? Can you do that?"

This had to be the weirdest conversation.

"No. Can you?"

That seemed to bring Levi up short. He paused, then started to move off.

"Okay. I'm gone. You do what you gotta do. Don't worry 'bout me sayin' nothin'."

"Nothing to say anything about."

"Sure."

"Um . . . why'd you stop me before?"

Levi stopped and turned. "Don't rightly know. You don't seem like a bad guy, and I guess I ain't got no love for a rich uppity sort like Carson Toliver, 'specially one that Saree says is all dark inside."

"Yeah. She told me that too. What's it mean?"

"You wouldn't understand."

"Try me."

"It's her talent. She sees people in colors."

"But she says she can't see me."

"Yeah, I know. Right strange, that."

Strange? How about out-the-wazoo weird?

"Yesterday I saw her touch Toliver's locker and act like she was burned, even though she said it was cold."

"Well, if she can touch something that's real near and dear to someone, she can see all sorts of colors."

"But she didn't mention a color, she said 'cold.' "

Jack saw him shake his head in the shadows. "Never heard her say anything like that before. I'll have to ask her. See you tomorrow."

He merged with the shadows and was gone from view. One strange guy. Worst of all, he knew. Jack didn't want anyone to have even a clue that he was involved. Lucky for Jack that Levi was a piney and they kept pretty much to themselves.

He turned back to the parking lot. He hoped he didn't fall asleep waiting. Man, he was tired.

2

Not a single mention of Weezy on the bus this morning. Which was good, because Eddie wasn't wearing his headphones. Like everyone else aboard, he was talking about what, if anything, Carson Toliver would find in his locker this morning. Stevie Ray Vaughn couldn't compete with that.

Jack allowed himself a single pat on the back: mission accomplished.

Well, *partly* accomplished.

He'd succeeded in shifting the focus of talk away from Weezy, but Carson Toliver hadn't paid enough for what he'd done to her—for laying his filthy hands on her, and for compounding that by spreading lies about her.

Not nearly enough.

Jack wasn't sure where to go from here, but maybe he was getting ahead of himself. He'd yet to see how this morning's drama at the locker would play out.

Carson Toliver versus the Mystery Marauder.

The *mystery* part was important. Crucial. Jack ached to tell someone what he'd been up to. He and Toliver were the two most talked-about people in school right now. Everyone wanted to know who the mysterious prankster was, and why he'd chosen Carson Toliver.

The *why* was another thing that had to be kept secret. Any connection to Weezy would turn attention back to her and her connection to Toliver, undoing what Jack had accomplished thus far.

Zip the lips, he told himself. And keep them zipped. And pray Levi Coffin did the same.

3

The boys' room usually had a fairly steady stream of traffic first thing in the morning, but today it was virtually deserted. He had a pretty good idea why. He relocked the window—maybe for the last time—and hurried to the senior locker area.

He found what seemed like half the school there, all clustered around Toliver's locker. Jack wasn't tall enough to see over, and couldn't get close enough for a clear view.

Then Toliver showed up behind him, passing nearby as he elbowed his way through the crowd.

"Coming through!" he cried with authority. "Move it, people! Coming through!"

People moved aside, because there'd be no show without Toliver. Jack leaped into the void in his wake, staying as close as he could without touching him, and managed to make it almost to the front.

Yesterday Toliver had quoted the old proverb, *Fool me once, shame on you; fool me twice, shame on me.* Jack wanted to ask who got shamed after you were fooled a third time.

Toliver stopped before his locker and turned to the crowd. "Don't you people have anything better to do?"

Almost as one the crowd roared "NO!" and then broke into laughter. Even Toliver laughed a little. Using the same flourish as with his combination yesterday, he produced the keys to the lock.

"Somehow some wiseass stole the combination to my last two locks, but that's not gonna happen this time." He waved the keys. "No combination, and I've got the only keys."

But I have shims, Jack thought as the crowd cheered. He'd brought along the lock-pick kit last night, in case the shim failed, but hadn't needed it.

Toliver added, "So whoever you are, up yours."

Another cheer went up, then faded as he turned and inserted the key into the bottom of the lock. He gave it a twist, popped the shackle, and removed it from the latch.

Like a magician waving a prop, he turned and held up the lock, then he reached for the door handle.

Jack chewed the inside of his cheek. Now the moment of truth.

After watching Toliver and his friends leave earlier this morning, and waiting a few minutes to be sure they didn't sneak back, he'd made his way to the locker with the marbles packed in a cardboard box. He'd set the box on the floor of the locker and tilted it forward by wedging one of Toliver's sneakers under its back end. Then he'd cut a wide flap in the box's front panel. Holding it closed, he shut the door against it. The weight of a hundred marbles lay behind the flap. The only thing holding it closed was the locker door. When that opened, the flap would drop and . . . marble avalanche.

Or so Jack hoped.

Even if it didn't open, Jack could still claim victory, because he'd gotten past the new lock. Toliver had been invaded again. He'd know it, and so would everybody else.

That was part A. The success of part B depended on the success of part A, but was otherwise out of his hands; he'd need a little cooperation from Toliver for that.

He watched Toliver grasp the door handle and, just for a heartbeat . . . hesitate.

Yes! Jack thought. You've got a new lock, you've got the only key. You should feel you've got everything under control, but still you've got this nagging doubt.

Toliver yanked open the door and a multicolored cascade clattered from his locker, bouncing and rolling in all directions. He leaped back in surprise and landed on some of the marbles.

His soles rolled . . . his feet kicked . . . his arms windmilled . . . he looked like he was trying some sort of spaz break-dance move . . .

And then he went down, smack on his butt, making part B a complete success.

The crowd burst into laughter. Even Jack had to smile at how ridiculous he looked as he tried to get up and slipped again. Only by grabbing his locker door did he prevent another fall.

The crowd roared louder.

And that was when Toliver lost it. *Really* lost it.

His face was already crimson, but now he looked like Bruce Banner about to go Hulk. His lips pulled back in a snarl as he bent and picked up handfuls of marbles and began hurling them at the crowd.

"You think it's *funny*? Having a good laugh, you sons of bitches?"

The crowd flinched and ducked as the marbles peppered them. A good many turned and began moving away. One kid thought it was funny and kept laughing. Toliver grabbed him and shoved him against the lockers.

"What's so funny? What are you laughing at? You know something about this? Huh? Huh?"

The kid was small and Toliver kept slamming him against the lockers.

Suddenly Mr. Kressy appeared and yanked him back.

"Cool it!"

Toliver cocked a fist and for a second Jack was afraid the Toliver temper would overcome sanity and he'd take a swing.

"Don't even dream about it," Mr. Kressy said, staring him down.

Toliver lowered his arm and backed off a step.

Mr. Kressy looked around, then down at the marbles scattered on the floor. The kid Toliver had been manhandling scooted off.

"What is going *on* here? Are these yours?"

Toliver shook his head. "No way."

Shaking his head, Mr. Kressy strode away, saying, "I'll call a custodian."

The remainder of the crowd began breaking up, a lot of the kids looking at Toliver strangely, and giving him a wide berth, like they would a dangerous animal.

With a roar Toliver turned and began kicking his locker again and again. Something popped out and hit the floor where it spun like a top for a few seconds, then stopped.

A little silver ring.

Toliver picked it up, studied it a second, then started turning in circles with that haunted look in his eyes again.

"Who?" he shouted. "Who, damn it! *Who?*"

Something else in his eyes now too: The same *hunted* look he'd seen in Weezy's eyes the other night.

Now you know how it feels, Big Shot. Like it?

Jack eased away with the rest of the stragglers.

He wondered at his feelings. Everything had worked out according to his best-case scenario. The marbles had poured out and Toliver had slipped on them.

So why didn't he feel better about it? Where was that

ecstatic elation he'd felt after the first two pranks? Today had been the most successful of all, goading Toliver into showing his true ugly colors and tarnishing his phony armor. He'd tried to smear Weezy, make people look at her differently, and now it was happening to him.

But instead of up, Jack felt sour. Maybe because this morning's gag had turned ugly.

"Gotta be someone from North," he heard a guy say.

"Yeah," said another. "And it seems to be working. You see how he got? Man, he was like crazy."

"Well, it *was* kinda funny—doing that crazy-legs thing and falling. Just hope it doesn't lose us the game."

"That happens, whoever's behind this, man, his ass is grass."

"You got that right."

Jack stopped and let the others pass. He felt as if he'd just had a sign from above:

Quit now.

It was Friday. He could make the end of the week the end of Operation Toliver. That had a nice symmetry to it. Plus, it had stopped being fun.

And if the Badgers lost the game because Toliver was too on edge to focus, it would be his fault. Well, not *all* his fault, but some of it could be laid at his doorstep.

That was why no one could ever even suspect he was behind this.

And then he spotted Levi coming his way, nodding knowingly.

"Oh, yeah," he said as he passed. "You got a talent. I know you do."

What?

He prayed Levi would keep his mouth shut.

4

In civics class, Mr. Kressy had returned to the subject of a first principle, asking, "Has anyone come up with a solid touchstone belief to which all your actions must answer?"

Various principles had been put forth—including "Do unto others . . ." by someone who had been absent last time—but all were shot down for one reason or another.

Jack gave it a try, going with Dad's idea. "How about everyone has a right to life, liberty, and the pursuit of happiness?"

"Absolutely!" Mr. Kressy said, snapping his suspenders. "One of the finest passages ever written! But *why* do we have those rights? Whence do they spring? Think: What does every human on this planet have in common?" He paused. When no one answered, he threw up his arms. "We're all *alive*! We all have life!"

"I don't," Matt Follette said. "Trust me, I've got *no* life."

As usual he got a laugh, but Mr. Kressy wasn't amused this time.

"This is serious. We're getting to the crux of everything. Your life—whose is it? Yours or someone else's?"

A chorus of "Mine" rose but a girl somewhere behind Jack said, "Don't our parents own us?"

"If they own your life, that means they can do whatever they want with you. Anyone here believe that your parents have a right to kill you, or sell you into slavery?"

The class was silent. The answer was too obvious.

"Of course not," he said. "*You own your own life*, and that fact should form the cornerstone of how you live your life."

"I don't get it," someone said. "How does that work?"

But Jack was getting it, taking the next step, and the step after that.

Mr. Kressy said, "If everyone owns their own life, it guarantees them liberty and the pursuit of happiness. Note that 'pursuit' is a very important word there—it means you can seek happiness, but it's not guaranteed. Happiness isn't a right, it's something you must achieve. Owning your own life means no one can interfere with that ownership by initiating force against you. It also means the opposite: You have no right to initiate force against another. In a nutshell: You have a right to swing your fist anywhere and anytime you wish, but that right stops at someone else's nose."

"What if someone attacks you first?" Jack said.

"Good question. Since it's your life, you have a right to defend it."

Jack pressed on. "What if you see someone attacking someone else? Can you step in?"

"Another good question. By defending others' rights to their own lives, you defend your right to your own." He beamed at Jack. "You're thinking. Good man."

Normally Jack would have basked in the praise, especially from his favorite teacher, but his concerns lay outside the classroom.

He had a right to his own life . . . it was so obvious, yet he'd never consciously formed the concept. Now that he had . . .

Toliver had attacked Weezy. She couldn't strike back, so Jack had struck for her. Would he have been justified using the bat that night? Yeah, probably, since Toliver had already opened the door to violence by physically attacking Weezy, but what Jack had done to him instead—without laying a finger on him—had proven so much worse.

"So in the coming months, as we hear lots of talk from the president and his challengers, let's hold up their ideas to the touchstone of owning your own life. We can decide if their ideas enhance or diminish that ownership, and by that we can judge whom we wish to support. Remember, it's all a tug-of-war about control: Who has power over your life—you or the government?"

As the end-of-period bell rang he raised his voice.

"A U.S. senator named Daniel Webster once said, 'There are men in all ages who mean to govern well, but they mean to govern. They promise to be good masters, but they mean to be masters.' We'll keep that in mind as we listen to the palaver."

Despite the frustration of not having fully dealt Toliver what he deserved, Jack felt an inner glow as he gathered up his books.

"The right to my own life," he muttered. "I like that."

"I like it too," said a girl's voice.

He looked around and saw Karina standing behind him, smiling.

"But not everybody feels that way," she added.

"Who wouldn't?"

"Whole nations and religions don't think that applies to women, only men."

"Yeah, you're right. Even here they couldn't vote a hundred years ago."

Her smile broadened. "You know about the Nineteenth Amendment?"

"Um, yeah."

Weezy had mentioned it a few weeks ago.

5

In the caf, Jack was eating a ham sandwich with a group from his homeroom when Cristin came up to the table and started rapidly sliding her feet around while making spastic movements with her arms.

"Cristin?" Karina said. "What are you doing?"

She grinned. "A new dance. It's called the Carson."

That cracked up the table, Jack too.

Oh, yeah. Easy Weezy was history.

Jake Shuett came running up. "Carson's by his locker and wants everybody there! He says he's got a big announcement!"

Jack was first out of his seat and on his way as dozens of others rushed from the caf. He managed to snag a spot near the front of the crowd centered around Toliver and his locker.

He'd returned to his usual cool, calm, and collected self as he held up a new lock—a non-combination model.

"Take a look at this everybody: brand-new."

Then he held up a tiny nail.

"See this? An upholstery tack."

He then pulled a small hammer from his back pocket and tapped the tack into the keyhole at the bottom of the lock. The hammer returned to the pocket to be replaced by a small plastic vial.

"Krazy Glue."

He put a few drops of the glue into the keyhole around the tack. Then he turned the lock right side up and emptied the rest of the glue into the shackle hole. He inserted the shackle through the latch in his locker door, then snapped the lock shut.

He turned to the crowd.

"It's over. It ends here. No more games. This clown will not be getting into my locker again. We've all had some laughs, but it's over. The last laugh is on him."

We? Jack thought. I don't remember you laughing.

"Nobody," he continued, "but nobody is getting past that lock."

"But what about you?" somebody called from the crowd. "How are you getting past it?"

"Let me worry about that," Toliver said. "I've got it covered. See you all at the game tonight to watch us whip some Greyhound butt."

A cheer went up. Jack had to admire the way he worked the crowd.

"And then we'll all meet back here Monday morning for the grand opening."

Another cheer as he wove through the throng and headed for class. With that, the crowd fractured and dissolved. A few of the guys hung back and approached locker 791. They stood in a small knot, staring at the lock. Jack joined them.

"Man, nobody's getting past that," one said as he upended the lock and stared at the nail in the gooey keyhole.

"No kidding," said another. "I've played around with Krazy Glue. Once that stuff sets, it's there to stay."

"I can get past it easy," said a third kid.

"How?" the other two asked in unison.

"Hacksaw."

All three nodded.

"Yeah, that'll do it," the first said. "But we'll all know as soon as we see it, so there'll be no surprise. Carson's got him beat."

As they wandered away, Jack hung back, lost in thought.

A challenge had been issued.

Jack had already called it quits, unilaterally ending the operation, but Carson Toliver wasn't letting it go. He'd thrown down the gauntlet.

Jack could still walk away. He'd stopped the talk about Weezy.

And yet . . .

If Toliver walked in here Monday morning with his locker untouched, he'd have a moral victory. He'd have proven that he could stop the pranks whenever he wanted. He'd be back on top. Even if Jack returned to pranking him later, it wouldn't be the same.

Sure, he could sneak back with a hacksaw and cut the lock off, but that was so crude. Like throwing a bomb. No finesse, no style. Toliver was perceived as having style, so Jack had to show even more. He couldn't be a bomber; he needed to be a sniper. Needed a surgical strike. Resorting to a hacksaw would be an admission of defeat. It said, Yeah, you beat me—I couldn't open your lock.

Plus, cutting the shackle would kill the mystery of the moment and banish that instant of exquisite uncertainty when the door began to swing open.

Uh-uh.

Jack couldn't allow the challenge to go unanswered. One more time . . . he had to get into Toliver's locker one more time.

Mr. Big Shot had to walk in here Monday morning and find the lock on 791 just as he'd left it. But when he opened the door he'd find the surprise of his life.

But how to make that happen?

The lockers were steel and bolted to the wall. No way in through the back, and he'd need an acetylene torch to cut through the top. The door was the only way in.

Jack stared at the two-inch wide, laminated-steel Master padlock, saw the glue pooling around the shackle hole. Once it was fully hardened, he'd never get a shim in there. And with a nail glued into the keyhole, picking the cylinder was impossible.

Levi wandered by then and spoke out of the corner of his mouth.

"Well, I guess that ends your pranks."

Pranks! Jack wanted to lash out at him. These weren't pranks. They might look like it, but they were the only course Weezy had left open to him.

But of course Levi had no inkling of Jack's higher purpose. He thought he was just goofing on Toliver. Best to play it that way.

"You might be right. Fun while it lasted, though."

"Yeah. But not even you can get past *that* one."

Don't count on it, he thought, although he had no idea how on Earth he was going to pull it off.

Then he spotted Saree down the hall and remembered what Levi had said when they were hiding a few hours ago.

. . . if she can touch something that's real near and dear to someone, she can see all sorts of colors.

What would be near and dear to Toliver. Not his locker . . .

His Mustang.

Yes!

Jack was desperate for any clue as to how to get to Toliver. If Saree did have some weird "talent," maybe she could help. He didn't see how it could hurt.

He nudged Levi and pointed toward Saree. "Think she'd be interested in what colors she can see around Toliver's car?"

Levi looked at him, then at Saree.

"She might be."

"Talk her into it and meet me by his 'stang."

6

Jack grabbed the lock-pick kit from his backpack and raced to the parking lot. With the lunch period coming to a close, no one was about. When he first got the kit from Mr. Rosen, he went around his house picking every lock he could find. That included the family cars. Cars were easy. Their door locks tended to have big pins that responded smoothly to a little raking.

He had Toliver's Mustang open in twenty seconds and had the kit hidden away before Levi and Saree showed up.

"What do you want me to do?" she said, hanging back and staring at Jack.

"You said his locker was cold. Is his car cold too?"

She took a hesitant step forward and gingerly touched the hood with her fingertips. After a second, she pressed her palm flat against it.

"No . . . it's warm."

Yeah, well, of course it was warm—he'd just driven to a hardware store for the lock and glue.

Jack pulled open the passenger door. "How about inside?"

Levi gawked. "He left it unlocked?"

Jack didn't look at him, but scanned the parking lot instead, check for anyone who might spot them.

"Sure looks that way."

"You and locks," Levi said with a chuckle. "You got a talent, all right."

Jack gestured Saree toward the front passenger seat. "See any colors there?"

Said aloud, the question sounded ridiculous. What did he expect to get out of this? Probably nothing—the girl seemed a little off her rocker—but he couldn't see a downside to trying.

She bent, looked, then shook her head. "No."

"Maybe if you sit inside."

She looked at Levi who shrugged and said, "Go ahead. But make it quick. We gotta get back to class."

As Saree slipped into the seat, Levi turned to Jack. "Why you so tore up about this guy, anyway?"

Jack had figured this was coming, but hadn't come up with an explanation he could use.

"Red," he heard Saree say. "It's all red."

"It's personal," he told Levi.

"I figgered that. But what you 'spect to get outta this?"

"Well, I've got him thinking he's haunted. Can we leave it at that?"

Levi nodded slowly. "I reckon we can. But about your talent—"

Jack heard Saree making noises like "Uhn-uhn-uhn!" and when he looked her eyes were rolled back in her head and she was twitching like she was being electrocuted.

"Get her outta there!" Levi shouted.

They both pulled her out and the noises and twitching stopped as soon as she was free of the car. Her eyes fluttered open as they started to lay her on the ground and she pushed herself up to standing. She leaned against the neighboring car, panting, a wild look in her pink eyes.

"Red! All red! Blood!"

"Blood?" Levi said. "Whose?"

"I don't rightly know." She rubbed both hands over her

face and eyes. "He hurt somebody there. Hurt them bad. He's got blood on his hands."

Jack stood stunned, speechless.

Blood on Toliver's hands? Not Weezy's. She'd just been bruised and scared—bad enough, but no blood. So if not Weezy's, whose?

"Levi?" Saree said, her voice quavering. "It's piney blood."

7

Between the final bell for dismissal and boarding the bus home, Jack squeezed in a trip to the boys' room to unlatch the window. He didn't know what he was going to do about Toliver's latest lock, but if he came up with something, he wanted to be able to act on it.

As he exited the stall he let out a yelp of surprise when he almost bumped into Levi.

"How long've you been waiting here?"

"Long enough. Figgered this'd be your last stop. Listen, this 'piney blood' thing's got me riled."

It had been nibbling at Jack too. Gnawing was more like it. The whole episode had been majorly upsetting. But when he stepped back and took a hard look at it . . .

"How do you know there's anything to it?"

"Saree said—"

"She doesn't *know*. It's just a feeling she's got. She doesn't know who, she doesn't know when—"

"That don't matter. She knows what she knows, and I gotta do something about it."

Uh-oh.

"Like what?"

"Don't know. First thing I do is ask around and see if anyone knows of a piney who's been banged around by a towner. Second is, I join forces with you."

"Oh, no," Jack said, backing away. "No way."

"Why not?"

"Because, like I said, it's personal."

"Well, hell, if he hurt a piney, it's personal for me too."

"You don't even know if he really—"

"Pineys stick together—well, when they ain't feudin'."

Jack pulled open the door and stepped into the hall. "Sorry. Not gonna happen."

Jack hurried for the bus, thinking how Levi Coffin was becoming a real problem.

8

"Aren't you done yet?" Eddie said as he watched Jack rake up the grass clippings.

"Almost."

"Well, hurry up so we can—uh-oh. Here comes Gargamel."

Jack glanced up and saw Mr. Drexler stepping out the Lodge's back door in his white suit.

"Gargamel dresses in black."

"Yeah, but this guy looks like he eats Smurfs for breakfast."

Mr. Drexler held up a wooden box. "Take a break and come over here. Both of you."

Jack didn't hesitate. Mr. Drexler might be strange, but he was standing on the shady side of the building and Jack needed a cool-off. Eddie held back a few seconds, then walked his bike over.

As Jack approached, Mr. Drexler leaned his cane against the door frame, then removed the top of the intricately carved box and held it out.

"Take a look at this. I believe you will find it entertaining." A soft, white glob lay within. "Hold out your hand."

When Jack did so, Mr. Drexler flipped the box over and dropped the glob onto his palm. It felt cool and squishy, and looked like vanilla pudding in a thin, clear skin.

Then, as Jack watched, it began to change color, moving slowly from white to deep blue.

"No surprise there," Mr. Drexler muttered.

"Weirdacious!" Eddie said.

Mr. Drexler looked at him. "You're Louise Connell's brother, aren't you."

Eddie swallowed. "Um, yeah."

He looked jumpy. Jack understood. The Lodge had always weirded him out.

"I haven't seen her around. Is she well?"

Eddie seemed stuck for an answer.

"She's home," Jack said, figuring Weezy's problems were none of the man's business.

Mr. Drexler nodded, then said, "Let your friend hold it, Jack."

Eddie put his hands behind his back. "Nuh-uh. Too weird."

"Come on," Jack said. "Don't be a wuss."

With obvious reluctance, Eddie cupped his hands before him, looking ready to drop the thing the instant it touched him. But he didn't. After Jack dropped it onto his palms, he held it and jiggled it.

"It's like Jell-O. Sort of—hey, it's changing color."

Jack had already noticed the dark blue fading. The glob turned a paler shade of blue . . .

"Will wonders never cease?" Mr. Drexler said. "Give it back to Jack."

Eddie did, and the glob turned dark blue again.

"Must be because my hands are hot and sweaty," Jack said.

Mr. Drexler held out the empty box. "Do you think so?"

Jack placed it back in the box and watched it return to white.

"I don't get it," Jack said. "What is it?"

"A crude sort of meter. It measures a certain . . . inner quality."

"Did we pass?" Eddie said.

Mr. Drexler's cold blue gaze remained fixed on Jack as his thin lips curved upwards at the corners. Jack couldn't quite qualify it as a smile.

"Passing or failing would depend on who is conducting the test, and what result is sought."

He replaced the lid.

"Show over."

He turned and walked back inside.

"Oh, he's weird, Jack," Eddie said in a hushed tone. "*Majorly* weird."

Jack couldn't disagree.

9

Eddie had moved on and Jack had just dumped the last of the clippings into a plastic bag when he heard Mr. Drexler say, "That's enough for today. Come have a drink."

He looked over toward the Lodge and was surprised to see that two chairs had been set out in the shade. Mr. Drexler sat on one, leaning on his cane. A can of Pepsi sat on the seat next to him.

Jack wanted nothing more than to head home for a shower, but that Pepsi was calling his name. As he walked over, Mr. Drexler lifted the can and held it out to him. Jack popped the top and took a long, cold, bubbly chug.

"Thanks."

The man patted the seat of the chair next to him. "Sit."

Jack complied. He closed his eyes and savored the cool shade.

"Look at all the little people at play."

Jack opened his eyes and saw Mr. Drexler gesturing with his cane down the slope toward Quaker Lake. People sat or sunbathed on blankets by the water's edge. With the arrival of an Indian summer, Mark Mulliner had brought his rental canoes back to the lake. People paddled them to and fro under the bridge.

"I guess they look little from here."

"They don't merely look little, they *are* little. In every sense."

Jack glanced at him. "I'm not following."

"There are two classes of people in this world: the Movers

and the Moved, the High and the Low, the Wheat and the Chaff, the Select and the Hoi Polloi."

"Hoi polloi?"

"It's Greek for 'the many.' It refers to the masses. The low folk."

Jack shrugged. "I guess it's always that way—high and low. Some people are smarter than others or work harder than others, some people want it more, and other folks want it less or don't want to spend the time and effort chasing it."

Mr. Drexler's eyebrows rose, almost framing his widow's peak. "My dear boy, I am not talking about ants and grasshoppers, nor about success and endeavor. You can't *earn* your way into the Mover class. The proverbial sweat and hard work and stick-to-itiveness will not move you up. Nor can you *buy* your way in. One must be *born* to it."

"You mean, like royalty?"

"Royalty is more about prestige, and the *perception* of power rather than the actual wielding of it. True power is knowledge, and that is what separates the Movers from the Moved: knowledge."

Jack nodded. "Yeah. 'Knowledge is power.' I've heard that before. But anyone who works at it can get knowledge, right?"

Mr. Drexler *tsk*ed. "Do not confuse knowledge with information. Certain knowledge can be trusted to only a few."

Jack had no idea where this conversation had come from or where it was going, or why they were even having it. But it seemed important to Mr. Drexler. He was really into it.

"Why not just spread it around?"

"Because, as you said, knowledge is power, and if everyone has power, then no one has power."

"You mean, no one would have power over anyone else."

Mr. Drexler's eyes lit as he pointed the silver head of his black cane at Jack. Was it really wrapped in rhinoceros hide?

"Exactly!"

"But isn't that the best way?"

He snickered. "That's what the Moved—the hoi polloi—and their naïve, egalitarian apologists would have you think, but that's not the way the world works."

"But isn't knowledge simply truth? Shouldn't everyone know the truth?"

"No-no-no," he said with a vigorous shake of his head. "Absolutely not. Only the Movers can handle certain truths, only they are entitled to share them."

"You're talking about secrets, then. Secret truths."

"Of course. Only a select few share them. It's been that way throughout history."

Jack gave him a sidelong look. "Like what's under the Lodge?"

"You mean what *was* under the Lodge." Mr. Drexler frowned. "It's lost now, thanks to you."

Jack bristled at that. "Wasn't my fault that the lake—"

Mr. Drexler waved a hand. "Water under the bridge, so to speak. I was referring to secrets much larger in scope."

Weezy's pet theory leaped into his brain. "The Secret History of the World."

"If you mean that certain truths have been kept secret and passed on throughout the history of the world, yes, that is so."

"But when Weezy mentioned it you called it a . . . a . . ."

"A 'wild imagining'? Yes, I did. Because that's the way the Moved have been conditioned to see that theory, and that's the way they must go on seeing it. Because the Moved cannot handle the truth. In fact, at the risk of sounding like I'm quoting purple prose, the truth would drive some of them stark raving mad. So in a sense it is for their own good that they remain in the dark."

"But what *is* the truth?"

Mr. Drexler stared at him. "Do you really want to know?"

"Of course. Doesn't everyone?"

He shook his head. "No. Not really. Your father, for one. He didn't care to learn."

The words rocked Jack.

"My father?"

"He was invited into the Septimus Order but declined."

Jack had known that, but . . .

"Wait . . . so what you're saying is that the Septimus Order knows the Secret History of the World."

Drexler gave a soft *heh-heh,* maybe as close to a laugh as he ever got. "No one knows the entire Secret History, but the Order is privileged to be keeper and guardian of some of those truths. I believe you qualify for membership, in fact I believe you would be an asset to the Order, but you're not eligible at this tender age. In the future, however, should you be invited, do not be so foolish as to turn down access to those secret truths."

"But what do *you* do with them?"

That pseudosmile again. "Use them, of course. Put them to work. Once you are a member, and progress through the ranks, you will learn how."

An inane thought popped into Jack's head: Would he find the secret to opening Toliver's lock?

"Until then," Mr. Drexler added, "I'm afraid you must remain among the Moved."

The conversation was beginning to make Jack uncomfortable. Lots of people thought they had special knowledge. He'd once seen an ad in a comic book for "Secrets of the Rosicrucians" and had looked them up. They thought they had special knowledge, but they let anyone in. Somehow he doubted that people advertising in comic books knew real secret truths.

But according to Weezy, the Ancient Septimus Fraternal Order was truly ancient. So maybe they did know things no one else knew. Or maybe they just thought they did.

If they really knew something, did Jack want a piece of it?

Damn straight.

But right now he had more immediate, real-life concerns.

He rose and placed the empty Pepsi can on the chair cushion.

"Thanks for the drink. I'd better get to the weeds."

"The beds can wait until tomorrow," Mr. Drexler said, standing. "As long as the grass is cut—that is the important thing. Come back then."

"But I thought you said—"

"The gathering I mentioned? They'll begin to arrive soon, so I want you and your mower gone."

"What's this gathering about?"

He gave Jack an intense stare. "You ask too many questions. Only members may ask questions, and even they do not always receive an answer. You are not a member. Your concerns about the Lodge are to be limited to the grounds and nothing more. You can finish up your duties tomorrow. Perhaps we can talk a little more then."

Jack couldn't fathom why Mr. Drexler wanted to talk. It

wasn't like he was trying to convince him to join the Order—he'd already said he was too young.

Was he trying to talk him into something else?

Without being called, Eggers appeared and picked up one of the chairs. As he returned it to the Lodge, Mr. Drexler moved a few steps closer to the lake, where he stood with his hands on his hips, staring at the "little people."

Watching him, Jack had a strange thought about the bombings in Beirut and the trouble in Grenada and all the rest of the turmoil in the world. Could the Septimus Order have something to do with that? Could they be using their secret truths to manipulate events? Were they the method behind the madness?

Nah. That was Weezy talk. Nobody, not even the Septimus Order, had that kind of power.

10

"Sounds like a load of elitist crap to me," Dad said.

"Tom," Mom scolded. "Not at the table."

Jack had just related a nutshell version of his conversation with Mr. Drexler. He glanced across the table at Kate, who smiled and winked at him. They always made fun of Mom's tender ears.

She'd served what he and Kate called a "Mommy meal": roasted chicken and potatoes, plus buttered green beans.

Kate was home for the weekend, and so the dinner table held four tonight. His older sister had started medical school at UMDNJ in Stratford the same week Jack had started high school. Her apartment there was less than twenty miles away, so it was no big deal for her to visit. Jack hoped she came home often. She was one of his favorite people in the world.

His brother Tom, on the other hand, was finishing law school up north in Jersey City and probably wouldn't be back until Thanksgiving. Jack could definitely wait to see him again.

Kate was slim with pale blue eyes and faint freckles. While away she'd cut her long blond hair back to a short, almost boyish length. It gave her an entirely different look, one that would take Jack some getting used to.

" 'We hold these truths to be self-evident, that all men are created equal,' " Dad said.

Jack's father and Kate shared the same blue eyes. His hair

was thinning. He sipped from a can of Carling Black Label beer.

"They really aren't, Dad," Kate said. "Created equal, I mean. Some are mentally retarded or physically defective from the get-go."

"I'm well aware of that, but that's not the point. This Lodge fellow is talking about people who believe they're entitled to special benefits and privileges and considerations simply because they are who they are. Congress is full of them."

"But they must think you're entitled too," Jack said. "I mean, the Lodge invited you to join, right?"

Dad nodded. "Yeah, they did. But something about the place and the people . . ." He shook his head. "I don't know. It didn't smell right."

"Smell?"

He smiled. "In a figurative sense, not . . ."

"Olfactory," Kate said.

"Right. Anyway, there was this smug undertone running through everything. Rubbed me the wrong way."

"Mister Drexler showed me this glob of stuff that changed color when I held it."

"Turned blue, right?" his father said.

Jack hadn't expected that.

"How did you know?"

"Haskins—you know, the freeholder who died—was a VFW member and he brought something like that to one of the meetings and passed it around. Mostly nothing happened till it got to me and then it turned dark blue."

"Me too!"

"Come to think of it, shortly after that I was invited to join the Lodge."

"Do you think it's some kind of test?"

Dad frowned. "Test of what?"

Jack couldn't imagine.

"I guess it's secret. You said you blew the Lodge off because 'Too many secrets can wear you down,' remember?"

Dad rubbed his jaw. "Can't say as I do."

Jack waggled his eyebrows, Groucho style. "What other secrets do you have?"

Dad gave him a look, then turned to Kate. "You know, Kate, I think I'm getting to like your hair short."

Talk about changing the subject!

"Well, thanks, Dad," she said. "It was kind of necessary, what with my labs and all. Especially the cadaver lab. I couldn't get the formaldehyde smell out of all that hair."

Jack straightened in his seat. "*Cadaver?* As in dead body?"

Kate nodded. "Four students to a body. We're dissecting it."

"Kate, really," Mom said. "At the dinner table?"

"Can I come see? Have you cut it open?"

"Just the back of the neck so far. We—"

Mom tapped her plate with her fork. "I insist we talk about something else. Please."

"Okay," Dad said, focusing on Jack, "let's get back to this job at the Lodge. You sure you're not taking on too much? The store, the other lawns . . . I don't want your grades to suffer."

Jack shrugged. "So far the teachers are taking it slow and the work's pretty easy. By the time it gets harder, I'll be freed up. Mister Rosen says after Halloween he won't need me anymore till spring, and once we get a good frost, I'll have nothing to mow."

"Got it all worked out, eh?" Dad said, nodding.

Jack sensed his approval and it warmed him.

He grinned. "Pretty much."

Except how to get past Toliver's lock.

He suddenly realized that what he'd done to Toliver had made him, for a short time and in a very limited sense, a Mover.

Then again, no. Not according to Mr. Drexler's meaning. Everything that had happened around Toliver's locker had originated with Jack, not from some secret knowledge someone said he was entitled to.

Jack said, "Maybe some days you're a Mover, and maybe some days you're one of the Moved."

"Why be either?" Kate said.

Jack looked at her. "What do you mean?"

"Why not just opt out and refuse to be part of the game? Step aside and play your own game with your own rules, and screw the rest."

Mom frowned. "Kate!"

Jack sat there, stunned as epiphanies exploded in his brain like a fireworks finale. Neither a Moved nor a Mover be . . . refuse to play . . . step off the board and liberate yourself from the game . . .

Dad harrumphed and said, "Sounds like anarchy to me."

But it sounded wonderful to Jack.

11

Jack's dad dropped him and Eddie off in the parking lot, and they had to walk around the side of the high school to get to the football field. They were about halfway there when Jack spotted Levi standing under a stand of trees, gesturing to him.

Aw, jeez. Now what?

He didn't want to talk to him with Eddie around—who knew what might slip?

"Catch up to you later," Jack said.

Eddie nodded. "Okay. Sure."

He didn't look at Jack. His gaze was fixed on the hot dog stand.

Levi faded back into the shadows as Jack approached.

"I checked around," he said when Jack reached him.

"About what?"

"A piney getting bloodied up by Toliver—or someone like Toliver, just in case whoever he beat on didn't know who he was."

"And?"

"And nothin'."

"So Saree was wrong."

"Saree ain't wrong. That feelin' she got was too strong. We pineys gossip a lot, and we got a grapevine like you wouldn't believe, but it ain't perfect. May just be someone who ain't in contact, or who ain't talkin' 'cause they're shamed. If we knew whose blood it was, there'd be piney justice comin' Toliver's way."

Jack had heard of pine justice—it was swift and to the point and didn't involve the legal system.

But all this confusion looked like good news for Jack.

"Guess you'll just have to wait for someone to speak up."

"Like hell. If Saree says there's piney blood on his hands, then there's gonna be another kinda blood on his head. Or at least on his car."

"What are you talking about?"

"I brought along some blood."

Jack felt his stomach curdle. "Blood? Can I ask—?"

"Deer." He gave Jack a look. "We get our meat on the hoof in the Pines."

"And you're going to pour it on him?"

"If I can find a way."

That had to be the dumbest idea Jack had ever heard.

"You get caught, there'll definitely be piney blood on his hands."

Levi nodded. "I reckon there will. That's why I was thinking maybe that fancy car of his would be better."

"Go with that thought . . . but include me out."

Levi laughed. "Don't worry. This is a piney matter, and you ain't a piney."

Jack was wishing he'd never brought Saree out to Toliver's car and was about to say so when he noticed the beat-up binoculars hanging from Levi's neck.

"What are those for?"

"To watch the game. Should be starting soon. Let's go."

12

Jack and Eddie found spots high and to the right. SBR fans occupied the south stands—naturally—and NBR the north. Levi had drifted off. Jack scanned the crowd, hunting him. He finally spotted him standing at the lower corner of the SBR stand by himself. Jack didn't remember ever seeing him at the games before—for the most part, the pineys didn't seem to take much interest in school sports—but then again, he'd never looked for him.

The game began and it soon became clear that Toliver wasn't himself. His strength was his passing game—he threw bullets with pinpoint accuracy—but he was off tonight. The ones that weren't high or low were late reaching the receiver.

Jack's gaze kept drifting from the game to Levi. Blood . . . how stupid. He could ruin Jack's whole plan if he got caught. Had to find a way to talk him out of it.

As he watched, he noticed Levi peering through the binoculars, but only now and again. By the time the second quarter rolled around, Jack realized that he was using them only when South had the ball, and even then, only when Toliver dropped back to pass . . .

. . . which he was doing right now.

Toliver shot a bullet to his wide receiver. As Jack watched it arc through the air, he swore he saw it lift in midflight—not much, just enough to make it go high over the raised hands of the receiver who jumped and stretched for it. He got his fingertips on it, sending the ball wobbling through the air *and into the hands of one of the North defenders*.

Interception! Crap!

The player ran it back for a touchdown. As NBR celebrated, Jack noticed Toliver screaming at his receiver.

Temper, temper . . .

He had to be frustrated. Not one completion so far in the first half, and time was winding down.

He shifted his gaze to Levi and . . . was that a smile?

Jack stopped watching the game. Instead, he divided his attention between Levi and the game. Levi followed every Toliver pass with his binocs, and each time the ball behaved strangely. Nothing big, just little shifts like the wind might cause.

But the air was still.

The half ended with another NBR interception. The teams left the field with the Greyhounds leading seventeen–zip.

"What's up with Carson?" Eddie said. "I've never seen him like this."

A kid in front of them turned around. "It's gotta be because of somebody messing with his locker. His concentration's off."

The kid next to him said, "If he's really any good, the locker stuff shouldn't bother him."

"Well, either way," said the first, "whoever's been doing it oughta be strung up on the school flagpole."

Jack didn't like the sound of that.

"Gotta be more to it than rigging his locker," Jack said.

"Yeah? What else is different? Unless he's throwing the game, and he'd never do that."

"Right," Eddie said. "Never."

"No way," Jack added, and meant it.

Carson Toliver might have a dark, ugly side, but one of the things he would most want in this world was victory over NBR. So what was happening?

Jack looked at the lone figure standing at the corner of the stand.

Levi? He kept talking about "talents" . . . could he . . . ?

Nah.

While Eddie hit the refreshment stand again, Jack spent the remainder of halftime mulling ways to convince Levi to leave Toliver to Jack. The mood of the SBR crowd was dark. A couple of shoving matches started between South and North kids but were quickly broken up. Jack hadn't come up with anything by the time the Badgers and Greyhounds returned to the field.

"Okay, Carson!" Eddie yelled. "Do it! Show 'em what ya got!"

But all Toliver had was more of the same. And Levi kept tracking every pass with his binocs. SBR fans wailed as Toliver threw another interception, his third of the game.

As the offense came off the field, the coach pulled his quarterback aside and spoke to him. Whatever he said threw Toliver into a rage. He pulled off his helmet, grabbed it by the face mask, and began smashing it against the bench. He kept it up until it cracked, then started walking off the field. The coach grabbed him and shoved him toward the bench, where he sat with his head in his hands.

Jack suspected what had happened, and that was confirmed the next time the offense took the field: Toliver remained on the bench.

Levi turned and started to walk away.

"Be right back!" Jack said as he leaped to his feet and started down through the crowd.

"Bring me some popcorn!" Eddie called after him.

Jack caught up to Levi by the school.

"Where you going? The game's not over."

"Yeah, it is." Levi slowed his stride but didn't stop. "We lost."

"What do you think of Toliver's passes? Pretty weird the way they went off course."

"Wind can do strange things to a football."

"Except there's no wind."

Levi shot him a sidelong glance. "Maybe it's a haint. If he thought he had one after him before, he's probably sure of it now."

"Haint?"

"Yeah. You know . . . a ghost."

Oh, right. Toliver had asked Mrs. C about someone being haunted . . .

And then a beautiful idea hit Jack, perfect, complete in every detail . . . a way to tighten the screws on Toliver and keep Levi in line.

"You said you had blood . . . ?"

13

One of the things about living in a small town was that people tended to know their neighbors, maybe too well sometimes. Everyone knew something about what everyone else was doing. And they recognized strangers. No outsider could cruise the streets without being noticed. As a result, folks tended to be lax about security. The Tolivers were no exception.

Jack led Levi through the orchard to the rear of the Toliver house. The place was dark. Jack checked the garage—empty. The parents were at the game, watching their son. Jack remembered Carson's window from Monday night. A twist of Levi's penknife popped the screen out of its groove, and the unlocked window lifted easily.

A part of Jack screamed that this was crazy, but he'd done crazier things, so he didn't listen, and didn't hesitate. They had to get in and get out ASAP. No telling how long they had.

Jack went through first, and took the mason jar of blood Levi handed through the window. He checked out the room as Levi clambered through.

"Look," he whispered. "A mirror. Perfect."

"For what?"

"For leaving a message."

"Why're you whispering?" Levi said, a nervous laugh nibbling at the edge of his voice. "Ain't no one here but us chickens."

"That's true, but I'll keep whispering, if you don't mind."

"Don't mind ay-tall. Okay, how 'bout we write, 'You got piney blood on your hands!!!' That'll spook him."

Remembering the KISS rule, Jack shook his head.

"Nah. Let's just make it 'Blood on your hands' and leave it at that. If he really does have blood on his hands, he'll know what it means. If not, the rest won't matter. But if you put 'piney' in there, he'll start looking at the pineys in school."

"Good thought. You want to write it?"

Dip his finger in clotted deer blood. Uh-uh.

Jack handed back the jar. "Um, no. You do it."

"Hopin' you'd say that."

Levi unscrewed the top, stuck his finger in the jar, and went to work. When finished, he stepped back and surveyed his work.

"What y'think?"

Even in the dark room, the message of the glistening letters was clear.

BLOOD
ON
Your
HANDS

"Yeah, that'll do. Let's get out of here."

They climbed out, lowered the window, fitted the screen back into place, and retreated to the orchard.

"What do we do now?" Levi said.

"We find ourselves a spot where we can see without being seen, and we watch what he does when he sees the message."

Jack had told Eddie he was leaving early. Mr. Connell was

supposed to pick them up after the game and Jack didn't want anyone getting all worked up because they couldn't find him.

It turned out to be a short wait before Carson and his folks pulled up in their respective cars. Jack could hear raised voices, arguing about something.

"Give me the binocs."

Levi handed them over, saying, "Okay but don't hog 'em."

Jack raised them to his eyes. "We'll see what he does, then move on. We don't want to get caught when the cops show up."

"Why'll the cops come?"

"If you found a message written in blood on your bedroom mirror, wouldn't you call the cops?"

"Nope. Pineys don't call cops. Cops don't pay us no nevermind anyhow."

"Really?"

"Really."

"That's not right."

"That's why we got piney justice."

Jack saw the bedroom light up and focused through the window. He watched Toliver step into the room, freeze, and then half fall against the dresser before the mirror. It looked as if his knees had given out on him. With his hands braced on the dresser, he stared at the mirror, then straightened and ran from the room.

Jack lowered the glasses and handed them to Levi.

"He saw it, he's spooked, he's gone to tell his folks. Time for us to disappear."

"Wait a second," Levi said, raising the glasses. "We got time before we gotta skedaddle. I want to see what his folks do. Maybe they know about it. Maybe they're in on it."

Jack was about to say that they didn't know for sure if there was anything to this "piney blood" thing in the first place, but decided not to bother. Levi seemed to have complete faith in Saree's "talent."

"Hey, he's back!" Levi said. "But he's alone. And guess what he's doing."

He handed Jack the binocs. Jack looked and saw Toliver spraying the mirror with what looked like Windex and wiping away the blood.

He felt a chill settle across his shoulders as he lowered the glasses.

"He didn't tell his folks . . . he's not calling the cops . . . that means . . ."

"Yeah," Levi said. "He's guilty. He *does* have blood on his hands."

Jack couldn't see any other conclusion.

"Yeah, but whose?"

1

"Why so glum, chum?"

Jack looked up from his bowl of Cap'n Crunch and found his father staring down at him from the other side of the kitchen table. He was wearing his steel-rimmed reading glasses and had the morning paper folded under his arm. Mid-morning sunlight bathed the backyard beyond the screen door behind him.

Jack had slept in—the first uninterrupted night's sleep since Tuesday. He'd almost forgotten how great it felt to wake up rested. But that didn't soften Toliver's reaction to the blood, or help open his lock. He couldn't tell Dad about those, so he chose the most obvious.

"We got killed last night. Bummer."

"The football game? Glad to hear this."

Jack nearly choked. "That we lost? You're glad?"

He laughed. "No, just glad you care. Good to see you getting involved over there, school spirit and all that."

Jack twirled a finger in the air. "Rah. Rah."

"I'm serious, Jack. We've discussed your loner tendencies before and how I think you'll regret it later on if you give in to them. You know what I mean, so I don't see any need to open the subject again."

That was a relief. Dad's heart-to-heart talks, though rare, usually made him uncomfortable.

"Your high school years can be some of the best of your life. Trust me, the more you put in, the more you'll get out. I'm glad to see you're into the Badgers."

Jack didn't respond. What could he say to that? Besides, his head was filled with too many other matters.

How to explain Toliver's rotten performance, and the weird behavior of his passes? Not that the guy hadn't needed a comeuppance, but the rest of the school had been rooting for a win. A lot more people than Carson Toliver had been disappointed last night.

"Any plans for the day, Jack?" his mother said as she entered the kitchen.

Yeah, he thought. I'm going to waste more time trying to find a way around that spiked-and-glued lock.

Maybe he should just forget Toliver's challenge and let him have his locker victory Monday morning. Looked like it was going to work out that way anyway. He'd hit a wall on that lock.

But he said, "Just have to finish weeding the beds at the Lodge, then cut the Bagleys' lawn. Mister Rosen said he'd need me for only a couple of hours today."

For nap time, most likely.

"Well, you'll be on your own for lunch, I'm afraid. Kate will be out with Jenny Styles most of the day, and your father and I will be shopping in Cherry Hill for a new suit."

Dad rolled his eyes. "Be still, my heart."

Jack knew he hated shopping, especially for clothes.

"Oh, stop it, Tom. You need a new suit. You wear one every day. Actually, you could use two new ones."

"Jane, I trust your taste implicitly. Why don't *you* go and—"

"Don't be silly. A suit has to be fitted." She turned to Jack. "We'll be back about four. We've got leftover chicken in the fridge."

Jack nodded absently. He'd just thought of something: Dad's lockbox.

He kept it in the top of his bedroom closet. Toward the end of the summer Jack had fixated on it after he'd heard Mr. Bainbridge's "Deadeye" remark. He'd been convinced then that his father had been some sort of ace marksman and that the box had to contain memorabilia—medals, papers, *secrets*—from the war Dad would never talk about. He'd tried and failed to pick its little lock a number of times. Starting high school, the pyramid quest, and then the Cody Bockman thing had distracted him, but now he was being handed a golden opportunity.

He still had the lock-picking kit. He could take another stab at opening that little box while Mom was dragging Dad from store to store.

First he had to finish up at the Lodge.

2

"So, have you given any thought to our conversation yesterday?"

Mr. Drexler watched Jack weed the foundation beds along the Lodge's front.

"A little."

Mr. Drexler smiled. "Excellent. Conclusions? Opinions? Expansions? I'm all ears."

After batting this around with his father and Kate last night, he felt more comfortable continuing with it. Because he'd remembered some things Mr. Kressy had said in class.

"This Mover-and-Moved situation . . . it sounds wrong."

"Wrong? As in incorrect, or immoral?"

"Immoral, I guess."

"How could it be immoral? It's nature, it's woven into the very fabric of existence."

"But nobody has a right to control other people."

"Ah, but they have, and they do. Right and wrong do not enter into the Mover-Moved equation. It's all merely a question of which you were born to be."

Mr. Drexler seemed to be enjoying this. Jack wished he could feel the same. He readied his big question, inspired by Kate.

"What if you refuse to be either?"

Mr. Drexler gave a full-fledged grin this time, showing teeth as white as his shirt.

"Surely you're not thinking of autonomy! That's pure fiction. Everything is determined."

Jack refused to buy that.

"I don't have to play. I can step off the chessboard and refuse to be a Mover or be Moved."

"So you can. But free will is an illusion." He leaned closer and lowered his voice. "I'll let you in on a secret, Jack, a truth that a few people have suspected and even fewer have accepted: Even the Movers are being moved."

He straightened and paused, as if to let that sink in.

"Should you manage to escape the board and onto the table—not at all an easy feat, I assure you—you need to realize that the table itself is being moved; and if you jump down to the floor, that the floor is being moved. Ultimately it all works back to the Prime Movers."

"Prime Movers? What are they?"

"No one knows. No one will ever know. But they're there. And we're their property. No one moves the Primes. Sometimes you can have a say in which of those Primes moves you, but you are moved nonetheless. One way or another, we are all ultimately among the Moved."

Jack stared at him. He'd never heard this view of the world before, and didn't like it. He couldn't, wouldn't buy into it.

"How do you sleep at night, Mister Drexler?"

"Very well. Extremely well. Because, through the Septimus Order, I have become privy to what your girlfriend calls 'the Secret History of the World.'"

"She's not my girlfriend," Jack said, but Mr. Drexler ignored him.

"I have seen how existence works, I know where the battle

lines are drawn, and I am comfortable with the side with which I am aligned. So yes, I sleep well at night." He leaned closer, his eyes bright. "But what of you? How will you sleep knowing what you now know?"

"Just fine. Because I don't *know* anything more than before. This is all just talk, just opinion."

"Ah, but opinion based on secret truths, truths to which you may become privy in the future. The easy way is through the Order. The other way is through experience, and that can be *most* painful."

He gave a quick, two-finger salute, then turned and strolled away, swinging his cane as he walked.

Jack tried to concentrate on the weeds, but he kept picturing a chessboard, and himself as a pawn someone was moving around.

He hated the picture, and knew he'd be seeing it again as he tried to get off to sleep tonight.

3

With the Bagleys' lawn done, Jack had some time to himself before he had to show up at USED. He scarfed down the left-over chicken, then grabbed the lock-pick set and bounded upstairs to his folks' bedroom. After Jack's birth back in 1969, the house had needed another bedroom. So his folks had finished off the attic, turning it into a master bedroom suite, and leaving a first-floor bedroom to each of the three kids.

He found his father's metal lockbox in its usual place on the top shelf of his closet. He reached up and dragged it out, but this time a few papers it had been sitting on slid out with it. He took a quick glance at them—some kind of old bills— and set them on the bed. Then he sat cross-legged on the floor and opened the pick set. He was inspecting the selection of tension rods when he heard a car in the driveway.

Kate? She was supposed to be out with her friend.

He rose, padded to the window, and peeked out.

What? Oh, crap! His folks were home, and already halfway to the door!

He leaped to the lockbox and fumbled it back onto the shelf just as the back door slammed. He heard their voices as they came through the kitchen. They were hurrying, and now they were coming up the stairs!

Jack couldn't get caught up here with a lock-picking kit. But he had nowhere to go except the bathroom, and that was out of the question. The only safe hiding spot was under the bed. He dropped to his knees and was about to slip under when he noticed the papers on the bedspread. He snatched them and took them into hiding with him.

A heartbeat later he heard his father say, "I swear, Jane, we must be getting senile."

"I know," she said. "How could we forget?"

Jack watched their feet walk by the bed.

"Well, in our defense, we made the date weeks ago."

"Yes, but I've had it written big as day on the calendar. And I always look at the calendar. How could I have missed it?"

"We're not late yet. There's still time."

Time for what? Jack wondered as he lay on his belly, barely breathing.

He watched his father kick off his shoes, saw his slacks hit the floor. He could see his mother's feet stepping out of her dress.

What were they undressing for?

His father's feet approached his mother's. They stood toe to toe.

"Hey," he heard him say softly. "Jack's gone." He heard a kiss. "Why don't we—?"

"We don't have time for that."

Jack's stomach clenched. They weren't talking about sex, were they? No-no-no!

"We've got time enough." Another kiss. "And if we're a little late, the Gillilands can simply warm up a little longer."

The Gillilands—his folks played tennis with them now and then.

And they *were* talking about sex! This couldn't be happening. His parents didn't still have sex, did they? They couldn't! Hell, Dad was fifty-three! They were too old!

Tennis! Jack thought, trying for mental telepathy. *Play tennis! You don't want to be late for tennis!*

"Tom . . ."

The feet disappeared from view as a weight settled on the bed.

NO-NO-NO-NO-NO! This can*not* be happening!

"How often do we have the house to ourselves like this, hmmm?"

"Jack might come home any minute."

"But he probably won't, and he certainly won't run up here as soon as he comes in the door."

Another kiss.

Jack covered his ears and squeezed his eyes shut. Oh, God, how long before the bed started bouncing? He gave up telepathy and tried for teleportation—anywhere. Anywhere in the world but here.

And then Jack sensed some of the weight leave the bed. He opened his eyes and uncovered his ears. He saw his mother's stockinged feet on the floor again.

Yes!

"Tom, really. Nice as it would be, I don't want to spend the game feeling all, you know . . ."

He covered his ears again. He was *not* hearing this.

Finally his father's feet reappeared.

Saved!

Finally they were gone.

He'd watched as stockings and dark socks were replaced by white socks and slipped into sneakers, and watched those two pairs of sneakers leave.

He waited for the sound of the car starting and rolling out the driveway, but it never came. Could be because he was under a bed. He decided to take no chances. He'd wait.

To kill the time, he looked at the sheets of paper that had fallen off the closet shelf. They were dusty and looked pretty old, like they'd been up there a long time.

One was an old photo, faded and creased. It showed a guy wearing a kilt, a fuzzy hat, and holding a rifle. He recognized his mom's handwriting at the bottom: *Uncle Joe*. He vaguely recalled her mentioning him a couple of times. He looked like he should have been holding bagpipes instead of that old-fashioned rifle.

The rest were old bills, mostly from the time they remodeled the house. The last one caught his eye, though—a medical bill, and it had his father's name on it. He knew he shouldn't look, but also knew he couldn't not look, so his hesitation lasted about ten seconds. Maybe less.

The letterhead said Kurt Welsch, M.D., and it was a bill for surgery performed on his father back in 1968. The procedure was listed as *repair of spontaneous recanalization of right vas deferens post 1962 vasectomy*.

Huh?

Jack had no idea what it meant but it sounded serious as all hell. He reread it twice but it still made no sense. Whatever it was, his father had survived it. The surgery had been fifteen years ago and he was still going strong.

Fifteen years . . . 1968 . . . he hadn't been born yet.

He wriggled out from under the bed and paused, listening. No sound from the house. He crept over to the window where a quick peek revealed an empty driveway. He had the place to himself again.

He returned all but one of the papers to the top of the closet. He was going to keep the medical bill for a while, at least until he figured out what it was talking about.

His first stop was the dictionary. He was pretty sure he knew what a vasectomy was but he looked it up anyway: *Surgical division or resection of all or part of the vas deferens usually to induce sterility.*

Yeah. Okay. And the vas deferens was . . . ?

A sperm-carrying duct especially of a higher vertebrate that in the human male is a thick-walled tube about two feet (0.61 meters) long that begins at and is continuous with the tail of the epididymis and eventually joins the duct of the seminal vesicle to form the ejaculatory duct.

Swell. That was a big help.

He went to the encyclopedia and found an illustration that showed a tube coming off the testicle and running up and . . .

Wait. Dad had that *cut*?

Jack's knees locked together of their own accord.

Yow and *ow*!

So wait . . . the bill indicated that Dad had had a vasectomy in 1962 . . . had himself sterilized seven years before Jack was born.

Well then, how had he fathered Jack?

Jack didn't want to do it, but saw no way around it now. He was going to have to talk to Kate about this.

But first he had to get over to USED.

5

As he guided his bike onto Quakerton Road, Jack spotted a familiar car on the Quaker Lake bridge: A light blue Mustang GLX was heading toward Old Town.

Jack wondered if Toliver was alone, or maybe had another unwitting girl with him. But it was midafternoon, not the usual time for funny business. Maybe a stop at Mrs. Clevenger's to ask about being haunted again? Because if he suspected he was being haunted before, he had to be thoroughly convinced now.

Jack looked at his watch. He had time for a quick detour before Mr. Rosen's nap time.

He followed the car over the bridge into Old Town, past the Lodge and Mrs. Clevenger's house. Well, so much for that idea. He rode past the old graveyard and the supposedly haunted Klenke house to odd-looking Lester Appleton's truck, parked as usual next to the Lightning Tree.

The Mustang stopped, so Jack stopped. He watched Toliver get out with an empty bottle in his hand. He gave it to Lester, who filled it with clear liquid from a big brown jug. Money changed hands.

Doubly illegal, Jack knew. Still years from twenty-one, Toliver was underage to buy liquor. But that didn't stop Lester, and when Jack thought about it, why should it? Lester was already breaking a bunch of laws just by distilling his applejack moonshine, so adding one more by selling to a minor was no big deal to him.

But the town wouldn't feel that way. Nobody reported

the applejack trade in Johnson and other Pinelands towns. The cops knew, but it was part of the life cycle of the Pines, a private matter, not subject to the rules and regulations common to the rest of the state or even the country. Nobody would dream of blowing the whistle. That would be like sticking a knife in a dying way of life.

But the quarterback of the high school football team buying applejack . . . that would make waves. Especially after last night's performance. People would get upset. They'd blame the applejack and wouldn't look the other way on that.

Is this my doing too? Jack wondered. Had the locker rigs and the bloody words driven him to drink?

But from the way Toliver and Lester chatted, and the way Lester clapped him on the arm, it seemed pretty clear this wasn't their first transaction.

As Toliver returned to his car he spotted Jack and froze. Their eyes met and locked for a few heartbeats, then he slipped into the front seat and started the engine. He turned the car around and pulled to a stop beside Jack.

"What did you just see?" he said, giving Jack a hard look. He had circles under his eyes, like he hadn't slept. His air of superiority seemed less natural and more forced today. And his eyes . . . definitely haunted.

Jack looked right back. "Nothing."

He was tempted to add, *Nice game last night,* but decided against it.

"Good," Toliver said. "See that you keep it that way." He reached for the gearshift, then looked back at Jack. "Hey, I've seen you around."

Yeah, Jack thought. I'm the guy who showed you up at the circus last month.

"I go to SBR."

"Right. A frosh. You pal around with Weezy Connell."

You mean "Easy Weezy"? Jack wanted to say, but bit it back. Couldn't risk giving his feelings away. So he simply nodded.

"Yeah."

"Where's she been lately?"

"Home."

"Yeah?" His stare bored into Jack. "She ever talk about me?"

"Now and then."

"Really? What she say?"

"Not much, except she used to think you were a great guy."

Toliver looked gut-punched for an instant, and Jack wondered if it was because he regretted what he'd done to her, or because after the locker episodes and the blown game, lots of other kids in school might be feeling the same.

But he recovered quickly and gave a who-cares shrug. "That's life, I guess."

Jack wanted to punch him. Instead he decided to rub it in a little.

"Want me to say hello for you?"

"Don't bother." He pointed to the bottle of applejack on the passenger seat. "And don't bother saying anything about this either. Or else."

Jack felt his anger rise. He wanted like crazy to say, *What's that red spot on your hand? Could it be . . . blood?* But that would be stupid. That would give everything away.

Instead, he said, "Or else what?"

Toliver's smile was cold. "Or else I make your first year in SBR a living hell. And if you don't think I'll do it, try me."

With that he hit the gas and roared off.

Jack watched him go, wondering how he could have felt even a little bit sorry for the guy.

Let him off? Let him have his little victory on Monday? No way.

Jack had been ready to declare a truce, but now he was back in full war mode.

But to win the war he had to get past Toliver's latest lock. And to do that he'd need another close look at it.

That meant another trip to the school. Tonight, most likely.

6

Later that afternoon, as Jack was pedaling away from USED along Quakerton Road, he heard a car toot. He looked and saw Kate waving as she passed.

He started to wave back, then remembered the piece of paper folded in his back pocket.

"Kate!" he cried, releasing the handlebars and waving with both arms. "Kate!"

As she slowed and pulled over, Jack hopped off his bike and leaned in the passenger window.

"I need to talk to you."

"I'm headed home. We can talk—"

"I can't talk to you about this at home."

She frowned. "Are you in some sort of trouble?"

"Nothing like that." He pulled the medical bill from his pocket and hopped into the passenger seat. "But you can't tell anyone about this."

She cocked her head. "I don't know . . ."

"Please, Kate. It's nothing bad. It's just . . . you just can't let Mom and Dad know I found this."

She held out her hand. "No promises until I see it."

Jack hesitated, then figured if he couldn't trust Kate, who could he trust? She'd be cool with it.

He handed it to her. "I found this at home."

Kate looked it over, a frown deepening as she read it.

"Where'd you get this?"

"Can we just say I was somewhere I probably shouldn't have been, and leave it at that?"

She glanced at him. "More like 'definitely' shouldn't have been, I'm sure." She reread the paper. "This is very personal."

"I know. I just want to know what it means."

" 'Repair of spontaneous recanalization of right vas deferens post 1962 vasectomy,' " she said, reading. "I have an idea what it means but I'm not sure."

"But you're in medical school."

She laughed. "For a little over a month! I've got four years of studying ahead of me before I can qualify to be even an intern. But Jenny's in her second year. Maybe she can clear it up."

"When can you call her?"

"I'll have to wait till no one can overhear, but I'll get to it as soon as I can." She looked at the paper again. "I'd like to know what this is about too."

7

"Dad, you were a soldier, right?" Jack said as he helped Mom clear the table before dessert.

His father and mother were still in their tennis clothes—they'd beaten the Gillilands. He'd grilled burgers on his trusty Weber. He refused to buy a gas grill, insisting that charcoal was the only way to go.

Dad looked at him. "You know darn well I was."

Yeah, he did. He kept pestering his father for war stories and was continually frustrated.

"Right. Was your father a soldier?"

He shook his head. "No. Too young for the First World War, too old for the Second."

"But your grandfather was in the Spanish American War," Mom said.

"Yes, he was. On San Juan Hill." He looked at Jack. "Why the sudden interest?"

"Just curious as to how many soldiers were in the family."

He *was* curious, but that wasn't why he was asking now. Kate had sneaked off to the phone in her room to call Jenny Styles about the recanalization thing and Jack wanted to keep his folks in the kitchen, far out of earshot.

Plus he wanted to know about that photo of Uncle Joe.

"How about your dad, Mom?"

She shook her head. "No. Too young too. But his older brother, your great-uncle Joe, was a career soldier in the Black Watch."

Black Watch? That sounded cool.

"What's that?"

"A Scottish regiment," Dad said. "Reputed to be some of the fiercest fighting men in history. They used to wear kilts into battle, and because of that their enemies named them the 'Ladies from Hell.'"

Jack laughed. "My uncle was a Lady from Hell! How cool is that?"

Mom pulled a gallon of Welsh Farms peanut butter swirl ice cream from the freezer and handed it to Jack.

"There's warriors on both sides of the family."

"And thank God we'll have no more," Dad said, looking at Jack. "At least in your generation."

He felt mildly insulted. "What do you mean?"

"The draft's gone, and if we can avoid war for the next ten, twelve years, you'll be too old should some idiot bring it back. I don't want anyone shooting at my son."

Kate returned then. She looked at Jack with a tiny shake of her head.

What did that mean? Jenny didn't know either?

Jack cocked his head toward the back door and wandered over there, pretending to look out at the backyard. Kate joined him for a second.

"She's out for the night," she whispered. "I'll call her in the morning."

Jack nodded and stayed at the door as Kate drifted away.

Okay. He was disappointed, but only a little. He could wait till tomorrow.

His thoughts drifted to tonight—or early tomorrow morning, rather—and his planned trip to school.

That lock . . . how was he going to beat that lock?

8

His folks had gone to bed earlier than usual, so Jack decided to get an early start. But just before midnight, as he wheeled his bike into the garage, he caught sight of a glow in the cornfield next door. He stopped and stared in wonder as a softball-size glob of yellow-white light skimmed along the tasseled tops of the stalks, heading east . . . toward the Pines.

A pine light. What was this one doing out here, out of the woods?

He walked around to the back of the garage to keep an eye on it and saw it meet up with another light. They circled each other twice, then continued toward the Pines.

He felt an urge to follow but held back. Heading into the Pines alone at night was risky. Weezy always knew where they were, but no way he could get hold of her. He wished again for a *Star Trek* communicator.

He found the Big Dipper in the moonless sky and followed its leading edge to Polaris, the North Star. Good. If he got lost, the stars would guide him home. All he'd have to do was keep heading west and eventually he'd run into a town, a farm, or Route 206. So, besides wasting a little time, he couldn't see much downside in following. And the upside . . . well, you never knew with the Pine Barrens.

He hopped on his bike and followed the pair. Once in the Pines they picked up others. This reminded him of the time he and Weezy had followed a group of lights—she called them lumens—during the equinox last month.

Lights of all sizes mingled and circled one another as he

followed them along the starlit firebreak trails through the trees. They led him to a place he recognized: the clearing beyond the spot where Toliver had attacked Weezy.

He stopped his bike near the dead zone and watched as the lights got organized. They formed a line and began swooping down on the bare area amid the trees. They seemed to disappear into the sandy soil for a second or two before reemerging farther on; then they soared back above the trees and looped around a big oak that stood above the pines, only to return for another dip into the barren sand. They flowed around in a continually moving figure eight.

Jack watched, awed and fascinated, until they dispersed and drifted off in all directions.

What was that all about? Was that why nothing grew in that spot? Did the lumens somehow sterilize it?

Questions, questions, questions, but none so pressing as how to open Toliver's lock.

1

A little after one A.M., Jack pushed his bike through the brush and onto the shoulder of Route 206. As usual he emerged opposite the Lonely Pine Motel. In the dim blue light from the roadside neon sign he again made out Miriam's old station wagon in its same spot before room three.

She said she'd be there till Sunday. Well, Sunday was here. He imagined her waiting alone with her baby since Tuesday in that tiny room. The poor woman had to be stir-crazy by now.

He was about to push on when he saw a shadow moving along the motel's front walk, passing the doors one by one until it stopped by number three.

Walt?

Could be, but Jack couldn't make out any details. The light from the sign didn't reach that far. All he saw was a man-shaped blob of black.

The shape stood silent and unmoving before room three. Then, with a suddenness that made Jack jump, three loud knocks echoed through the night. Seconds later the pair of double-hung windows to the right of the door lit. The curtains parted in the middle and Miriam's face appeared, then quickly vanished. The door opened, letting light escape into the night.

Jack recognized the figure now.

Even if he hadn't, Miriam's cry of "Mister Erskine!" would have been enough. She was dressed in some sort of bathrobe. She pulled him in and shut the door.

Jack stood frozen, staring. He knew he should be heading down the road toward school, but he couldn't take his eyes off the door to room three. What was going on in there? Obviously Miriam believed that Walt had some sort of healing power—she'd said so loud and clear that afternoon in USED. But did Walt believe it too?

He must, or else why would he have come? But why at this hour of the morning? To keep it secret? Or was there another reason?

After Miriam had peeked out, she hadn't closed the curtains all the way. A bright blade of light sliced into the darkness. Jack moved toward it, drawn like the moths already fluttering against the glass.

He knew he shouldn't do this—he felt like a Peeping Tom—but the situation was so bizarre, so far-out, he had to see what would happen between Walt, Miriam, and her baby.

He leaned his bike against the rear bumper of the station wagon and tiptoed toward the window. Gravel scraped under his sneaker as he stepped onto the walk. He stopped, ready to duck away should anyone take a look. But no one seemed to have heard, so he crept the rest of the way and crouched outside the window.

Through the one-inch gap in the curtains he saw Miriam standing by an unmade double bed, holding her sleeping baby. Walt stood opposite her, looking stiff and awkward.

"I can't believe it," she said, tears running down her cheeks. "I can't believe you came. I'd given up hope."

Jack was surprised he could hear her so clearly, then realized the window sashes were raised a couple of inches, probably to let a little air circulate in the tiny room.

"I don't want to give false hope," Walt said, his voice thick and hoarse.

His eyes seemed clearer that usual, but his gaze was darting all over the room, settling everywhere but on the baby.

"It's not false, Mister Erskine—"

"Call me Walt."

"Okay . . . Walt. I know it's not false hope." She raised her left arm. "I'm living proof."

"Yeah, but that was then, this is now."

Yeah? Jack thought. Did Walt just say *yeah*?

He wasn't denying it as he had back in the store. It seemed like now that they were alone, their shared secret could come out.

"I believe in you."

"Belief isn't enough, miss."

She smiled. "My name is Miriam."

"Okay. Fine. But this is gonna take more than belief. The timing has to be right, and I don't know if it is. I think it is, but . . ."

Her smile faded. "Oh, it must be. It must! My little Tammy needs you so bad!"

"I know," he said, finally looking at the baby. "That's why I came. But I need something first."

"Oh? Oh, yes." She turned and pulled an envelope from her shoulder bag. She extended it toward Walt. "It's not a whole lot, but it's all I've got. And if it's not enough . . ." She averted her eyes. ". . . if you want anything else from me, you can have that too."

Walt looked at her as if she was handing him a timber rattlesnake.

"I don't want anything from you but a promise."

She stared at him. "A promise? What—?"

"This never happened. If this works, you've got to promise me that you will never tell a living soul about me. Even if it doesn't work, this never happened, right?"

"If that's what you want—"

"It's what I *need*. If this works, people will notice, and they'll want to know how and why and where and when and, worst of all, *who*. The who is me, and I just want to be left alone. So, do I have your word?"

She nodded. "Yes. Absolutely."

"Do you swear on the life of your daughter?"

"I do. And if it makes you feel better, only a couple of people have seen Tammy. The doctor who delivered her is one, but I'll never see him again. And my ma, but she already knows about you. I'll hide Tammy away through the coming year, and won't let anybody see her till her new arm's fully grown. That way there'll be no questions to answer."

Walt sagged and seemed to shrink inside his coat.

"Okay," he said, his voice barely audible. "Let's get it done with."

Miriam dropped the envelope onto the bed and began pulling at the folds of blanket around the baby. In a few seconds the fleshy little flipperlike flap that passed for the baby's left arm was exposed.

Walt pulled the black leather glove from his right hand. Jack had seen his bare hand only once before . . . last month . . . with Cody . . .

He held his breath as Walt's trembling hand inched through the air toward her. What would happen? Thunder? A flash of light? A weird glow?

The hand hesitated, fingers hovering an inch from the

flipper. Then Walt took a deep breath and pressed his palm against it.

No light, no sound, but the baby stiffened and her eyes flew open as she began to wail. Walt snatched his hand back and stared dully at the baby.

"You did it!" Miriam cried over the high-pitched crying.

Jack wondered how she knew. Her baby's flipper looked the same as ever.

Walt mumbled something as he turned toward the door.

"No. It worked. I know it did." Tears streamed down her cheeks. "I felt it through Tammy. I'll never forget that electric-shock feeling. You did it. Thank you, thank you!"

With the door halfway open, Walt turned and gave her a strange look.

"For what?" His gaze drifted to the crying baby, then he said, "Oh . . . yeah."

They held the pose, Walt staring at the baby and Miriam staring at Walt for what seemed a long time, then he turned and stepped through the door.

Jack had been so mesmerized by the scene, he'd forgotten to move away from the window. He leaped off the walk and crouched behind the wagon's front fender. Hearing Miriam's voice, he dared a peek over the hood.

"Mister Ers—I mean Walt! Please come back. Tammy's stopped crying and we can sit and talk. I just want to know how you—"

"Going home," he said without looking back.

But Jack saw that he'd started walking south on 206. Johnson was north.

Miriam called after him a few more times, then gave up. Jack heard her sob as she stepped back and closed the door.

Jack's brain was spinning from what he'd just seen. What *had* he seen? That was the question. Had anything really happened, or was it all in the minds of Walt and Miriam?

And where was Walt going? Had he somehow got turned around and lost his sense of direction?

Jack didn't like revealing himself, out and about at this hour, but he couldn't leave Walt walking in the wrong direction.

2

"Hey, Walt?" Jack said as he glided up behind him on his bike. "It's me, Jack."

Walt stopped and turned. "Jack? That really you?"

Jack realized he probably couldn't see his face in the dark.

"Yeah, Walt. Where are you headed?"

"Home."

"You're headed the wrong way." He jerked a thumb over his shoulder. "Johnson's back that way."

"It is?"

He didn't seem all there. Then again, he never seemed all there, but tonight he was less there than usual.

"Want me to show you a shortcut back?"

He nodded. "Yeah. A shortcut would be good. I'm tired."

The shortcut would not only be quicker but would keep them off the road. Jack didn't want to be spotted.

They crossed 206 and started walking north. Walt was sort of shuffling. Jack walked his bike beside him, not wanting to admit that he'd been watching, but feeling like he was going to explode if he didn't ask about it.

Finally he took a deep breath and said, "I . . . I saw what happened back there."

Walt kept looking straight ahead. "Where?"

"At the Lonely Pine . . . in Miriam's room."

"What did you see?"

"I saw you touch the baby."

Walt looked down at his right hand—his *ungloved* right hand.

"Oh man." He pulled a glove from a pocket and wriggled his hand back into it. Then he looked at Jack. "How could you . . . ?"

"I saw you go in. I . . ." Might as well get it out in the open. "I peeked through the window."

"Shouldn't've done that. It's not right. People got a right to their privacy."

He was absolutely right. Seemed like Jack had been prying into a number of privacies lately.

"I'm not proud of it, but I just had to look. And I've got to ask: Can you heal people, Walt?"

He didn't answer right away, just shuffled along. Finally he said, "Kind of."

Jack felt a surge of excitement. If this was true, if such a thing was really possible . . .

"What do you mean, 'kind of'?"

"Okay, yeah. I've done it."

"How?"

"Don't know. A dying grunt passed it to me in Nam, not long after we took back Hue. I was set to end my tour and I couldn't wait to get home. I think it wanted to come to America."

"It?"

"Yeah. The healing power. It worked when it wanted to. It came and went when it damn well pleased. When it came, I couldn't turn it off; and when it was gone, I couldn't turn it on. But I found a way to put it to sleep."

He pulled a pint bottle from the side pocket of his fatigue jacket, unscrewed the cap, and took a long pull.

"Applejack?" Jack said.

"Any kinda booze. It won't work when I'm half lit."

"That's why you're always drinking? So you can't heal?"

Jack felt disappointment tingeing his wonder. "But Walt . . . think of the good you could be doing."

Walt took another gulp, and Jack resisted the temptation to knock the bottle from his hand.

"You don't understand, Jack. There's a price to pay. It's yin and yang, man, like a cosmic scale that's gotta be balanced, like TANSTAAFL."

"Tan-what?"

"TANSTAAFL. It's from a sci-fi book I read. It stands for 'There Ain't No Such Thing as a Free Lunch.' And that's what it is with this thing, this power inside me. The healings don't come free, Jack. Somebody pays, somebody always pays. And that somebody is me."

"I don't get it."

"Neither do I. But when I found I could knock it out with hooch, I started drinking every day."

Jack was confused. "But . . . then . . . does that mean you didn't heal the baby?"

"I think I did. I could feel the power awake and ready, felt the little shock when I touched her."

"But the applejack—"

"I kept thinking about that baby and knew I couldn't let her go through life like that, so I put the booze aside today. It woke up. Now I gotta put it back to sleep."

Just like last month, when Mrs. C had told him to stop drinking because he might be "needed."

He took another swig as they reached the turnoff into the woods. Jack glanced ahead and saw a deer lying on the shoulder, its head twisted at an unnatural angle. Big roadkill. He hadn't noticed it when he'd come out, hadn't looked that way. A thought struck.

"Can you heal that?" he said, pointing.

Walt looked, made a face, and shook his head. "Nope. Sorry. Can't raise the dead. Tried a coupla times, but no go. Just as well." His voice thickened. "Who knows what price I'd have to pay for something like that."

He sobbed and the sound tore Jack's heart. He touched his arm.

"Walt?"

Another sob, then, "I've paid a big price, Jack. I've lost so much of me I can't even remember what's gone. I could have had a good life. I didn't start out as the brightest bulb in the box, but I had some good wattage. Now I'm just a dimwit drunk who's hanging on only so I can pass it on to the next guy."

"Next guy?"

"Yeah. Supposedly this thing has hopped from person to person through the ages. Mrs. Clevenger knows all about it. She told me." Walt turned to Jack. "For a while I had this weird feeling that the next guy, the guy I'm looking for, might be you."

A lump of ice formed in Jack's gut. His tongue suddenly felt like old leather.

"Me?"

"Yeah. But Mrs. C said no. It ain't you."

Jack relaxed. What a relief.

He pushed his bike off the shoulder and through the brush that hid the trail.

"Come on, Walt. I'll take you home."

Didn't look like he'd get to the school tonight. Too bad Walt didn't have a touch that could cure a sick lock so it could open.

3

"Hey, lazy pants. Wake up."

Sounded like Kate's voice . . . coming from far away.

Jack opened one eye and peeked over the edge of his bedsheet. Yeah, Kate's voice, but not so far away. She stood in his bedroom doorway, wearing cut-off shorts, a Philadelphia Eagles T-shirt, and a smile.

"You going to sleep all day?"

"Sounds like a plan," he mumbled, closing his eye.

Walking Walt home had taken a long time. He didn't know when he'd sneaked back in the window, but it couldn't have been too long ago.

"I talked to Jenny."

Jack opened both eyes. "Yeah? What she say?"

"Not here. I'm going to take a walk down to the lake. Meet me there."

"Can't you give me a hint?"

She smiled. "All I'll tell you is it's verrrrry interesting. And it explains a lot of things."

Then she winked and closed the door.

Jack flopped back on his pillow and stared at the ceiling. He felt exhausted.

Sleeeeep . . . I need sleeeeep.

But how could he sleep after what Kate had just said? And that wink hinted at all sorts of secrets and mysteries revealed.

With a groan he pushed off the covers and rolled out of bed. His jeans and rugby shirt from the early morning excursion lay on the floor where he'd dropped them. He slipped them back on, shoved his feet into his Vans, and headed for the bathroom to throw some water on his face.

Walking through the kitchen a few minutes later, he realized he was famished. A look at the clock told him why: a quarter to ten. He hadn't eaten in more than twelve hours.

He grabbed a couple of Eggos from the freezer and popped them into the toaster. While they were heating he pulled the carton of milk from the freezer. He glanced around. No one in sight. He had the container halfway to his mouth when his mother breezed in. He lowered it and turned to get a paper cup from the pantry.

"How's my sleepyhead miracle boy?"

Miracle boy . . . how could he make her stop calling him that?

"As miraculous as ever, as in not at all."

She beamed. "Oh, but you are."

He shook his head as he filled the cup with milk. She'd never stop. Never.

The Eggos popped up. He pulled them out and dropped them on the counter. He slathered one with Skippy Super Chunk, then pressed them together. A little melted peanut butter leaked out one side.

"That's not a proper Sunday morning breakfast," she said. "I'll scramble you some eggs."

"Thanks, but I'm gonna take a little walk down to the lake." He banged out the back door, peanut-butter Eggowich in one hand, milk in the other. "See ya later."

A beautiful morning—hazy sunshine, gentle breeze, birds calling back and forth between the trees. He angled across Jefferson to North Franklin and walked toward Quakerton, munching and thinking about last night.

A few hours ago he'd been pretty well convinced that Weird Walt could truly heal people with a touch. But they'd been in the woods then, and such things are easier to believe in the wilds at night. Now, in the light of day, surrounded by the everyday ordinariness of Johnson, it seemed crazy.

Walt had told a fascinating story, but that was just talk. What had Jack actually seen? Nothing.

He passed Adams—Weezy's street. He had to see her today, but later. First, Kate.

Repair of spontaneous recanalization of right vas deferens post 1962 vasectomy explained "a lot of things"?

He wanted to know just what sort of things.

4

He'd finished his Eggowich by the time he found her. She sat on a lakeside bench with some sort of textbook in her lap, staring at the water and what Mr. Drexler had called "the little people." Any more canoes on the lake and there'd be gridlock. Mark Mulliner would be smiling tonight when he counted his rental money.

"Whatcha reading?"

"Histology."

"Let me guess: the study of snake noises."

She gave him a gentle slap on his thigh. "The study of tissues—all microscope stuff."

"Sounds like a page-turner."

She laughed. "For me it is. It's fascinating."

"As much as the recanalization of a vas deferens?"

"*Spontaneous* recanalization—that's the important part."

He did his bad Ricky Ricardo imitation. "Hokay, Lucy. 'Splain it to me."

She closed her book and half turned to face him. The breeze ruffled her short blond hair.

"Do you know what a vasectomy is?"

He nodded. "Male sterilization. You cut the vas deferens."

She laughed. "I'm impressed."

"I looked it up yesterday."

"Figured. But the vas is more than simply cut. Its cut end is cauterized—burned so it will scar shut—and then stitched for extra measure. Everyone wants to be absolutely sure that no sperm will get into that tube."

Jack shrugged. It seemed obvious. "Otherwise, why bother doing it at all?"

"Exactly. But rarely—very rarely—the two cut ends meet up and form a new connection, a new passage that allows sperm through and undoes the sterilization."

Jack frowned. "But if it's cut and burned and stitched, how . . . ?"

"It happens," Kate said with a shrug. "Dad wasn't a unique case. It's been documented a number of times, most often shortly after surgery, but also years later. And it's not so surprising when you think about it, since everything in our body, in our genes, in our very being, is aimed toward reproduction. It's second only to self-preservation. A vasectomy is, in a sense, the creation of a vacuum, and nature abhors a vacuum."

Jack thought of the margarine commercial where the lady says, *It's not nice to fool Mother Nature!*

He tried to picture the two cut ends wriggling toward each other and fusing, but had trouble. It required picturing Dad's scrotum, and his mind rebelled.

"So think about it," Kate said.

"I'd rather not."

"No, really. According to the bill, Dad had had a vasectomy in 1962. That would be a year after I was born."

"Yeah, it would. You think they had their boy and had their girl, and decided to call it quits?"

She shrugged. "Seems obvious. They were both in their thirties already. The older the mother, the greater the chance of birth defects. The birth control pill was brand-new back then, so it was probably the smart thing to do."

"Easy for you to say. You were already born."

The thought that he hadn't been wanted popped into

Jack's brain. He knew it was childish, but it was hard to ignore. Getting sterilized meant they didn't want any more kids. Therefore his folks hadn't wanted him.

He shook it off before woe-is-me violins could begin whining in the background.

"But listen—six years is a long time to wait before recanalization. Think what Dad must have thought when Mom told him she was pregnant."

That hadn't occurred to Jack.

"Mom? Oh, he couldn't have even—"

"I'm sure it crossed his mind. How could it not? Here he was, certified sterile for six years, and suddenly his wife is pregnant. But a simple sperm count cleared things up, I'm sure."

Jack took a breath. "Okay. So I'm an accident."

She slapped his arm. "A much-loved accident."

Yeah, well, he couldn't argue with that. His family life was nothing if not tranquil. At least so far. All that might change if his folks learned he'd been sneaking out at night and breaking into the high school, or snooping through their room and trying to get into Dad's lockbox.

It was risky business, but sometimes you had to break the rules.

"So, we've learned that this bill means Dad had a vasectomy in 1962 that reversed itself in 1968 and was then redone by this Doctor Welsch. Fine. But you said it explains lots of things. What? It doesn't explain anything to me."

Kate grinned. "It explains why Mom calls you 'miracle boy.' "

Her words hit like a hammer against the side of his head.

"Oh, God! It does!"

All his life he'd wondered about that, but she'd never had a good answer. Now he knew why she couldn't explain it to him. By some—in her eyes—miracle, her supposedly sterile husband had become fertile again to give her a surprise baby.

"It also explains why you've been her favorite since the day you were born, something that did not endear you to your big brother."

Jack shook his head. He fought a smile but it broke through.

"I guess I *am* a miracle boy."

In a way it was a relief to realize that he wasn't expected to perform a miracle sometime in the future. The miracle was already behind him.

Kate rose and kissed him on the top of his head, then handed him the folded bill.

"I'm glad you found it. I don't know how you got your hands on it and I'm not sure I want to, but I'm glad to know what I know. As I said, it answers some questions." She tousled his already messed-up hair. "Heading back?"

He shook his head. He had some thinking to do.

"Not yet. Think I'll stay here. Catch you later." As she started to move away, he laughed and said, "And tell the folks their accident says hi."

Kate came back and leaned close, shaking a finger in his face. She wasn't smiling.

"Don't make me sorry I explained this to you. I don't want to hear you refer to yourself as an 'accident' again. Okay? Please?"

He realized he'd upset her, and Kate was the last person on Earth he wanted to upset.

"Okay. Deal. Never again." Anything for Kate.

She smiled. "Great. See you home." Waving, she walked off.

Jack slouched on the bench. Now that the "miracle boy" mystery had been cleared up, and a family secret revealed, he felt an oddly peaceful feeling settle over him. But it didn't last long.

The lock . . . Toliver's damn lock. He couldn't find any way past it.

He stared at the water and the canoers for a moment, then let his eyes drift closed. Maybe he could dream up a so-lution if he caught another forty winks. If nothing else, he needed the sleep.

5

"Some things that seem like accidents are not."

Jack's eyes popped open at the sound of a voice to his right. He thought it sounded like—

"Oh, hi, Mrs. Clevenger."

The old woman sat next to him on the bench, her black scarf around her neck despite the warmth of the day. Her three-legged dog sat at her feet, panting as he stared at Jack.

Once again, where had these two come from? When he'd closed his eyes, they'd been nowhere in sight. Had he napped?

She turned her dark eyes on him. "I couldn't help overhearing."

Overhearing from where? he wanted to say. You weren't in eyeshot, let alone earshot.

But then, she might have been screened by one of the trees or the people wandering around.

"Overhearing what?"

"About the 'miracle' of your birth."

Jack suddenly felt uncomfortable. "That was private."

She smiled. "But spoken in such a public place."

Couldn't argue with her on that.

"Yeah, well . . ."

"As I said, some happenings that appear accidental are not." She lowered her voice. "Like your father's return to fertility, perhaps."

Jack looked around. Now he was *really* uncomfortable.

"I don't think that's something to talk about outside the family."

She laughed. "Nor *inside* the family, I gather. Not to worry, no one will hear us. This is a conversation between an old woman and a teenage boy. No one is interested."

They could be very interested, Jack thought, if the old woman is rumored to be a witch.

"Still . . ."

She leaned closer. "You should realize that 'miracles' very often happen for a reason."

"What sort of reason? My father—"

"There are times when something needs to happen, and so what needs doing gets done, no matter what. Obstacles are removed, plans are undone, sometimes in a 'miraculous' or 'accidental' fashion."

She was sounding a little too much like Mr. Drexler now. Movers and Moved . . .

"What are we talking about here? *What* needed doing?"

"You, perhaps."

"Me? Who needs me?"

"Perhaps no one. Perhaps the entire world. An important word to remember in this case is 'perhaps.' "

Jack felt like he'd entered the Bizarro World, but that wasn't a complete surprise with Mrs. Clevenger. She always seemed to talk in circles.

She held up a finger. "A singular event occurs. A threatening event. It triggers other events, defensive moves. Perhaps one of those moves was your conception."

"Me?" Unease wormed through his gut. "Why me? What for?"

She shrugged. "Maybe for nothing. Maybe as a contingency. Maybe just one of a number of contingencies for use against a potential future threat. Perhaps you will face that threat, perhaps not."

He forced a laugh. "What comes next? You tell me I have hidden magical powers that I must use only for good?"

She didn't seem to think it was funny. She shook her head. "You have no magic, but you are special in your blood and in how you use your brain."

Jack had heard enough. She was a crazy old woman who had a knack for sounding like she knew more than she really did. He wasn't going to learn anything useful here—because *useful* right now meant finding a way to open Toliver's lock.

He hopped up from the bench.

"Nice talking to you, Mrs. Clevenger, but I've gotta go."

"Of course you do. You're a busy young man. Go on about the business of being a boy. Now is the time to enjoy every day. For one thing is certain about joy—it never lasts."

Now there's a cheery send-off, Jack thought as he turned away. But a thought popped into his head and he turned back.

"Say, you wouldn't know how to dissolve Krazy Glue, would you?"

She didn't even blink as she said, "Acetone."

"Really?"

"Really."

"Cool!"

6

Jack picked through the entire inventory of the lock section in Spurlin's Hardware until he found a two-inch, laminated-steel Master padlock exactly like Toliver's. In fact, he found three.

He carried all of them plus two tubes of Krazy Glue to the front counter.

Mr. Spurlin grinned and said, "What's up, Jack? Building a new Fort Knox?"

He was a chubby guy with a salt-and-pepper beard.

"Just replacing some old locks."

This was a potentially risky move. Jack didn't know where Toliver had bought his lock. Could have been right here. What if he came back for another and found them all gone? He might ask and Mr. Spurlin might say Jack had bought them. Might even mention the Krazy Glue too. And then Jack's ass would be grass.

Even though the chances of that happening were way remote, Jack was still uneasy about it. If he could drive he'd have bought his supplies in another town. But with only a bike, it was Spurlin's or nothing.

As he paid for the locks and glue, he pointed to the tubes and said, "If I, um, spill some Krazy Glue, what's a good way to get it off?"

"Wicked stuff. Keep it off your hands. It'll glue your fingers together like you wouldn't believe. Did you know it was used to close battlefield wounds in Nam?"

Jack had heard something like that.

"Yeah, but what takes it off?"

He frowned and scratched his jaw. "Acetone's the only thing I know."

So Mrs. Clevenger was right.

"Got any?"

"Afraid not. But most nail polish removers are basically acetone. Use some of that."

He was sure his mother had some.

Operation Toliver was not dead yet.

As soon as Jack got home he set up shop in the garage. He spread the classified section of the Sunday paper on the battered workbench, borrowed a hammer and a couple of little tacks from his father's toolbox, some nail polish remover from his mother's dresser, and went to work.

The first thing to do was test the shims. Once he found one the right size, it opened the lock without a hitch.

Okay. He knew now if he could get past the glue, he could open the lock.

Next step: Duplicate what Toliver did—Toliverize the locks. So he tapped a tack into the keyhole of one of them and followed it with some Krazy Glue. Then he filled the shackle hole with glue and snapped the shackle into it. He did the same thing with a second lock and put both aside to set.

He left the third as it was in case he needed an untampered lock for reference.

He'd promised Mr. Rosen three hours at USED today. That would give the glue plenty of time to set and cure. He'd tackle the locks then.

8

Later, Jack returned to the garage straight from USED. He had a bad feeling as he inspected the two Toliverized locks. The Krazy Glue had cured for hours now, forming a clear, hard seal around the tacks in the keyholes and around the shackles. He went to work on them.

He tried to force the shim inside but no use. And no surprise. He'd expected that.

As he unscrewed the cap on his mother's bottle of nail polish remover, the chemical stink wrinkled his nose. He took one lock and brushed some acetone on the keyhole and on the rim of the shackle hole. Then he waited. He gave it five minutes, then tried the shim.

No go.

The acetone seemed to have softened the surface of the glue enough for the shim's point to scrape it, but that was it. The solvent had had no effect on the deeper levels.

Same with the keyhole. Jack could not budge the tack.

Maybe he'd have to use more acetone and leave it on longer.

He slathered the same areas of both Toliverized locks with nail polish remover, then stood back.

How long to wait? He'd go nuts standing here counting the minutes.

Well, he'd planned to stop in on Weezy today. Why not now?

He grabbed his bike and wheeled it out of the garage.

9

"Oh, Jack," Mrs. Connell said with a smile when she opened the front door. "I'm glad you're here."

"Is Weezy around?"

Her smile faded. "Around? Of course she's around. Where else would she be? She's up in her room, as usual. Go knock on the door, but I can't guarantee she'll open it."

On his way up the stairs Jack heard the sounds of a football game from the TV in the living room. The Sunday afternoon game. He'd been so wrapped up in vasectomies and Toliverized locks that he'd forgotten all about the NFL. His Eagles were playing the Baltimore Colts.

He knocked on Weezy's door and got no answer, so he knocked again.

"Hey, Weez, it's Jack."

Her voice came faintly through the door. "I'm kinda tired, Jack."

"I've got news—good news. You'll really want to hear this."

A few seconds later the door opened and Weezy stood there, looking pretty much the same as the last time he'd seen her. Except maybe a little paler, if that was possible.

"What news? What about?"

Jack lowered his voice to just above a whisper. "About 'Easy Weezy.' "

Her face contorted and she started to close the door. "I don't want—"

"Wait." Jack blocked the door with his foot. "It's good news. Very good news."

She allowed it to swing open again.

"All right. But just for a minute."

He ducked into the dimly lit room—as usual, the shades were drawn—and she shut the door behind him.

"I could use some good news," she said. "But I can't see anything about 'Easy Weezy' being good."

"How about if nobody's saying it anymore? Wouldn't that be good?"

"That's only because I'm not around. All I have to do is show my face again—just once—and it'll be a different story."

"No way. Because the only thing on people's minds now that has anything to do with Carson Toliver is his locker."

Weezy gave him a strange look. "What are you talking about?"

Jack gave her a quick rundown of the surprises in To- liver's locker—the toy spider, the spring snake, the marbles— and his increasingly furious reactions, capped by his rigging a supposedly unopenable lock.

"The thing is, Weez, opening his locker has become an event. It's all anybody's talking about—'What's gonna be in Carson's locker this time?' That's all you hear. 'Easy Weezy' is old news—*way* old news."

Weezy stood silent a moment, then, "Who do you think's doing it?"

The last thing Jack wanted to do was lie to Weezy.

He really, really, really wanted to brag that he was the guy and that he'd done it for her because no one dumps on a friend of his without paying a price. He knew it sounded like something out of a lame western, but that was the way he felt.

But no way could he tell her or anyone else. At least not

now. Maybe next summer, after Toliver had graduated and moved on, he could let her know, but not before. She might let something slip.

"The 'who' is another constant topic of conversation. Nobody's got a clue as to who or why someone would want to make a fool out of the wonderful and glorious Carson Toliver. Or how. Nobody knows how he's getting into the locker, or when."

Weezy folded her arms. "What makes you so sure it's a 'he'? You don't think a girl could be capable?"

"I didn't say that. I just—"

"But anyway," she said, waving her hands, "it doesn't mean I won't be hearing 'Easy Weezy' if I show up."

"Trust me, Weez: That's over."

Her expression softened. "Are you sure that's not just wishful thinking on your part?"

"Even Eddie will tell you."

Weezy closed her eyes. "He's never mentioned 'Easy Weezy.' I don't know how, but I gather he's never heard it."

"That's because of his headphones and the fact that no one's going to say that about his sister to his face. Especially since it died down once you weren't around. But let me get him up here. He's got no wishful thinking going on, so we'll see if he has the same impression I do."

Jack stepped out into the hall and called down the stairs to the living room where Eddie was watching the game. He arrived a few minutes later.

"Wow," he said as he entered Weezy's room. "I'm allowed to enter the Bat Cave?"

Jack jumped in before Weezy could respond. "I was just telling her about what's been going on at school. Besides

Toliver screwing up the NBR game, what'll everybody be talking about tomorrow morning?"

Eddie's eyes widened. "You kidding? The crap going on with his locker."

He then launched into a tirade about how somebody from NBR had been pranking Toliver to psych him out of the game.

Jack watched Weezy's face as Eddie rattled on and saw a look of growing awe.

"It's true then? It's all anyone's talking about?"

"True," Jack said, then turned to Eddie. "Where are you going to be first thing tomorrow morning?"

"You kidding? Right by Carson's locker with everybody else. I bet the whole school'll be there, waiting for him to open it."

Jack said, "What do you think he'll find inside?"

Eddie's grin was fierce. "Nothing! Nobody's getting into that locker. He's got the bastard beat!" He sobered. "Just wished he'd beat him one day sooner. Maybe we would have won the game."

Weezy's voice dripped scorn. "That's all it took to make your boy hero blow the game? A couple of jokes and he falls apart?"

"He didn't fall apart! It just messed up his concentration!"

She shook her head. "I don't know. He never seemed that . . . fragile. Got to be more than that. And who says it has to be NBR? Maybe it's personal."

"Against Carson? He's the coolest guy in school. Everybody likes him. You'd know that if you weren't hiding here in the Bat Cave."

Color flushed into Weezy's pale cheeks. She looked ready to explode.

"I think you're wrong, Eddie," Jack said. "I think Toliver's going to have another little present waiting in his locker."

"Wanna bet? Five bucks says no way."

Jack nodded. "You're on." He turned to Weezy. "How about you, Weez? Gonna miss seeing Carson Toliver get smacked down again?"

Eddie looked at her. "What've you got against Carson?"

"Nothing," Weezy said quickly, then stared at Jack. "But that's tempting. That's very tempting."

Eddie waved his hands in the air and danced in a circle. "Hallelujah!" he cried with a Foghorn Leghorn drawl. "She's steppin' out—Ah said, she's steppin' outa th'darkness and inta th'light! Hallelujah!"

"I didn't say I would," Weezy told him. "I *might*. And then again, I might not."

Eddie hurried from the room, still in preacher mode. "Hallelujah! If Sister Weezy—Ah say, if Sister Weezy can leave the Bat Cave, the Eagles—Ah say, the Eagles can beat the Colts!"

Jack laughed, but Weezy only shook her head.

"He's such a dork," she said.

"And he's wrong about Toliver's locker. There *will* be a surprise inside. And then he'll go from honcho to loser."

Her eyes narrowed and she seemed to be studying him as she replied. "How can you be so sure?"

Uh-oh. Had to be careful here.

"Because whoever this Mystery Marauder is, he's beaten Toliver every time. Why should this be any different?"

"Well, from what you told me about the lock . . ."

"Yeah. It's a tough one, but I'm betting he'll get around

it." He touched her arm. "You should be there to see. You really should."

He wanted her to see it. Toliver had become a Big Bad Boogie Man in her mind. If she saw him taken down in front of the whole school, maybe he'd go from Boogie Man to plain old booger.

She kept staring at him. "I probably should."

He grinned. "Then you're coming back to school?"

"I'm . . . I'm not sure. You've got me thinking about it, but if you're wrong about the 'Easy Weezy' thing—"

"I'm not. I guarantee it."

As soon as the words left Jack's mouth, he wished them back. He could *not* guarantee it. And if Toliver opened an un-booby-trapped locker tomorrow, people might start remembering "Easy Weezy."

He prayed the nail polish remover was working.

"So . . ." he said slowly, "are we going to see you at the bus stop tomorrow?"

"I don't know. I'll have to see how tomorrow feels."

He guessed that was as much of a commitment as he was going to get, so he didn't push.

On his way downstairs he heard Mr. Connell in the kitchen.

"Eddie told me Weezy says she might go to school tomorrow."

Mrs. Connell said, "Oh, that's wonderful!"

Jack paused, waiting to hear them credit him with the miracle.

But instead Mrs. Connell said, "Doctor Hamilton told us the pills would take at least a week to work. It's only been a few days."

"I'm not going to complain if they work quicker. Are you?"

"Heavens, no!"

Jack hurried the rest of the way down the stairs and out the front door.

Pills? The doctor had put Weezy on medication?

That must have been where she and her mom had gone on Wednesday. Jack didn't know if he liked the idea of Weezy being drugged up by her folks. Then again, after what Jack had heard outside her house Monday night, maybe she needed it.

Poor Weezy . . . what was wrong with her?

10

Oh, crap.

Jack stood at the workbench in his garage and tried to force the shim into the shackle hole of one of the Toliverized locks. It wouldn't budge. He tried the second with equal lack of success.

The nail polish remover had done nothing.

He turned the locks over and tried to pry out the tacks.

Nothing!

He cocked his arm to hurl one of them across the garage but stopped himself. What would that prove?

Think! Think! Think! he told himself as he began pacing back and forth. There has to be a way.

But he kept coming up blank until his pacing took him past the hacksaw hanging on a nail in the wall. He stopped and stared at it. Then he turned and looked at the extra tube of Krazy Glue on the workbench.

Maybe . . . just maybe . . .

He grabbed the saw and went to work on the shackle of one of the Toliverized locks. The thin blade quickly cut into the shiny metal. He stopped and stared at the grooves in both sides of the loop, then continued until the curved top fell off.

Okay, with that cut off, he'd be able to open the locker. But a big question remained: After he'd done his business inside and reclosed the door, would he be able to Krazy Glue the shackle back together again?

He applied the glue to the cut edges and pressed them

together, holding them in place for a couple of minutes. When he let go, the bond held . . .

But the result looked terrible. No way that patch job would fool anyone, not even from ten feet away.

"Crap!"

Now he hurled the lock across the garage. It bounced off the opposite wall with a solid *thunk!*

What was he going to do? He had to open the lock and close it again with no sign that it had been touched. Nothing less would do.

And it wasn't going to happen, because it was impossible. At least with the tools at his disposal.

Fury and frustration exploded within. He was looking around for something to kick when he heard his mother calling from the back door.

"Jack? What are you doing out there?"

"Just messing with stuff."

"Weezy's on the phone."

Weezy?

He trotted inside and grabbed the receiver from the counter where his mother had left it.

"Hey, Weez. What's up?"

"I have got to get out of here. Want to go for a ride?"

He glanced out the window. The sun had set, dark was falling, but there was still light left.

"Sure. Meet you at the corner."

11

Jack found Weezy waiting on the corner of Adams and North Franklin.

"Thanks for coming. I'm going stir-crazy in the house but my folks didn't want me out alone. And really, I didn't feel like being alone."

"Any time. But I thought they wouldn't let you out."

"I told them I'm going to school tomorrow and so they said okay."

"Are you?"

"I think so."

Jack decided to leave it at that.

"Where to?"

"Let's just ride. I need air."

"Air?" he said with a laugh as they rolled toward Quaker-ton. "Since when does Weezy Connell need air?"

She smiled. "It's night air, mister. *Night* air."

"That explains it."

Jack wondered if the after-sundown timing was because she'd be less visible.

They cruised down toward the lake and into Old Town.

They were passing the Lodge when the sound of a car on the rickety boards of the bridge made them turn. A new Mustang convertible was coming their way.

"Ohmigod!" Weezy whispered, shrinking behind a tree trunk. "It's him!"

Jack felt fury rise again. Weezy shouldn't have to be afraid of anyone. He watched the car cruise toward the end of Quakerton, then turn into the Pines.

"He's gone," he said. "I don't think he saw us."

"Was he alone?"

Jack shook his head. "Don't know."

"He could have a girl with him . . . someone who doesn't suspect . . ."

Jack didn't know where it came from, but he felt a fierce urge to follow the car.

In Mr. Kressy's class he'd offered "do the right thing" as a guiding principle. Well, the right thing wasn't to turn a blind eye to what might be happening, or about to happen.

"Maybe we should follow."

"No way," Weezy said. "I don't want to be anywhere near him."

"You don't have to be. If he's got a girl with him, we know where he's going."

"And what do we do when we get there?"

"Make sure he doesn't treat her like he treated you."

"And how are you going to do that?"

"I don't know. I'll think of something."

He hoped it wouldn't come to that, but he couldn't stand here and simply hope for the best. Someone had to stop the guy.

"Maybe she was one of the ones calling me 'Easy Weezy.' Maybe she's got the same thing in mind he has. He's Mister Hot to most of the girls."

"If that's the case, then it's none of our business." He looked at her. "Coming?"

She shook her head. She looked cowed. "I can't."

"It's okay. I understand. See you tomorrow."

Jack kicked off and started pedaling. He'd gone maybe a hundred feet when he heard a noise. He turned and saw a grim-faced Weezy riding half a dozen feet behind him. He nodded. She nodded back.

12

Dusk had faded toward night, making it easy to follow Toliver's taillights without being seen. He drove slowly, weaving back and forth along the sandy firebreaks. Jack suspected he might be heading back toward the dead zone. He told Weezy about his solo trip into the Pines and the strange behavior of the lights.

"You followed lumens *without* me?" she said. "That's not fair!"

"I had no way of letting you know, and last time I tried to get you into the woods you blew me off."

"Sorry I'm such a jerk."

Jack could tell by her tone she meant it.

"Have you ever heard of anything like that?"

She shook her head. "Never. But then, nobody knows anything about lumens. Some 'experts' say they don't even exist."

Jack started to reply just as Toliver slowed near the hidden, rutted path.

"Let's hold up here."

They stopped and watched as he pulled into it.

"What now?" she said in a low voice.

Jack gave that a moment's thought, then . . .

"We ditch the bikes and follow on foot."

Jack pushed his bike into the underbrush. It wouldn't have hidden it during the day, but here in the dark it was fine. He turned and found Weezy still standing next to hers.

"I'm scared. That was where . . ."

"It's okay, Weez. Wait here."

He heard her take a deep breath. "No. I'm coming."

She hid her bike next to Jack's and followed him onto the hidden path. He walked the right rut, she the left.

They found the car parked facing the dead zone. The engine was off but the headlights stayed on. The wash from the lights silhouetted only one head in the front seat. Toliver appeared to be alone.

Suddenly the driver door swung open. Jack and Weezy dropped into a crouch. Weezy's hand was cold and damp where she clutched his arm.

Toliver got out of the car and staggered toward the mysterious clearing. When he stepped into the headlight beams, Jack spotted a familiar-looking bottle dangling from his right hand. Only a little clear liquid sloshed within.

He stepped through the ebony spleenwort and into the open area. With the headlights casting weird, elongated shadows beyond him, he stumbled around, kicking at the bare earth.

"What's going on?" he shouted to no one. "What's going ON?"

Jack watched in amazement. What *was* going on?

Toliver dropped to his knees and looked for a moment as if he might be praying.

To whom? Jack wondered. Or to what?

Was he somehow connected to this place where nothing would grow, where animals wouldn't walk and ants wouldn't nest?

Then he began pounding the dirt, screaming, "Stop it! Stop it! Stop it!"

He fell silent but stayed on his knees. Then he screamed again.

"You're ruining my life! It was an accident! I didn't mean it! Leave me alone!"

"Who's he talking to?" Weezy whispered.

All Jack could think of was Toliver asking Mrs. Clevenger about someone being haunted, and Saree's words about piney blood on Toliver's hands, and now here he was in the Pines, talking to the air about an accident and for someone or something to leave him alone and—

Weezy's grip on his arm tightened.

"Listen! He's . . . he's crying."

Sure enough, tortured sobs were coming from the clearing. Abruptly they broke off as Toliver lurched to his feet.

"You're not gonna ruin my life! No way! I'm not letting you!"

Then with a wordless scream that made Jack jump and Weezy squeeze his arm even harder, he threw his bottle and smashed it against the big oak beyond the clearing.

As he began to stagger back to his car, Weezy tugged on Jack's arm and the two of them hurried back to the firebreak trail in a crouch. They hid in the brush until the Mustang rolled by, heading back toward Johnson.

They freed their bikes and followed Toliver's weaving path. The guy was drunk as a skunk and should have been anywhere but behind the wheel. Jack wondered if he'd make it home before ramming a tree. But he was driving slowly.

"What did we just see?" Jack said.

"I have no idea."

"One thing's for sure: That's one screwed-up guy."

"I already knew that," Weezy said. "But he's losing it. Completely losing it."

"Sounds to me like he's already lost it."

She was silent a moment, then, "I think I want to see what happens at his locker tomorrow."

Jack's heart leaped, but only for an instant. Then it crashed.

Great that Weezy was going to be there, but Jack had no way past that lock.

The big show was going to be a bust. Operation Toliver was going to go down in flames.

Crap.

He stood in the garage and stared in dismay at the workbench. He'd sawed through the shackle of the second Toliverized lock, but very carefully this time, making as clean a cut as possible, flush against the top of the body of the lock. Then he'd glued it back together, but no go: The seam still looked way too obvious.

He stepped back to the other side of the garage, but he could see it even from there. And the light would be better in the locker area.

He was forced to admit it: Toliver's lock had beaten him. The major coup he'd planned was out of the question.

But that didn't mean Toliver was home free. No way. One way or another he was going to find something ugly in his locker tomorrow. Jack would saw off the lock, place the surprise, then glue the shackle back together. He had a chance, a very slight one, that no one would notice the seam. Maybe it looked obvious to Jack just because he knew it was there.

Nah. No use in kidding himself. If no one else spotted it, Toliver surely would when he got close. And he'd point it out. And then the ugly surprise would no longer be a surprise, merely ugly.

Toliver would have a moral victory: He'll have forced the Mystery Marauder to abandon sleight of hand and resort to naked force.

Crap-crap-crap!

Jack walked back to the workbench but halfway there he

froze as the solution, blinding in its simplicity, hit him like a wrecking ball.

He could do it.

Yes!

1

Jack sat on the school bus and stared glumly through the window at the teeming rain.

He should have been buzzed with the prospect of Toliver discovering the surprise he'd left him, but just the opposite. Maybe it was the weather. Maybe because he was dead tired after his trip to the school at two A.M.

Nah. He knew what it was.

Weezy hadn't shown up at the stop this morning. Neither had Eddie, for that matter.

He'd been doing this for her and now she'd let him down.

No, that wasn't fair. She didn't know he had anything to do with it, so he couldn't take her staying home personally. Still, he thought he'd brought her around last night.

Last night . . . how weird was that? What had Toliver been doing in that dead zone? Kneeling and screaming . . . to whom or what? The ghost he'd thought was haunting him? If he'd only said a name, it would have cleared up so many questions.

But one thing was clear: He was losing it. He'd sounded inches away from a nervous breakdown. But he'd probably be his usual fine-and-dandy self when he walked into school this morning.

Jack shook his head as the bus turned into the school lot. The world continued to make less and less sense.

He pulled up the hood on his yellow nor'easter slicker and ran through the downpour, straight from the bus to the locker area where a crowd had already gathered. He skipped the trip to the boys' room to lock the window. He wanted a good vantage point. He found one and settled in to wait.

During the next few minutes, as more and more buses emptied, the hallway became packed in both directions. Jack wished Weezy were here.

"Hope you've got your five bucks ready."

Jack turned and found Eddie squeezed in behind him.

"How'd you get here?"

Eddie made a face. "The Weezster. First she's gonna go, then she's not gonna go, back and forth, back and forth. Finally it got so late we missed the bus, so my mom drove us."

" 'Us'? You mean she's here?"

He jutted his chin toward the other half of the crowd on the far side of the locker. "Right over there—the Bat Lady herself."

Jack looked and found her right away—a small island of black in a sea of color. He caught her black-lined eyes and gave her a grin and a little salute. Her face remained grim as she responded with the slightest nod. He could tell she was wound tighter than a magneto coil.

Eddie nudged him. "About the five bucks?"

Jack didn't want to cheat Eddie out of his money, so . . .

"I'm canceling the bet."

"Hey—"

"I thought about it and you're right."

"That Carson's got him beat?"

"Yeah, or maybe the guy's given up bothering him. Either way, nothing's gonna be in that locker."

A kid standing in front of them half-turned their way.

"You're probably right," he said. "Too bad."

Eddie frowned. "What's that supposed to mean?"

"After the way he blew the game, I hope there's a can of yellow paint waiting to tip on him."

Hmmm . . . Jack thought. A little anti-Toliver sentiment. Interesting.

"There he is," Eddie said, pointing. "The man himself."

Jack looked, and sure enough, here came Carson Toliver, carrying a duffel bag. He was pale, with baggy, bloodshot eyes, but putting on a game face for his audience.

"He doesn't look so hot," Eddie said.

It's called *hungover,* Jack thought. And in Toliver's mind, it's called *haunted.*

And on the subject of haunts or "haints," where was Levi?

Jack scanned the crowd but couldn't spot him.

"Happy Halloween, everybody," Toliver said in a slightly hoarse voice.

He dropped the duffel in front of the locker and grabbed the lock. He bent to inspect the shackle hole and the key-hole, then turned and showed a sickly grin to the crowd.

"Just as I left it—spiked and glued up the wazoo." If he expected a laugh, he didn't get it. "I guess the jerk knows when he's beaten."

"Too bad NBR didn't," a voice called.

More anti-Toliver sentiment. Was he feeling something like what he'd put Weezy through?

"Okay," he said. "I deserved that. I'd like to apologize for my performance Friday night. I was sick and didn't realize it until too late."

"You still don't look so hot."

Toliver gave another sickly grin. "Better than I felt Friday night, believe me. I apologize for not taking myself out of the game before it even started. It won't happen again, I promise."

This earned a smattering of applause and even some cheers. Jack tightened his fists and closed his eyes. The guy knew how to work a crowd. He was winning them back. Give him more time and he'd have them in the palm of his hand.

"What about the locker?" called another voice. "How are *you* gonna get in?"

Another smile, a tad more real. He figured he'd won this battle. "Didn't you ask me that on Friday? Don't worry—I've got it covered." He squatted and unzipped the duffel. "Time for the grand opening."

He removed a long-handled bolt cutter and held it up to another round of cheers. With two quick snaps he severed the shackle, and the lock clattered to the floor. Then with a flourish like a magician opening a box to reveal that his vanished assistant has reappeared, he bowed and yanked open the door.

A moment of stunned silence as the crowd saw the inside of the locker, then a chorus of shouts and screams as they pushed and tripped over one another in a rush to get as far as possible from the bloody and partially flattened possum roadkill swinging by its ratlike tail from the top shelf.

Jack remembered wondering as he'd hung the poor dead possum in the locker if maybe he was overdoing it. But this was the swan song of Operation Toliver and he needed a grand finale. Had to go out with such a bang that if Toliver ever mentioned "Easy Weezy" again the words would drown in a sea of memories about spiders and snakes and marbles and "doing the Carson" and roadkill and the Mystery Marauder Carson Toliver could not keep out of his locker.

Toliver's dramatic bow had moved his line of sight away from the locker. When he noticed the reaction he looked up. And when he saw the possum, he fell backward to land on his butt, where he stayed staring in mute, openmouthed horror at the dead creature above him.

And now Jack stared too because he'd just noticed a pink hair band around the thing's neck.

Where had *that* come from?

Then the possum's tail slipped free and it tumbled to the floor, landing with a sick *splat!* Jack heard a retch and another splat as a girl near the front blew breakfast.

Yep, he'd overdone it.

He felt bad for her. She wasn't the target—just the guy she'd been cheering for a second ago.

But Jack couldn't take his eyes off the hair band. Where had it come from? It hadn't been there at two A.M. Someone else must have gotten into the locker after him. But how? And who?

He looked around for Levi, and finally found him, but his face was as surprised as those around him. No question, he was seeing the possum for the first time too.

Still on the floor, a wild-eyed Toliver whimpered and scrabbled backward like a crab. When he finally regained his feet he pushed violently through the crowd and ran full tilt down the hall, wailing like the hounds of hell were after him.

2

"Aw, man," Eddie said, looking a little shaken after Toliver was gone. "This is creepitacious. It's like supernatural. How'd anyone get past that lock?"

"Maybe they took the door off," Jack offered, trying to sound as perplexed as Eddie. He'd considered and discarded the door-removal solution as impossible days ago.

"How? The hinges are on the inside."

"Oh . . . yeah. I guess it's going to remain a mystery."

At least Jack hoped so.

"The other mystery is who'd do something so crummacious to Carson."

Jack shrugged. "Someone who doesn't like him, I guess."

"Well, duh. Thanks for the news flash."

Shaking his head and grumbling, he stalked off toward his first class.

Jack turned back toward the locker and found himself face-to-face with Weezy.

" 'Easy' who?" he whispered.

She nodded. "You were right." She leaned closer and lowered her voice. "You?"

Oh, crap.

He gave her an are-you-kidding? look. "What? A lowly frosh like me messing with Carson Toliver? I'd have to be crazy."

Her gaze bored into him. "I suspected you were behind it. In fact I was almost sure you were behind it. It's the kind of thing you'd be so into."

She knew him. God, how she knew him.

"Well, yeah, it's exactly the thing I'd have loved to do. You know, give the creep his comeuppance. But . . ." He shrugged. "You know."

"I was watching you," she said. "If there was anything in the locker, I wanted to see your reaction. If you'd known what was coming, I'd have been able to tell." She glanced back at the dead possum on the floor. "But you looked as shocked as everyone else."

True—but his shock was because of the hair band. Where in all of creation had it come from and how had it got around the possum's neck?

"Well, I was. Too bad I canceled my bet with Eddie."

"Yeah. You'd have earned an easy five." She looked at him. "Just as well it wasn't you, I guess."

"Why?"

"Because then I'd have to consider you my knight in shining armor."

Whoa. Not that that would be terrible or anything, but . . . whoa.

"Again, why?"

"Because if it was you, you'd have done it for me, right?"

"Uh, right."

"And that would have changed things between us."

Jack swallowed. "I kind of like things the way they are."

She smiled. "Me too." She looked at the locker again. "I still can't figure out how anyone got past that lock without cutting it off or boring into the locker, and neither happened. What gives? I can't imagine."

Jack could.

The solution had been so simple he didn't know why he hadn't thought of it earlier.

"Only the Mystery Marauder knows."

She was staring at him. "You've got this funny look on your face. Are you sure you had nothing to do with—?"

The bell for first period rang.

"Gotta move," he said, giving her a little wave as he moved off.

Talk about being saved by the bell.

Instead of heading for class, he detoured toward the boys' room to lock the window for the last time. As he entered he sensed someone following him. He turned and found Levi Coffin staring at him with wonder in his mismatched eyes.

"You got a talent," he said, pointing a long, spidery finger. "Ain't no doubt about it. I thought maybe you could think a lock open, but—"

"Think?"

"Yeah. You know, just think about pushin' the innards around so's everything's lined up and *bang,* it's open."

"I wish."

What was he talking about? Magic?

"But ain't no amount of thinking was gonna open a lock with all that glue gunkin' up its innards. So how'd you do it? What's your talent?"

"I don't have any talent. I swear."

Levi stared at him. "Maybe you just don't know about it yet, but you got one."

Maybe he's right, Jack thought.

Maybe it was simply not quitting. Maybe it was just hanging in there and looking at a problem every which way until he found a solution. Maybe his talent was seeing a solution where other people didn't.

Like Toliver's lock. The simplest thing, in hindsight. He'd

removed it by sawing through the shackle, just as he'd done on the test locks at home. After putting the roadkill inside—on the way to the school he'd kept an eye out for a suitable specimen and hadn't been disappointed—he resecured the locker with the leftover identical padlock he'd bought at Spurlin's. Then he'd tacked it and glued it just as Toliver had. The result was indistinguishable from the original, which presently was lying in the weeds and brush somewhere off Route 206.

Nothing magical about that.

"You plannin' any more larkin' on that boy?"

Jack shook his head. "Don't think I can top this one."

"I don't reckon you can neither—except maybe findin' whose piney blood is on his hands. Your talent good for that?"

Jack didn't want to get into what he and Weezy had witnessed last night.

"I've got no talent, Levi. I'm just a regular kid."

Levi stepped back toward the door, shaking his head. "No you ain't. You ain't regular ay-tall. But if that's the way you wanna play it, fine. But while I'm looking for a hurt piney, I'm gonna figger out what your talent is. And when I do, you're gonna tell me how you did that lock."

No, Jack thought. I'm never telling anyone.

"Guess what?" Eddie said as he plopped down next to Jack in the caf.

Two thick ham and cheese sandwiches, four big chocolate chip cookies, and two containers of milk filled his tray. His headphones hung around his neck.

Jack was still psyched from the locker-area show this morning. How could he not be? Every class had been abuzz with talk of the incident—either about Toliver's over-the-top reaction or speculating on how the Mystery Marauder had gotten past that unopenable lock. Jack had been sorely tempted to tell them—or rather, presenting it as a theory of how it *might* have been done—but that would have been terminally risky, and in Eddie-speak, stupidacious.

Even the teachers got into the act. They'd heard about the roadkill in the hallway and kept asking what it was all about.

Jack swallowed a bite of his own sandwich and said, "You're donating your Walkman to charity."

Erik Burns, sitting across from them, laughed. "The headphones'll have to be surgically removed!"

Eddie made a face. "Yuh, right. Guess again."

"How about a hint?"

"Okay. Guess who left school before first period and hasn't been seen since?"

"Toliver?"

"Give this man a prize."

Jack took another bite and thought about how fitting it

was that the guy who'd made Weezy afraid to show her face around school was now afraid to show his. Almost poetic.

"What goes around, comes around," he muttered.

Eddie looked at him. "What's that supposed to mean?"

"Nothing."

Matt Follette, sitting next to Erik, said, "Did you see him this morning—*crawling* away from his locker and then running like he'd seen a ghost? I mean, I know it was gross, but it wasn't that bad."

"He's had a rough week," Jack said, concentrating on his sandwich instead of looking at Eddie. "Maybe it all got to him. He'll be back tomorrow, acting like king of the hill again."

Eddie shook his head as he took a Godzilla bite of his sandwich and spoke around it. "I don't know. I think the Locker Magician knocked his crown off."

" 'Locker Magician'?" Jack laughed. "Is that what they're calling . . . him."

Oh, man—he'd almost said "me."

"That's what *I'm* calling him." He shook his head. "I don't know . . ."

"Don't know what?"

"I got a bad feeling about this. I mean, him running off and not coming back."

Jack felt a tingle of unease.

"Bad feeling how?"

"I don't know . . . like something bad's going to happen."

Jack didn't like the sound of that one bit, but he shook it off. Eddie was hardly a psychic. Anything but.

But Toliver had been acting unhinged last night. Jack hoped he wouldn't do anything rash like run away.

Eddie's words followed Jack the rest of the day.

4

"Well," Jack said as he and Weezy walked up Quakerton Road, "how'd it go today?"

All around them, trick-or-treating Darth Vaders, Princess Leias, and Ewoks traveled door to door among the more traditional ghosts and witches. Jack had been dying to pull Weezy aside all day but never had the chance, and it wasn't something they could talk about on the bus. Now, with Eddie a few paces ahead, lost in his headphones, he finally had the chance.

She shrugged. "Pretty good."

Not exactly a rave review.

"No mention of 'Easy Weezy'?"

She shook her head. "No. How could there be? All everyone was talking about was Carson-Carson-Carson."

"Not even one snide comment?"

"Nope. In fact, no one even asked where I was—I mean, if I'd been sick or anything. It was like I hadn't even been gone. In fact, it was like I hadn't even come back."

Jack couldn't help feeling a little annoyed.

"Well, which do you prefer: all the attention last Monday, or all the inattention this Monday?"

She smiled. "Oh, today was better—definitely better. And it made me see some things."

"Like?"

"Like who my friends are and who aren't." She hooked an arm through his. "And you're definitely a friend. The best friend I have. Maybe the best friend I'll ever have."

F. PAUL WILSON

Jack found himself strangely moved.

"Hey, Weez, I just—"

"No. It's true. Neither of us makes friends easily. And I know I set myself up by dressing like I do, but you don't care. You take me as I am. And I learned something else: No one is untouchable. Carson acted like he was and I bought into that. But he's not. Someone—what did you call him?"

"The Mystery Marauder. Eddie calls him the Locker Magician."

"Well, whatever his name and whatever his reasons, he showed everyone that Carson Toliver was just another kid, just like the rest of us. He's not so tough, and he's not untouchable. So that's why I think I'm going to report him."

"To who?"

"Whom."

"I know that. To whom?"

"The police. He attacked me. I was ready to let him get away with that. *Nobody* should get away with something like that."

Jack saw immediate problems.

"You'll have to tell your folks you snuck out."

"I know. And I know it will be my word against his, and because I have no proof, nothing will happen to him, but at least he'll be put on notice. He'll know a complaint against him is on file with the sheriff's office, and he'll think two or three times before he tries something like that again."

"If he can find a girl to go out with him after today."

She smiled. "And there's that too."

A sour note struck Jack.

"But aren't you afraid of starting up the 'Easy Weezy' stuff again?"

She shrugged. "It was partly my fault it started in the first place. If I'd reported him Saturday night when I had a torn blouse and some scratches and bruises, none of this would have happened. I don't think it'll start up again—not after today."

Jack hoped not. The main point of Operation Toliver had been to stop it.

5

"Jack?" his mom called from the kitchen. "See who's at the door, will you?"

Jack walked down the hall from his room and into the living room. A man stood outside the screen.

"Hey," he said, smiling. "Remember me?"

Jack looked him over. He had longish brown hair, wore an expensive-looking suit, and looked like he was in his late forties.

"Um, no."

He laughed. "I'm not surprised. I was in pretty sad shape last time you saw me."

"Wait," Jack said as recognition flashed. "You're the man—"

"Right! Ted Collingswood. You and your girlfriend rescued me from those godforsaken woods last month."

"She's not my girlfriend."

Mom entered then, drying her hands on a dish towel. "Who's not your girlfriend?"

Jack introduced them. She'd heard about the "rescue," of course. She invited him in.

"I can only stay a minute," he said, stopping just inside the threshold. He pulled a white envelope from inside his jacket. "I just stopped by to give you this."

Jack took it, lifted the unsealed flap, and pulled out a check. He didn't believe the amount the first time, so he read it again.

"Five hundred dollars!"

"All yours and you deserve every penny."

Jack felt giddy, ready to burst out laughing. Five hundred bucks! He'd conquered the Toliver dragon, and now this. What a day!

"Yow! I—"

"Oh, he can't accept that," he heard his mother say.

What? He couldn't believe his ears.

Mr. Collingswood said, "Your son saved my life. If he hadn't found me I'd have died in there."

"Well, from what he told me, you found him." She touched Jack's shoulder. "You can't take money simply for helping a stranger find his way. It would be like charging for directions."

Jack wanted to protest—after all it was *five hundred bucks!*—but knew she was right. Still . . .

"But Mom, if he wants to give it . . ."

"He's just being gracious and a gentleman. You did the right thing by helping him out, now do it again."

The right thing . . .

Jack had to force his hand forward to give it back.

Mr. Collingswood looked him in the eye. "You're sure?"

Jack shrugged. "Yeah."

If a reward had been offered and he'd gone looking and found him, no way he wouldn't take the money. But Mom was right. He'd been hanging out in the Pines on his own time.

The man shook his head. "What is it around here? Your girlfriend wouldn't take it either."

Mom said, "She's not his girlfriend."

He pulled out his wallet and removed a card.

"At least take this," he said, handing it to Jack. "If you ever need anything—*anything*—you call me. I owe you."

He shook hands with Jack, then headed for the Land Rover parked at the curb.

He glanced at the card. Everyone seemed to be giving him cards. Mr. Drexler, the strange Mr. Grossman, and now the normal Mr. Collingswood. Might as well start a collection.

He sighed as he watched the Land Rover pull away. "There goes five hundred bucks, Mom."

She was already halfway back to the kitchen. "You can always make money, Jack. You don't get many chances to help out a person in need."

Yeah, he thought, but wouldn't it be great to be able to do both?

Now *there* was a thought . . .

1

"All right, everybody, settle down," Mr. Kressy said. "I've got an important announcement to make."

Jack had just slid behind his desk. The bus trip to school had been what it should always be: uneventful. All the talk had been about the Carson Toliver show yesterday and how he'd stayed out the whole day. Not a single "Easy Weezy." Jack had to work hard to keep from grinning like an idiot.

Mission accomplished.

He focused on Mr. Kressy. Whatever announcement was coming must be important. He usually saved them for after attendance.

When everyone was quiet, he said, "Carson Toliver is missing."

Jack felt a cold lead weight form in his stomach as he re-membered Eddie's "bad feeling" yesterday.

"He left school yesterday morning after some incident at his locker—no need to go into that since it's all you've been talking about ever since—and never returned. No one knows where he went after that. He might have gone home, but no one can say so for sure since both his parents were out all day. He wasn't there when they came home and he never re-turned last night. His car is gone, but none of his clothes are missing, so he does not appear to have run away. The sheriff's department is searching for him but they've requested that we ask the student body if anyone has seen him since he left school." He raised his eyebrows and looked around. "Hmmm? Anyone?"

Jack sat frozen in silent shock and dread as the classroom erupted in a burst of excited chatter—talking to one another or asking Mr. Kressy for more information. He didn't have any.

Toliver . . . gone? Didn't come home last night? Where could he be? Where could he have gone without extra clothes?

Yeah, he'd been embarrassed, sure, but to run off like this . . . it seemed so out of proportion.

That was what bothered Jack the most.

All the earlier pumped-up feelings deflated with a whoosh, leaving him feeling small and cold and worried.

Had he pushed him too far?

2

Mrs. LeClaire, Jack's French teacher, dropped a hydrogen bomb right after lunch.

He knew something was wrong the instant he saw her. She looked pale, wobbly, and her eyes were red.

"I have terrible news," she said in a shaky voice. "Carson Toliver is dead."

As the classroom exploded with wails of shock and grief, Jack's blood turned to sleet. He saw the whole thing play out in his head: Toliver leaving school, buying some applejack or some other kind of booze, getting drunk, then racing along a back road and wrapping his car around a tree or a bridge abutment.

He closed his eyes and fought a wave of nausea.

In response to a chorus of kids asking *how, when,* and *where,* Mrs. LeClaire held up her hands to quiet things down. Quiet wasn't going to happen, not with a couple of girls crying, but the volume dropped enough to allow her to be heard.

"Here is what I know. A search has been on for him and a helicopter spotted his car in the Pines."

I knew it, Jack thought. I knew it, I knew it, I knew it!

"When the deputies arrived, they found him . . ." She covered her mouth and sobbed once into her hand. "They found him hanging from a tree. It appears . . . the police think he committed suicide."

The new outburst of dismay from the class dwarfed the previous one. Jack felt the room spin. Bile and acid surged into his throat.

Suicide!

No-no-no! It can't be!

He'd pushed him, tried to embarrass him, give him a taste of his own medicine, but he'd never intended to push him *this* far!

Carson Toliver was a bad guy, a violent phony. He'd earned a comeuppance, but he was only seventeen years old. He didn't deserve this.

It was Jack's fault he'd killed himself.

He'd pushed him too damn hard!

3

Except for some sobbing now and again, the school bus ride home was silent. Even Weezy looked dejected.

It had been tough just getting to the bus, what with passing Toliver's unlocked locker, and worse, seeing knots of weeping girls and stunned-looking guys.

"You've barely said a word," Weezy said after they'd been dropped off. "What do you think? How do you feel?"

She, Jack, and Eddie were making their daily after-school trek up Quakerton, with Eddie lost as usual in his headphones. Jack wondered if he was listening to something sad. Some of the dark, gloomy music Weezy liked would have been appropriate.

"How do I feel?" He searched for an answer. How could he tell her about the massive guilt weighing him down, hunching his shoulders, bowing his back? "I don't know. You?"

She shook her head. "Strange. I started out with a crush on him, then I was scared of him for what he tried that night, then I hated him—really hated him for the lies he told, and then I wasn't afraid anymore and was going to report him—"

"Did you?"

"No. I was going to do it today, but now . . . doesn't seem much point. You know, during all that Easy Weezy stuff I hated him so much I wanted him dead. I *wished* him dead. But now that he's really dead—killed himself, of all things—I feel really, really bad for him."

"Yeah. I know what you mean. Somehow, some way,

considering what he did to you and did to himself, he must have had some loose wires in his head."

Jack had begun telling himself that during the long afternoon. He hoped it might lessen the guilt. And it did, but not much.

"I know all about that," Weezy muttered.

Jack realized immediately what she meant, but hid any sign that he knew what she was talking about. He pretended he hadn't heard. But he wondered if Carson Toliver had been going to a psychiatrist. Maybe even the same one as Weezy.

"You saw how he was acting Sunday night. No way you can call that normal."

Weezy nodded. "Yeah. That was bizarre. I think the wheels were coming off then. Someone was making a fool of him, he blew the game, he was drinking, he was alone in the woods screaming at no one . . . all the signs were there."

"Of what?"

"Of a breakdown. Maybe we should have said something."

"How could we know? We're not shrinks."

They were passing USED. He was supposed to put in a couple of hours today. Usually he didn't mind spending the afternoon alone in a store full of musty old stuff, but today that was the last thing he felt like doing.

"Wait here a sec," he said as he trotted up to the store's front door.

He stuck his head inside and saw Mr. Rosen at the counter, reading the paper and listening to his classical music station.

"Mister Rosen, is it okay if I don't come in today?"

He looked up over his reading glasses. "Of course it's

okay. I heard about your friend at school. What a terrible tragedy." He shook his head sadly. "So young and yet nothing to live for? Such an awful thing to lose a child. His parents must be inconsolable."

Jack hadn't thought about Toliver's folks. His dad had a weekly TV show on the local channel. Thinking about them now made him feel even worse. He tried to imagine his own mother's reaction if someone ever came to the door and told her that her miracle boy had hung himself. His mind shied from the picture.

"Thanks, Mister Rosen."

"Take a couple of days already. It's slow now, so don't worry."

Jack waved and returned to the street where he resumed walking with Weezy. Eddie was way ahead of them now.

After a while she said, "Mrs. Morton told us something this afternoon."

"Who's she?"

"Social studies. Her husband's an EMT. He helped remove . . . the body. He said he had a note on him."

A suicide note? Jack stopped and grabbed her arm.

"What did it say?"

Please, he thought. Nothing about his locker. *Please!*

"She said he only got a glimpse at it, but he saw the words 'I hope you're happy.'"

" 'Happy'? Happy about what?"

She shrugged. "If it said, he didn't see it."

"About him committing suicide?"

"Jack," she said with a trace of annoyance, "I only know what she told me." She looked at him as they started walking again. "You're acting kind of strange."

He knew he was, but couldn't help it. He *felt* strange.

"It's not every day that someone you know hangs himself." Mentally he added, And you're possibly—*probably*—to blame.

She only nodded.

After a while Jack said, "Did Mrs. Morton say where he . . . where it happened?"

"No . . . but I can guess."

"Me too." He made a snap decision. "I'm going out there. Want to come?"

She stared at him. "Are you crazy? That's a . . . what . . . a crime scene or something. You can't go out there."

"Watch me."

They could shoo him away, but he wanted a look—*needed* a look—at where it happened.

"And you call *me* morbid."

"So you're not coming?"

She sighed. "Of course I am."

4

They found a sheriff's department patrol car and two state police cruisers parked on the firebreak trail near where he and Weezy had spied on Toliver's strange behavior.

Yellow crime-scene tape surrounded the big oak where the pine lights had performed their loop-the-loop.

His tongue felt dry as sand as he stared at the tree, wondering which branch Toliver had used, and what kind of rope, and how he'd gone about it, and what had been going through his mind the whole time up until the final . . .

Something flashed in the shade. Someone was taking pictures, but Jack couldn't see what the others were doing. Two sheriff's deputies stood outside the tape, watching. Jack recognized one of them as Tim Davis.

"Maybe we'd better go," Weezy said in a hushed voice.

Jack shook his head. "I want to see what they're doing."

He led her along the rutted path for a closer look. From the new angle he saw that someone was digging a hole near the tree. He wondered why.

No one had noticed them yet. If they could find a place where they could see without being seen . . .

He glanced around and saw the dead zone amid the ebony spleenwort. He remembered the vague uneasiness he'd felt in there before, but it offered perfect concealment.

He nudged Weezy and pointed toward the spot. She shook her head and pointed back to the bikes. Jack took her arm and guided her toward the clearing. She came along with no protest other than an unhappy expression.

As they arrived at the edge of the dead zone, Jack noticed a disturbance in the sand near its center. He pointed it out to Weezy.

"Look," he whispered as he spotted a line of scuff marks going toward it and coming away. "Footprints."

"Well, that makes sense," Weezy said. "That's where we saw him kneeling Sunday night."

Jack frowned. That sounded perfectly logical on the surface, but something wasn't clicking.

He was about to step through the spleenwort when he realized what was wrong and froze. Weezy angled to move past him but he stopped her.

"What's the matter?" she said.

"Don't you see? It—"

"You two!"

Jack whirled around at the sound of a voice behind them and saw Deputy Tim Davis. His eyes were invisible behind his sunglasses, but the rest of his face did not look happy.

"Why is it," Tim said, "that whenever anything strange happens, you two are never far away. What are you doing here?"

Jack said, "We were passing by and saw the cars."

He didn't want to tell him about following Toliver here.

"Why don't I believe you? I know you two like to trespass on Foster's land, but how did you just happen to end up here on this particular afternoon?"

Jack tried to change the subject. He jerked his thumb over his shoulder.

"We were just looking at something strange in that clearing." He turned and pointed. "See? The sand's messed up in one spot and there's one set of footprints going in and out."

Tim stared at the dead zone. "So?"

"So it rained like crazy yesterday. That means those footprints were made after the rain."

"Yeah," Tim said, nodding slowly. "That's exactly what it means."

He looked around at the ground and picked up a three-foot piece of broken branch.

"You two stay here."

With that, he stepped through the spleenwort and entered the dead zone. He dragged the tip of the branch through the sandy soil about a foot to the right of the footprint trails, around the area of disturbed sand, and then all the way back on the left side of the prints.

Then, staying outside the line, he went back and squatted by the disturbed area and started poking at it with the stick. Jack saw him stiffen as he lifted the stick. A dirty pink sock dangled from its tip.

He dropped the stick and hurried toward Jack and Weezy.

"Okay, you two," he said, his voice and expression tight. "Time to take off."

Jack couldn't take his eyes off the sock where it lay in the clearing.

"But—?"

Tim grabbed one of Jack's shoulders and one of Weezy's. He turned them around and began propelling them away from the clearing.

"No buts, no nothing. This whole area's about to be taped off. You don't belong here. Skedaddle home. Now."

"But Tim—"

"*Now*, Jack. This is serious. You can't be here. And don't think you'll get special treatment because of Kate. You push me, I'll arrest you."

Jack could tell from his tone that he wasn't kidding, but he had to tell him. He twisted free and faced him.

"That sock—I saw it or one just like it fall out of Toliver's locker last week."

Tim stopped. "You're sure?"

"Very sure. He grabbed it and stuffed it in his pocket."

Tim stood silent a moment, then said, "Thanks. That helps. But you're still outta here. Get!"

"Okay, I'm getting," he said, moving slowly, "but can I ask you about the suicide note?"

"Damn it!" Tim said. "Where did you hear about that?"

"Rumors." He didn't want to get Mrs. Morton's husband in trouble. "It said, 'I hope you're happy.' What does—?"

Tim raised his arms. "Where did you hear *that*?"

Jack ignored the question. "Did it say who he hoped was happy or why he did it?"

The answer was important to Jack. If he'd done it because of the locker tricks or because he'd blown the game to the Greyhounds, then the blame for Toliver hanging himself rested squarely on Jack's shoulders.

"I'm not telling you anything, Jack. I'm not even saying there was a note. This is an ongoing investigation."

"Please, Tim?"

He pointed back toward the firebreak trail. "Get!"

As they walked toward their bikes, Weezy said, "Why are you so interested in why he did it?"

"I just am." How he wished he could unburden himself to her. "He's the first person I've ever known who killed himself. Hopefully the last. I'd like to understand."

"We may never know. There could be a million reasons."

"Yeah, I suppose you're right."

Jack just hoped his locker wasn't one of them.

"And what do you think's going on in the dead zone? I mean, a sock?"

Jack shook his head. "I wish I knew. There's something really weird going on here."

"You think those were . . . his footprints?"

Weezy couldn't seem to bring herself to say his name.

"Toliver's? Yeah, I do. But why he buried that sock there I can't even begin to imagine."

Weezy said, "Maybe he was so completely out of his head that we shouldn't expect him to make sense."

Jack found himself unable to reply to that, because he was the one who'd helped drive him out of his head.

5

It hit Jack hard later on when he was alone. He kept seeing the shock and terror on Toliver's face when he saw that dead possum. Jack had reveled in it at the time, but now, knowing what it had led to, it sickened him.

If only he could talk to someone about it—someone who knew the whole story and could understand the guilt he was feeling.

His folks hadn't helped. Oh, they'd meant to, but their consolations were based on the assumption that Jack was down because he'd lost a schoolmate he'd looked up to. Nothing was further from the truth.

But it only got worse.

He'd struggled through his homework and finally finished it. Now he was trying to read a science fiction novel— one of Edgar Rice Burroughs's old Mars tales—in the hope that it would grab him and give him a break from thinking about Carson Toliver. It wasn't working. And then his mom called from the kitchen.

"Jack? Kate's on the phone."

Kate . . . good old Kate would help.

"Oh, Jack, I'm so shocked to hear about this boy at school. You must be feeling terrible. I'm so sorry."

"Yeah." Had to be careful. His mother was over by the sink, hanging on every word while pretending to be busy with something else. "No one saw it coming."

"I took a few psychology courses in college and that's too

*often the case. But usually, when you look back, there were
signs."*

"Um, someone was kind of harassing him." He needed
to bring this up somehow, and figured this was the best way.
"You know, breaking into his locker and leaving stuff. It
kind of embarrassed him. And then he had to be benched
during the game against North. Do you think all that could
have had anything to do with it?"

*"Could have. Mom told me he was the most popular boy in
school."*

Jack could feel his stomach tightening. Come on, Kate.
Help me out here.

"He was. Who could have thought that stuff would
make him, you know, kill himself?"

*"You never know, Jack. Some people who look like they've got
the world on a string are barely holding it together. They've
learned to hide all sorts of inner turmoil and put on a good front.
But when things start to go wrong, they can't cope. Things that
would simply upset you and me bring the world crashing down
around them. They decompensate, and some of them . . . some of
them see no way out, so they end it all."*

Jack closed his eyes and leaned against the wall. He'd
picked on a guy who'd been walking a psychological high
wire. He'd made him lose his balance and fall. The fact that
he hadn't known about the high-wire act was some defense,
but if Jack had stayed away from the locker, Toliver would
still be alive.

Then again, if Toliver had left Weezy alone, Jack wouldn't
have gone near his locker.

What a godawful mess.

"Thanks, Kate," he said, hoping he sounded sincere

through the growing wave of nausea. She'd tried her best. She didn't know the whole story. "You've been a big help."

Jack managed a little small talk with her, then hung up and wandered back to his room.

He could tell he had a long, sleepless night ahead of him.

A second bomb dropped the next day.

The bus to school was not as quiet as yesterday's ride home. The kids were talking, but only about Carson Toliver. No one was crying . . . yet.

In school Jack forced himself to walk by the locker, now draped in black bunting. Nearby he saw three senior girls in a tight group hug, sobbing. The sight built a lump in his throat.

The school brought in counselors who went from class to class and talked about coping with death and loss. Jack barely listened. He wished they were talking about coping with *causing* death and loss.

The teachers tried to teach but they knew the kids were only half there so they didn't pull any pop quizzes. Mrs. Schneider even canceled a history test she'd had scheduled.

All the kids who thought they were feeling about as bad as they could feel in school were wrong.

Things were about to get worse.

2

Jack knew something was up the instant Weezy dropped into the last empty chair at the table where he and Eddie were eating lunch. First off, sophomore girls didn't hang out with freshman boys, and second, her usually pale face was dead white—as white as Saree's. Even her lips were white. Which made the redness of her eyes even more startling.

"What's wrong?" Jack said. He knew she couldn't be this upset about Toliver now—not a whole day after the news.

She sniffed. "Didn't you hear?"

"Hear what?"

"Somebody just heard it on the radio. The police dug up a body in the Pines yesterday."

Jack nearly choked on his sandwich as the table went silent. His mind raced. Another Lodge member, like the one he and Weezy had found? Or . . . ?

"Do they know who it is?"

She nodded, tears welling in her eyes. "They say it's Marcie Kurek."

Jack felt a chill. Marcie Kurek . . . the sophomore girl who'd disappeared last year.

"Did they say where in the Pines?"

She shook her head. "No."

Jack looked straight into her eyes. "Do you think it could have been . . . ?" He didn't want to say where.

Weezy stiffened as if she'd been hit with an electric shock.

"Ohmigod!"

"What?" Eddie said. "What are you two talking about?"

A couple of the other kids at the table wanted to know too.

Jack leaned back. "Nothing."

"Bull!" Eddie said. "You guys know something. Give. What is it?"

Jack looked around the caf. He could see the news spreading from table to table like a wave. He heard screams from over where the junior girls usually sat—Marcie would have been a junior this year. Jack had never met her, and had seen her face only in newspaper photos shortly after she disappeared, but she had been talked about so much in the past year, he felt as if he knew her.

He closed his eyes and wished he could teleport himself into the Pines, because he knew—or at least was as sure as he could be without actually going out there—where they'd found Marcie.

School seemed like a prison now. He knew where he'd be headed as soon as he was sprung. He glanced at Weezy and knew she'd be with him.

3

But Weezy couldn't.

She had to go to Medford with her mother. She didn't say why, but Jack suspected it was to see that Dr. Hamilton. He'd spotted her in the car with her mother last Wednesday. A weekly visit?

The state police and the sheriff's department had only one car each in the Pines today. Jack recognized the license plate on Tim's unit. No surprise since he patrolled this section of the county.

He dropped his bike and hurried along the ruts. This time, in addition to the suicide tree, he found the entire dead zone taped off as well. Jack moved up as close as the tape would allow. A large hole, big enough to fit a human, had been dug in the center of the clearing.

I was right, he thought, feeling suddenly short of breath. She was buried right here . . . right where they found that sock.

He'd suspected it earlier, but now . . . to see . . . to *know* . . .

He looked around and saw Tim Davis walking his way, an angry look on his face.

"You're really pushing me, Jack."

"That's where you dug her up, right?"

Tim pointed toward the firebreak trail. "Out. Now."

Jack started to obey, then stopped and held his ground.

"Come on, Tim. You owe me."

His expression changed to surprise. "Because I once dated your sister? I don't think so."

"No, because I showed you where that sock was. You wouldn't have found Marcie without that."

"Yes, we would have."

"But who knows when? You were digging way over the by the sui—by the oak."

"How do you know that?"

"I saw it yesterday. Come on, Tim. It's only fair."

He stared at Jack a long moment, his eyes unreadable behind his sunglasses. Finally he sighed and looked around.

"Okay. It'll be in tomorrow's paper anyway. I guess I can give you a preview."

Jack had been putting the pieces together all day. He was reasonably sure of the answer, but asked the question anyway.

"Do you know who did it?"

Tim nodded. "Carson Toliver looks good for it. He's our number one suspect."

Jack said nothing. Like seeing the spot where they'd dug up Marcie—one thing to suspect it, quite another to hear it confirmed.

"You don't look surprised," Tim said.

"Yeah, well, that's what I thought."

Tim snapped off his glasses and stared at Jack. "The hell you did! No way you could put that together."

Based on the little Tim thought Jack knew, that would seem true. But Jack knew Toliver was capable of violence—though he'd never dreamed he would kill—and had seen him in the dead zone Sunday night. It had never occurred to Jack that Marcie might be buried there until he heard that she'd been found. Then the pieces had begun creeping together.

Blood on Toliver's hands . . . Saree had been right about

that, but wrong about the piney part. Marcie wasn't a piney. She'd lived in Shamong.

Unless there was another victim . . .

"Well, I'd seen Toliver with the sock you pulled out of that bare area. Did it belong to Marcie?"

Tim nodded. "Yeah, we found a ring and a sneaker too, all on the list of things she'd been wearing when she disappeared."

"What'd he do . . . keep them as souvenirs?"

"That's the odd part. The crime scene people say they were buried with her—on her—and had only recently been removed. Lots of 'products of decomposition' or something like that on them."

Jack swallowed. "You mean he dug her up and . . ."

"No. They say the body hadn't been disturbed since it was buried a year ago."

"That doesn't make sense."

"Tell me about it. The only thing we're missing from the list of what she was wearing is a pink hair band. We're getting a search warrant for his locker and his home."

Jack's mouth went dry. The pink hair band around the neck of the possum—only he hadn't put it there and hadn't seen it in the locker.

As a matter of fact, he hadn't seen the sneaker in the locker either. And the ring . . . it had fallen out with the marbles, but there'd been no ring in the box when he'd set it up.

An ice-footed spider scurried up his spine to his neck and settled there. Something was going on, something that couldn't be.

"Okay," Jack said, choosing his words carefully, "if the sock you dug out of the sand was the same one I saw fall out of Toliver's locker—"

"It was—or at least we're ninety percent sure it was. Here's what we think happened: He left school, went home, stole a bottle of vodka from the house, a coil of rope from the garage, came out here, got drunk, buried Marcie's belongings over there, right over her grave, then walked over to the tree and hung himself."

"Somewhere along the line he wrote a note, didn't he?"

"Right. Forgot to mention that."

"Can you tell me now if it said who he hoped was 'happy'?"

"From what we can tell, Marcie Kurek."

"Huh?"

"The note said: '*You win, Marcie. I ruined your life so I guess it's only fair you ruined mine. I hope you're happy.*'"

Jack felt his knees soften with relief. He could have kissed Tim, although that might have got him arrested.

You win, Marcie . . . That meant guilt over killing her had made him believe Marcie was haunting him, ruining his life because he'd ended hers. That, not losing the game, had driven him to tie a rope around his neck.

Maybe Toliver had brought her out here thinking she'd be easy, and she wasn't. Maybe he got rough with her like he had with Weezy, thinking she was playing hard to get, or maybe he simply wanted what he wanted when he wanted it, had always gotten what he wanted, didn't know the meaning of the word "no," and didn't care to learn. Maybe things got too far out of control and he had to silence her.

He remembered Toliver's words right out here Sunday night . . .

It was an accident! I didn't mean it!

Whatever happened, Marcie wound up dead and he'd had to hide her body. Why he chose that particular spot,

Jack couldn't say, but with nothing growing there, he wouldn't run into any roots, making the digging easy. Like digging at the beach.

Maybe killing Marcie awoke some sickness in him that liked what he'd done. Maybe it had driven him to kill a piney girl. And to bring Weezy here last week.

"You okay?" Tim said.

Jack yanked himself back to the here and now. He'd been fighting a wave of nausea at the thought of what might have happened to Weezy if she hadn't escaped from Toliver's car.

"I-I'm fine. I'd just like to know how that sock got from Marcie's grave to Toliver's locker without her body being disturbed."

"So would we all. But we've learned that someone was harassing him lately, someone who was able to break into his locker and leave surprises. We'd like to talk to that person."

Jack went cold. He'd covered his tracks well enough to keep anyone at school from tracing him—except Levi—but was that good enough to elude the police?

He needed to muddy the waters a little.

"Everybody would," he said.

Tim looked surprised. "They would? Why?"

"Because no one can figure out how he got into Toliver's locker the last time." He described what Toliver had done to his last lock, then added, "But whoever it was got into the locker anyway."

Tim shrugged. "All he'd have to do was cut off the lock."

Jack shook his head. "Toliver had to cut off the lock the next morning. And the possum was inside. How do you explain that?"

"I can't."

Jack made a point of taking a long, slow look at the grave.

"Maybe Marcie was doing it."

Tim grunted. "Oh, come *on*, Jack!"

"Well, from the sound of his note, Toliver seemed to think so. So until someone comes up with a better explanation, that seems as good as any."

Jack had said it as a spur-of-the-moment thing, but the more he thought about it, the better he liked it. Not that he believed it for an instant, but if he mentioned it here and there around school in a half-serious fashion, he bet it would catch on and spread like a midsummer wildfire in the Pines.

"If you think about it, Tim, it answers all the questions. No one could figure why the prankster was picking on the most popular and best-liked guy in the school, but revenge by Marcie answers that question. It also explains how the objects got off Marcie and into the locker, and how every lock was bypassed."

Tim's expression was incredulous. "You expect me to believe there's a *ghost* involved?"

"It fills in all the blanks. Got a better theory?"

"No, but I'm sure as hell not telling the sheriff a ghost story."

You won't have to, Jack thought. Because everyone else is going to believe it—or want to.

That was what living close to the Pines did to people. Strange things went on in that nearby wilderness, and after a while you either accepted them or moved away.

The Revenge of Marcie Kurek . . . Oh, people were going to love that story, and they'd tell it and retell it until it became an accepted part of Pinelands lore.

Jack, of course, knew better. He and he alone knew who had really broken into Toliver's locker and why.

Except . . .

Except for the sock, the ring, the sneaker, and the hair band . . . someone had to put them there. Jack didn't believe in ghosts, but if not Toliver—he'd looked genuinely shocked to see them—and not Jack . . .

Then who?

4

"I can't believe it," Weezy sobbed as she buried her face in her hands. "Carson Toliver killed Marcie?"

Dark had fallen and they were sitting on one of the benches by the lake. Jack had relayed what Tim had told him.

"Tim says, with the note and all, everything points to him. It'll be in the paper tomorrow."

She raised her head and looked at him. Her tearstained cheeks glistened in the glow of a nearby streetlight.

"But that means I could have been . . ."

"I know . . ."

He could have added "next" but no need. She'd already reached that conclusion.

She wrapped her arms across her chest. "I feel so scared and cold and . . . I think I'm gonna be sick."

Jack hesitated, then slipped an arm around her shoulders and pulled her against him. He felt her resist, then tremble and lean into him.

"You're safe, Weez. He's gone and I've got your back. It's over."

Except for the piney blood . . . if there was any.

"Should I tell the police what he tried to do to me? I thought it didn't matter once he was gone, but maybe it does."

Jack took an instant dislike to that idea.

"What would that accomplish? The police are convinced he's the killer. Putting yourself in the middle of this mess doesn't help them, and can only hurt you."

She snuggled closer, like a kitten trying to borrow a little warmth. Man, that felt good.

"You're right. You've been right a lot lately, Jack."

"Just luck."

Jack remembered an old saying that went something like, *The harder I work, the luckier I get.*

Then she asked the question Jack couldn't answer.

"But who was breaking into his locker?"

So he decided to start the ghost story with Weezy.

"Maybe it was Marcie Kurek, getting even."

He went on to explain his reasoning, just as he had to Tim.

When he was through, Weezy said, "I believe in a lot of things I can't prove, Jack, but I don't believe in ghosts."

"Not even a little?"

"Well, maybe people leave emanations behind when they die violently, but the whole ghost thing . . . people reappearing and looking like they did in real life . . . that's so bogus."

"Why?"

"A ghost is supposedly their spirit, so why should it look like their body? And why should it be *dressed,* for God's sake? That always makes me laugh. Why would a spirit dress up in clothes?"

Jack had to admit she had a point. It did seem stupid. But he wasn't backing down.

"Marcie didn't appear to anyone that we know of—I can't speak for Toliver, of course—but it answers all the mysteries, Weezy. How else do you explain what happened?"

She was silent a long time, still leaning against him, and Jack sort of wished the moment would go on and on. But then she straightened, pulling away.

"Yeah, it does. But it's too easy. Something's missing."

Uh-oh.

"What do you mean?"

"I don't know. Somehow I think it's more complicated than that." She rose and turned to face him. "I'm going to have to do some heavy thinking on this. I don't need an immediate explanation for everything. But I know there's one out there. I don't believe I can know everything—I'm not smart enough and I won't live long enough—but I'm pretty sure, given sufficient time and intelligence, everything is eventually knowable."

Jack agreed. But he wanted the ghost story out there, circulating.

"But just for the heck of it, why don't you ask your friends at school what they think about ghost vengeance?"

"I may just do that."

Yeah, spread it around.

She stared down at him. "Thanks for the heads-up. I'll be ready when the news hits tomorrow morning." She bent and gave him a quick kiss on the lips. "You're a good friend, Jack."

I try, he thought as goose bumps raised all over his skin.

He watched her walk away, then stared at the lake, watching the ripples reflect the single lighted window in the Lodge up on the rise.

5

"How interesting," said a woman's voice.

Jack jumped off the bench and spun to see Mrs. Clevenger and her three-legged dog standing behind him.

"Oh, hi."

She fixed him with her stare. "You speak a truth while thinking you speak an untruth."

"Huh?"

She stepped around the edge of the bench and seated herself. She patted the spot next to her.

"Come sit again."

"Gee, I don't know . . ."

"Sit."

She said it like she was speaking to a dog, but Jack had never heard her tell her dog to sit.

Still . . .

He sat.

"It is strange how things work in there," she said, staring east to where the Pine Barrens lay.

"I guess so."

She glanced at him. "It was not a question. I was not asking you to agree."

"Ooookay."

"A girl dies, murdered. She is buried and, in most other places, that would possibly be the end of that."

"Most other places? You mean most places other than the Pines?"

"And even in the Pines. Most of the Barrens is exactly

what it appears to be, but places exist within its million acres where, possibly, the usual laws do not apply."

"Like where?"

"Places where plants will not grow, where living things will not tread. And where dead things do not rest easy."

She didn't use Weezy's ooh-scary voice, but the effect was more real. Jack felt that spider on his spine again.

"You . . . you're talking about the place where Marcie was buried?"

"I am speaking only of possibilities."

"What's wrong with it? Why won't anything grow there? Was the ground poisoned?"

He thought about the pine lights dipping into that dead soil. Did they sterilize it in some annual ritual, or had they been drawn by Marcie?

"That would depend on what you mean by 'poison.'"

"Weezy says there was a building there once—a big one."

Mrs. Clevenger looked at him. "And how would she know that?"

"She says the ebony spleenwort is a clue."

"She is very wise, that one. Yes, a building once existed there, a long, long time ago."

"What kind of building?"

"Let us call it a temple of sorts. And let us assume that what went on in that building forever changed—one might say *tainted*—the place where it sat. It is not the earth itself, it is the *place*. Remove dirt from there and you will find it supports life very well someplace else. Move new fertile soil in and it will become barren—whatever you sow will not germinate, whatever you plant there will die."

Jack swallowed. This was so weird.

"And if you 'plant' something dead there . . . ?"

She shrugged. "Perhaps it will rest easy, perhaps not. Let us assume the poor Kurek girl was buried in such a place. Perhaps she rested quietly and would have continued to do so had not a certain sequence of events been initiated."

Jack realized what she was talking about.

"Toliver's attack on Weezy."

She nodded. "Violence begets violence. Raw fear and lust are potent emotions."

"Do they attract pine lights?"

She nodded. "You witnessed something few humans ever see."

How did she know that?

"What are they anyway?"

"They are known to some as lumens, but in essence, they are what they are."

Thanks for clearing that up, he thought.

"But what did it mean? What were they doing?"

"Who can explain the lumens? They remain mostly isolated and disconnected, but under certain circumstances— the autumnal equinox, for one—they become organized. Something triggered their activity."

"Weezy—"

"Her pain and terror—perhaps. As I was saying, the Kurek girl might have remained quiet had not her killer attempted violence upon another girl so near to where she lay."

"She woke up?"

"No, of course not. She is dead. Death is death, but sometimes death is not the end. A remnant became aware, and with that awareness came rage at the one who had so shortened her young life."

"Wait-wait-wait." This was too much like the ghost story

he'd made up. "He asked about someone being haunted. Are you saying it's true? That Marcie's ghost got into Toliver's locker and left those things for him?"

"I am saying no such thing. I am saying that if an object exists in one place, it can be moved to another."

"But something has to transport it."

She nodded. "I agree."

"But—"

She gave Jack an intent look. "Sometimes the living help by opening that which is closed."

It took a moment or two for that to sink in. And when it did, the meaning blasted through Jack like a winter storm.

Was she saying that whatever "residue" of Marcie had awakened had been able to follow him into Toliver's locker? But how could Mrs. Clevenger know about—?

Oh, crap. Had Walt told her about meeting him in the dead of night? Had she put it all together?

Or did she just . . . know? She seemed to know all sorts of things. If she knew about his father's vasectomy becoming recanalized, and knew about him watching the pine lights a couple of nights ago, then she could easily know about his secret trips to Toliver's locker.

Though she seemed harmless, even benign, this old woman gave him the creeps.

"Wh-who helped?"

She smiled. "Not to worry. I will tell no one."

Tim had said the sheriff's office would be looking for whoever had broken into Toliver's locker. He couldn't imagine them questioning someone everybody considered crazy, or believing her even if she went to them. Still, you never knew.

"The police—"

"The concerns of the police are of no concern to me. You acted nobly. Weezy is lucky to have such a friend."

Jack couldn't help a swell of pride at the compliment.

"So . . . is it over?"

She nodded. "The Pine Barrens are all about balance. They allow the scales to remain uneven for only so long, then they must be brought back into line. The scales are balanced."

"Are they? Someone told me something about piney blood on Toliver's hands."

"That would be Saree. She is right."

"Then—"

"It is over." She rose and leaned on her cane as she looked down at him. "I will leave you now. I know you helped the balance. I have no need to discuss it with anyone else."

With that she turned and walked slowly away, her dog following in its strange, three-legged gait.

He watched them cross the Quaker Lake bridge and disappear into the shadows of Old Town.

6

He sat a few moments longer, pondering piney blood and thinking about how his collection of secrets was growing: things he'd done that he wasn't supposed to do, things he knew that he wasn't supposed to know.

He glanced left and saw a figure approaching. He couldn't make out the face but no need to: A tall, slim man in a white suit could be only one person.

"Well, well," Mr. Drexler said, smiling his thin smile as he stopped next to the bench. "Look who's here, all alone. No friends?"

"All I need. How about you?"

He shook his head. "Friendship is highly overrated. The only difference between a friend and an enemy is that a friend will stab you in the heart rather than the back. The few times I've tried friendship I found its attendant duties, social and otherwise, quite burdensome. I much prefer to do without."

Jack had no idea how to respond to that, so he said nothing.

Mr. Drexler added, "Some people cannot bear being alone. Perhaps because when they are alone there is no one there. You do not appear to mind."

"Just because I'm alone doesn't mean I'm lonely."

He tapped the bench with the tip of his cane. "Excellent response. You've got you, and sometimes that's quite enough." He waved his cane around. "Quite an entertaining little town you've got here, Jack. Murder, suicide, a man named Weird Walt, and you. I shall miss it."

"You're leaving?"

"Your powers of deduction are positively Holmesian. I have accomplished my purpose. Time to leave this entertaining little town."

He kept calling Johnson entertaining. Why?

"Not to worry. Your gardening job is secure until the frost. I came to town merely to reorganize after the sudden departure of a number of members. My work here is done."

Departure of members? Yeah, departed as in dead. As for work, Jack hadn't seen him do any work. Hadn't seen him do much of anything except hang around and have meetings. The card he'd given Jack had said he was an "actuator" for the Ancient Septimus Fraternal Order, but who knew what that meant.

He grinned up at him. "Going to go actuate somewhere else?"

Mr. Drexler's smile was tight and tolerant. "I suppose one might put it that way. As you can imagine, this Lodge was in severe disarray after the events of August."

I'll bet it was, Jack thought.

The mysterious sudden deaths of four local members would tend to disarray things.

"But it's back on track now. The Order has other tasks for me."

"Where next?"

"Wherever I am sent." He twirled his cane. "Good-bye, Jack."

Jack rose and thrust out his hand. "Nice meeting you. And thanks for the job."

It hadn't really been nice meeting him—he was kind of

creepy—but he'd treated him well and fairly, despite the fiasco last month, and it seemed like the right thing to say.

Mr. Drexler's hand was cool and dry as it gripped Jack's and gave it a firm squeeze.

"Perhaps someday we shall be brothers in the Order."

"Um, yeah, perhaps."

Don't hold your breath.

As Mr. Drexler turned and strolled away, Jack headed home.

He was halfway up Franklin Street when he saw movement to his right and Levi Coffin emerged from the shadows.

Jack hid his surprise. This guy had a habit of seeming to appear out of thin air.

"You following me?"

"Nope," he said as he fell in step beside Jack.

"Well, you've got to be a long way from home."

"I am."

"Then how do you get around? Teleport?"

"What's that?"

Jack couldn't believe he didn't know, but explained anyway.

"That's when you make a thing disappear from one place and appear in another."

"*That's* your talent! You moved those things into Toliver's locker without openin' the door!"

"No. Wrong. I don't *have* a talent."

"Then how'd you know about this teleportatin'?"

"Teleporting. And everybody knows."

"Not everybody. At least not by that word. We call it 'moving.' "

" 'We'?"

"Yeah, well, never mind that. Came by to tell you some

news. I found out whose piney blood Toliver had on his hands."

"Whose?"

"Marcie Kurek's."

"No way. She wasn't a—"

"Yeah, she was. I never knew. Hardly anybody did, but when news came out she was killed, people who did know started talkin'. Turns out she was Noah Appleton's little girl. Noah got killed in a huntin' accident shortly after Marcie was born. Not too long after that her mama took up with this Kurek fellow from Shamong and married him. Left her kinfolk and never looked back. Even let this Kurek fellow adopt Marcie and change her name. That gal may've lived in Shamong, but she was born in the Pines, and once a piney, always a piney."

Jack shook his head. "So Saree was right."

He now understood what Mrs. C had meant when she insisted the scales were balanced.

"Yeah, her talent held true. And yours . . . if it ain't tele-portin', what *is* it?"

Jack held up his hands, palms out. "Enough. I'm not doing this again."

"Okay, okay. Have it your way. But I'm a-gonna figger out your talent. I'm a-gonna keep an eye on you, and when I catch you usin' it, I'll know."

Jack didn't like the idea of anybody watching him, especially a weird piney, but he stayed cool.

"Well, Levi, you've got an awfully boring life ahead of you. And what's with all this 'talent' talk? You got some sort of special talent yourself?"

He sensed a wall go up around Levi. He was still right beside him but it felt like he'd teleported ten feet away.

"We ain't allowed to talk about that."

There it was again: *We.*

"What do—?"

"Gotta go," Levi said, and trotted off toward the shadows.

"Hey, wait!"

"Be seein' you."

And then he was gone.

Be seein' you . . .

That sounded too much like *Be watching you . . .* and that gave Jack the creeps.

And who were the "we" he mentioned, the ones who weren't allowed to talk about supposed "talents"?

Jack wondered if he'd ever know.

<www.repairmanjack.com>

AUTHOR'S NOTE

For readers who wish to know a little more about Weird
Walt and the secret behind his odd behavior, I suggest the
2009 reprint of *The Touch*. The novel's prequel, "Dat Tay
Vao," is included. Together they offer a glimpse into the
gift/curse that rules Walter Erskine's life.

THE SECRET HISTORY OF THE WORLD

The preponderance of my work deals with a history of the world that remains undiscovered, unexplored, and unknown to most of humanity. Some of this secret history has been revealed in the Adversary Cycle, some in the Repairman Jack novels, and bits and pieces in other, seemingly unconnected works. Taken together, even these millions of words barely scratch the surface of what has been going on behind the scenes, hidden from the workaday world. I've listed them below in the chronological order in which the events in them occur.

Note: "Year Zero" is the end of civilization as we know it; "Year Zero Minus One" is the year preceding it, etc.

THE PAST
"Demonsong" (prehistory)
"Aryans and Absinthe"** (1923–1924)
Black Wind (1926–1945)
The Keep (1941)
Reborn (February–March 1968)
"Dat Tay Vao"*** (March 1968)
Jack: Secret Histories (1983)
Jack: Secret Circles (1983)
Jack: Secret Vengeance (1983)

YEAR ZERO MINUS THREE

Sibs (February)
"Faces"* (early summer)
The Tomb (summer)
"The Barrens"* (ends in September)
"The Wringer"
"A Day in the Life"* (October)
"The Long Way Home"
Legacies (December)

YEAR ZERO MINUS TWO

Conspiracies (April) (includes "Home Repairs")
"Interlude at Duane's"** (April)
All the Rage (May) (includes "The Last Rakosh")
Hosts (June)
The Haunted Air (August)
Gateways (September)
Crisscross (November)
Infernal (December)

YEAR ZERO MINUS ONE

Harbingers (January)
Bloodline (April)
By the Sword (May)
Ground Zero (July)
The Touch (ends in August)
The Peabody-Ozymandias Traveling Circus & Oddity Emporium (ends in September)
"Tenants"*

YEAR ZERO

"Pelts"*

Reprisal (ends in February)

Fatal Error (ends in February)

The Dark at the End (March)

Nightworld (starts in May)

*available in *The Barrens and Others*

**available in *Aftershock & Others*

***available in the 2009 reissue of *The Touch*

Starscape

Award-Winning
Science Fiction and Fantasy
for Ages 10 and up

STARSCAPE

www.tor-forge.com/starscape